An Unforeseen Love

Lock Down Publications and Ca$h
Presents
An Unforeseen Love
A Novel by *Meesha*

Lock Down Publications
Po Box 944
Stockbridge, Ga 30281

Visit our website @
www.lockdownpublications.com

Lock Down Publications
Like our page on Facebook: Lock Down Publications @
www.facebook.com/lockdownpublications.ldp
Book interior design by: **Shawn Walker**
Edited by: **Jill Alicea**

Stay Connected with Us!

Text **LOCKDOWN** to 22828 to stay up-to-date with new releases,
sneak peaks, contests and more…
Thank you.

Submission Guideline.

Submit the first three chapters of your completed manuscript to ldpsubmissions@gmail.com, subject line: Your book's title. The manuscript must be in a .doc file and sent as an attachment. Document should be in Times New Roman, double spaced and in size 12 font. Also, provide your synopsis and full contact information. If sending multiple submissions, they must each be in a separate email.

Have a story but no way to send it electronically? You can still submit to LDP/Ca$h Presents. Send in the first three chapters, written or typed, of your completed manuscript to:

LDP: Submissions Dept
Po Box 944
Stockbridge, Ga 30281

DO NOT send original manuscript. Must be a duplicate.

Provide your synopsis and a cover letter containing your full contact information.

Thanks for considering LDP and Ca$h Presents.

Dedication

Doowop Baby! I never thought I would be dedicating a book to you in this way. Cuz, you just don't know how hard this is for me. We talked, we laughed, and we cried plenty of days. Only you and I will ever know what those conversations were like. Sitting outside, waiting for you to walk up or hoping you would call one more time to say "Mimi Babyyyyy! I love you!" the thought alone makes me smile every time. You stifled me with this one cuz, but I know you are in good hands now. Keep watching over me, Kid. I'm gonna need it. I will love you forever and ever. And just like you wanted, your name will ring bells because long as I'm the Ghostwriter; I got you. I love you, Cuz.

Antwaun "Doowop" Turner

9/30/1985
-
July 3, 2021

Pronunciation of Names

Chade: Rhymes with made

Baylei: Bay-Lee

Meesha

Chapter 1

"Are you really about to go through with this shit, fam?" Chade asked his best friend Ahmad as they took a break from shooting around on the basketball court. "I mean, you've only known her what, six months?"

"To be honest, bro, it feels like I've known her a lifetime though. No matter the time frame, she is everything I want in a woman. Chasity is ambitious, loyal as hell, there whenever I need her to be. I give her anything she asks for because she deserves it."

Chade and Ahmad had been friends since the fifth grade. They were more like brothers, and everyone thought they were blood related. Neither of them felt the need to correct anyone when they made the reference. Now they were grown men, but the bond was still solid between the two. As a matter of fact, the whole crew was still tight as thieves. Besides Chade and Ahmad, there was Malik, Vincent, and Samir.

All five of the guys were lucky enough to beat the odds and they had graduated college without getting caught up in the streets of Chicago. They attended UCLA and walked across the stage as one. Instead of going back to Chicago, the guys opted to rent a home together so they could save money. Once they got on their feet, they all branched off on their own, but still had weekly guys' night to catch up on what was happening in their lives.

"I hear you, but you met her ass on social media! Those females are like the Army. They can be all the fuck they want to be behind that keyboard. I'm just saying, six months isn't enough time to be trying to get married, my nigga. You have to make sure there isn't a hidden agenda on her part. Chameleons are hidden all over. They hide their true selves often."

Ahmad laughed as he shook his head no. "Chade, my woman ain't shit like these other females out here in these streets. Chasity is the true definition of a self-sufficient woman that loves me, just as much as I love her. There's nothing that will change my decision. Charity will be Mrs. Sanford soon. You are my best friend and I know you're only looking out for me, but we have stood by one another for years whether we were right or wrong. All I need is your support, bro."

"You got it. I'm going to be there with bells on. I wanted to make sure there wasn't any doubt in your mind about walking down the aisle. I'll support you because you are my brother and that's what we do. You ready to get out of here?"

"Yeah, I'm hungry as hell from schooling yo' ass on the court. By the way, nigga, you buying."

"You ain't said shit but a word; even though you didn't beat shit. Just say you broke from this million dollar ass wedding you had to foot the bill for."

Ahmad stood and waited for Chade to stop laughing and get up off the bench. With the basketball under his arm, Chade led the way to their cars. Chade glanced at Ahmad and laughed as the two of them walked slowly down the street. There were plenty of people out on the hot sunny day. Chade was ass watching, which slowed his pace immensely, but that's what he did all day every day. Being that he didn't have a significant other in his life, he took every opportunity he could to bed a different woman and add to his herd.

"Why the fuck you looking at these women, Chade? You are forever getting women's hopes up to be with you, knowing they don't stand a chance. Those are the bitches you should be dogging out instead of our sistas."

"You got me fucked up. I would never stick my dick in a snow bunny. Don't play with me. You already know I don't roll like that. As far as me dogging out sistas, I've never done that either. Every woman I've smashed initiated that shit and I gave them what they were seeking."

Ahmad shook his head and hit the key fob to unlock his black-on-black Benz. Chade threw his ball in the trunk of his car before walking over to Ahmad's to figure out where they were going to eat. Letting his eyes scan the perimeter around them, Chade propped himself on the side of Ahmad's ride.

"Where are we headed? Because you know damn well I'm not feeling all these lil knuckleheads that's just hanging out around here."

"Man, Chade, I hate when you do that shit. You act like you didn't come from the meanest streets of Chicago." Ahmad laughed. "Ain't nothing different. Hell, I don't know why you spending all your money living in Anaheim when shit happens out there too."

"You're right, but I don't have to worry about getting jacked for the shit I worked my ass off for. Enough of that shit. Where you want to go eat?" Chade asked, changing the subject. The guys were always arguing about the streets of L.A. and Chade always stood on why he didn't want to live there.

"I want seafood. Let's go to Boiling Crab."

Chade's left eyebrow rose as he stared at Ahmad. "You would pick some pricey shit now that I'm paying. You ain't shit, fam, but I got you. Remember this shit when you make your money back from this high-priced ass wedding."

"The wedding didn't cost as much as you are portraying," Ahmad laughed. "Just because my fiancée wants to get married out of the country doesn't mean it was costly. And I'm not broke."

"Yo' ass better be lucky I'm due for a vacation. The flight alone is a hit to a broke nigga's pockets. You're lucky all your friends did well for themselves, because it would be you and Chasity all alone saying I do by ya muthafuckin selves."

"Shut the fuck up and meet me at the damn restaurant, cheap ass."

Ahmad left Chade standing outside his car doing what he did best; laughing like a damn hyena. It was really starting to get on his nerves every time Chade said something about his wedding. At times, it had Ahmad second-guessing himself about agreeing to the extravagant wedding Chasity wanted. But the love he had for his fiancée erased all doubt from his head.

Chade backed his money green drop top Camaro out of the parking spot and headed in the direction of the restaurant. Ahmad followed with a thousand things running through his mind about his upcoming nuptials.

Meesha

Chapter 2

Baylei Jefferson was frustrated as she continuously erased the lines to the architectural project. She was working hard to perfect it while sitting in her corner office at King's Architect. Baylei was selected for the position when the company first launched. It was a newly started company and it was black owned, which she loved.

Weston King was an entrepreneur who had learned everything he knew when he worked for a prestigious white-collar company that took him for granted. Wes, as he preferred to be called, took a liking to Baylei two minutes into the interview. Her skills were impeccable, and that's what Wes needed on his team.

Baylei was five foot six with a slim waist and a fat ass. Her light skin was smoother than a baby's bottom and her cocoa brown eyes were beautiful. The naturally long hair that she possessed on top of her head flowed to the middle of her back. She turned heads everywhere she went from both men and women, but she didn't give an ounce of attention to anyone. Baylei had a man and she enjoyed the relationship they had for the most part.

"I'm not going to let these lines beat me." Baylei whispered as she concentrated on getting the structure of the building just right. Her phone vibrated on her desk and she groaned as she glanced at the screen and shook her head.

"What's going on, Noah?" Baylei asked as she tossed her stylus on the desk beside her Mac computer after accepting the call.

"I wanted to make sure you were going to be home on time. We have dinner reservations with my parents tonight."

Baylei quickly went to the calendar app on her phone to check the date, mouthing the word "fuck" because she had forgotten all about the plans Noah had made. Baylei glanced at the work sitting before her and groaned lowly because she had less than a week to have the assignment turned in. Bad as she wanted to cancel, Baylei knew she couldn't.

"Are you still there?" Noah asked irritably.

"Yeah, I'm here and I'll be there. I have a few loose ends to tie together and I'll be on my way home to change. I promise, I'll meet you at the restaurant."

"Baylei, don't be late. You know how much this night means to my parents. It's their anniversary for fuck sakes!"

"I said I will be there. The longer you keep me on the phone, the longer it's going to take me to get out of here. And for the last time, watch how you talk to me!"

"Make sure you leave your ghetto mentality at the office. I don't know how many times I have to tell you about all that hood shit, Baylei." Noah didn't wait for Baylei to reply. He just hung up on her, which pissed her off more than the tone he used prior.

Laying the phone back on the desk, Baylei worked her heart out until about nine o'clock that night. Her eyes were tired from staring at the computer for hours on end after the conversation she'd had with Noah. The vibrations of her phone had been nonstop since she didn't make an effort to meet Noah and his family for the anniversary dinner. Instead of viewing Noah's text messages, she went to her social media message box.

ChanceLover: Good evening, Beautiful. You were on my mind and I felt a strong energy to reach out to you. I ran across this quote and thought of you. "Keep your head held high, your chin up, and most importantly, keep smiling. Life is a beautiful thing and there's so much to smile about."

Baylei smiled as she read the short message. She had been talking to ChanceLover for a few months and he always came through when she needed words of encouragement. His messages were always right on time and she looked forward to them. Baylei replied with a simple thank you and a smiley face emoji then shut down her computer. As she gathered all of her belongings, Baylei stepped out of her office and headed for the elevator.

"Miss Jefferson, you're here rather late tonight," Joe, her favorite custodian, yelled from the other end of the hall as he made his way to her. "You should've called me. I don't want you walking around in that garage by yourself at this time of night."

"Hey, Joe! I didn't think to call for your assistance. I'm just trying to get out of here and get home to my bed. Come on and take this ride with me." Baylei smiled as the doors to the elevator opened.

Joe reminded Baylei of her father and she became comfortable with him from the first day they met. Joe caught Baylei one morning when she didn't have a smile on her face. He turned the frown to a smile with a few simple words that her father used to tell her all the time. *"There's always sunshine at the end of the tunnel. Never allow anyone or anything to disrupt your peace. Long as you're happy, everything else will fall in place."* Their relationship blossomed from that day forward. Joe was her at-work protector and Baylei welcomed the love he continued to shine on her.

As they exited the elevator into the garage, Baylei hit the unlock button on her key fob. Walking two rows back, Joe opened the driver door of her Jeep Cherokee and ushered her inside. Once she was comfortable in the seat belt, Joe closed the door and Baylei turned the key, bringing her truck to life. She lowered the window and smiled at Joe.

"Thanks so much for seeing me to my car. I appreciate you, Joe."

"Lei Lei, I want you to remember to call me when you're leaving the office any time after dark. These knuckleheads are getting worse by the day. They are carjacking any and everybody nowadays. I'm too old to handle the news if something happens to you," Joe said sincerely.

"I promise to let you know. You have my word. Now let me get out of here so I can get home and do it all over again tomorrow. Give me that cheek, Old Man."

Joe leaned in so Baylei could kiss him on the cheek. "See you tomorrow, Little Lady, and drive safely," he said, stepping back as Baylei put the truck in drive and peeled out of the garage.

Five minutes into her commute, Baylei's phone vibrated in her purse, but she didn't bother reaching for it. She knew exactly who it was, and Noah would have to wait until she arrived home to get a response from her. Thoughts of Noah's attitude change filled her mind as she merged onto I-94 south towards her home.

A little over two years prior, Baylei met Noah at Starbucks. She spilled her Caramel Frappuccino over his Tom Ford suit jacket. After apologizing repeatedly and offering to get his suit dry cleaned, Noah requested her phone number as payment instead. From that day, they were inseparable. Everything was going great for the couple until seven months into their courtship, when Noah introduced Baylei to his parents.

John and Elizabeth Connery were sweet every time they spoke with Baylei over the phone. They gushed over their son's new love interest and the fact she had a prestigious career, ambition, and basically her own money. But everything went from sugar to shit when Noah and Baylei went to the Connery's home for dinner. The pleasantries weren't there as they sat around the dining room table and Baylei felt it from the moment she entered the home. From that point, Baylei knew she wasn't welcome in Noah's family.

Baylei voiced her concerns to Noah and he blew them off by saying his parents didn't have a say about who he wanted in his life. That was far from the truth because Noah subconsciously spewed racial comments toward Baylei on a regular basis, then apologized afterward. Baylei was over it all, and that was the reason she didn't bother rushing to the anniversary dinner that night.

Pulling into her driveway, she spotted Noah's car and Baylei counted to ten to calm herself. She wanted to have a level head before entering her home. Baylei and Noah didn't live together, but they had access to each other's homes. As she grabbed her briefcase and purse from the passenger seat, her front door opened with an upset Noah standing in wait for her to ascend the steps.

"I'm glad you've finally decided to get your head out of work," he said with attitude. Baylei ignored his snide remark as she attempted to walk past to avoid putting on a show for her nosy neighbors. "Baylei, you know how important this day was for me!" Noah growled snatching her by the arm.

"No, it was important for your parents!" she said, snatching away from him. "I had every intention of coming to the dinner until your choice of words put a halt to that shit. I'm tired of you trying to change me, Noah! Come on, in your parents' eyes, I'm not good enough for you. As a matter of fact, let's address the elephant in the building. I'm not white enough!"

"Why do you always use that as an excuse when it comes to my parents? Your race has nothing to do with the way my mom tries to interact with you!"

"Race has everything to do with it and you know it, Noah! Every time I spoke with your parents on the phone, they were so sweet and doting. There was a different vibe when they met me in person. My voice, background, and demeanor were the same. My appearance is what had them lost for words. I got nothing but bad vibes from that day forth. Your mother is very snobbish with me and I swear, I'm over that shit."

"My parents are not racist!" Noah's face turned three shades of red and he was damn near purple. "Your black ass is speculating, and I don't appreciate it at all."

"And there goes the apple falling not too far from the tree. The difference between you and your mother is the fact you don't give a damn about calling me a black bitch, saying I need to stop using ghetto words, or leave the hood at home when it comes to being in the presence of your people. That's a form of racism, Noah!"

"I don't say any of that!" His voiced echoed off the walls in the foyer.

"Noah, you just said my black ass was speculating." Baylei laughed in his face. "I'm done with this conversation. I didn't go to the dinner, and I'm quite sure you all had a wonderful time without the awkwardness of having the only black person in the building. Goodnight, Noah. Enjoy sleeping in your own bed tonight. Make sure to set the alarm on your way out."

Baylei turned to head upstairs to her bedroom, but Noah had plans of his own. He took Baylei's actions as disrespect with the way she dismissed him. Rushing behind her, Noah grabbed her by the back of the shirt and swung her around with force to face him. Without notice, he drew his hand back and slapped Baylei hard across her cheek.

Noah had never raised his voice at her, let alone his hand. The gesture shocked the hell out Baylei and she cowered away from him in fear.

"I'm so sorry, baby. I didn't mean to hit you," Noah apologized instantly reaching out for her.

"Don't touch me! Just leave, Noah. I'm done. Talking shit to me is one thing, but putting your hands on me is something I will not tolerate. Take your sorry ass home."

"But—"

"Aht aht, if you don't leave now, I'll call the police and have you escorted out!"

Noah opened his mouth, but then clamped his jaws shut when he saw Baylei fumbling around in her purse. Going to jail was the last thing he needed to do with the career he possessed. Leaving as he was told was the only way to diffuse the situation. Noah knew he crossed the line when he struck Baylei and he regretted his action as soon as it occurred. He felt like crap for hitting her because of something so minor. His mind was racing as he tried to figure out how to correct his wrong.

Chapter 3

"Damn, girl. Suck that shit." With his hands tangled in Bonita's weave, Chade balanced his weight on the tip of his toes as he received the best head of the week. "Stop looking up at me. Concentrate on the dick," he said, swiping his hand over her eyes as if she had died and taken her last breath.

The tingle in his balls was intense and Chade couldn't prevent his seeds from flowing down her throat. Holding on tightly to her head, he thrusted his hips until his tank was empty. Chade tapped the tip of his pole on her tongue and he groaned lowly while squeezing the last of his kids out the door. He stepped back with a smirk on his face and Bonita slowly laid back on the couch, spreading her legs wide.

"Come get some of this gushy stuff, baby." Bonita licked her lips and tweaked her breasts through the tank she wore. "I can't wait to feel you deep inside me."

"Look, Nita, you know I agreed to come over for a top off. I have things to do and fuckin' isn't on the list."

"That's bullshit and you know it. I'm good enough to suck ya dick, but you always find an excuse when it comes to fuckin'! Just leave. And no, you can't use my bathroom either. Go home to whatever bitch you lay down with at night."

Bonita stormed to the door and snatched it open. Chade shook his head and laughed while stuffing his meat into his pants. "Don't worry about calling me anymore. I'm removing myself from the situation before I expect too much more from you. It's been fun."

She scowled as she waited for him to leave.

Before Chade could get out the door good, the door was slammed hard behind him. Without a care in the world, Chade jumped in his ride and backed out of the parking lot of her apartment complex with his music blasting.

Chade had met Bonita in the McDonald's drive-thru, where she was a manager. She skinned and grinned in his face until he agreed to have a conversation with her. From that night on, Bonita became his personal head doctor.

Hitting the highway, Chade made his way to Vincent's house so he could shower and change clothes before they met Ahmad, Malik, and Samir at the tuxedo store for their final fitting. Chade still thought Ahmad was jumping the gun marrying Chasity. There was something about her that just didn't sit right with him, but there wasn't anything he could do except be there for his friend.

Chade may have brought up the fact that Ahmad met Chasity on social media, but that wasn't his main concern. He in fact was getting to know a woman online as well and he could honestly say, he wasn't trying to marry her ass. Chade's thoughts of the whole online dating thing was, a person could be whoever the fuck they wanted to be. Everything about them could be a lie and once the time came to meet in person, the woman could be the total opposite of who they portrayed themselves to be the entire time.

"Sometimes it feels like, everything, is passin' me by. Every now and then it feels like, my ship has gone and sailed away. But I, I gotta be strong. Gotta hold on, it won't be too long."

Chade was singing along with K'Jon's "On the Ocean" when a called came in on his phone, interrupting his jam session. "Talk to me."

"Nigga, where you at? We gotta roll out in an hour," Vincent's voice boomed through the speakers.

"Shut yo' impatient ass up. I'm on the road." Chade checked his mirror and merged into the right-hand lane. "I had to shake Bonita's ass before she tried to convince me to fuck her," he laughed.

"Which one is that? Wait, you talking about McDonald's, right?"

"Yeah, her. I'm never gon' fuck her. She smells just like a Big Mac. Ain't no way a female can take a shower and still smell like the food she sells at her job. All she can do is deep throat my shit while her slob run down my balls."

"I'm glad you make good money being a CPA because one of these days, one of your many females is going to fuck you up. Stop playing with these women, Chade. You playing a dangerous game out here."

"I'm too grown for games. Vince, you making it seem like I'm leading them on a wild goose chase. That's not the case. I let all these hoes know what it is from the gate. Sugarcoating shit is not my forte and you know this. I let each and every one of them know I'm not looking to settle down, and the panties still hit the floor when I walk through. It's not my fault; blame them for all that rah rah you talking. I may not ever settle down. For what, so I can be put on restrictions? Nah, I'm good."

"You thirty-two years old and still running around like a college student. It's time to give your mama some grandbabies." Chade laughed loudly in Vincent's ear.

"It's never going to happen, fam. Half of these females trying to get deep in my pockets and I'm trying to be deep in the pussy. It's a win-win baby. Get off my phone; I'm pulling in your driveway."

Chade threw his car in park and his phone rang, displaying "Deep Throat" on the screen. He declined the call from Bonita and reached in the back seat, grabbing his duffle bag. "That bitch was adamant about me not calling her greasy-smelling ass, but she hitting my line. Get the fuck outta here," he mumbled to himself as he got out of his ride. As Chade walked toward the house, he blocked Bonita's number.

Vincent stood at the door with a frown on his face as Chade jogged up the steps, walking right past his ass. He went straight to the downstairs bathroom and turned on the shower. Stepping under the stream of water, Chade thought about what Vince said, but it was short-lived. There was no way he would settle down with one woman after what he went through with Sheena. That one incident messed it up for any female trying to get close to Chade.

Refusing to dwell on his past, Chade washed his body thoroughly twice and rinsed before getting out. After drying off he brushed his teeth, then dressed in black jeans, a polo shirt and a pair of white Nikes. Brushing his wavy hair, Chade looked at himself in the mirror and smiled. Standing at six feet five inches, his dark skin was smooth like Nestle chocolate and complemented the golden glow of his light brown eyes.

Chade applied beard balm on his long beard and finished it up with a little bit of oil. He took very good care of the hair on his face because that's what women complimented him on first. Good thing he didn't shave his beard off a year prior.

As he exited the bathroom, his phone chimed in his pocket. Chade removed it from his pocket and saw a message from his social media inbox. Opening the message, he smiled when he saw LeiLeiBay, the culprit behind the message.

LeiLeiBay: I hope you are enjoying your day. Just wanted to say hello.

Chade tapped on the message and responded.

ChanceLover: I'm heading to the tuxedo shop for a final fitting for this wedding. I'll hit you up later once I get settle at home. It's good hearing from you. We'll catch up later.

"Are you ready to go, Lover Boy?" Vincent asked sarcastically, interrupting Chade's moment.

"Shut yo' ass up. Let me get out of your place before I have to beat yo' body. You're so damn irritating." Chade laughed as he walked toward the door.

Climbing into his car, he tossed his bag behind him and inserted the key in the ignition, bringing the engine to life. He and Vincent made it to the shop with time to spare, maybe because they were racing on the highway trying to see whose car was the fastest. Vincent placed a hundred-dollar bill in Chade's outstretched hand the minute he stepped out of his car. No words needed to be spoken. They'd been doing the same ritual for years and they knew the drill. Chade and Vincent entered the shop and the woman up front led them to the back where the rest of the guys were.

"Mister Lover Man, Shaba!" everyone sang when they spotted Chade.

That was their theme song for him because of his lifestyle with the women. It didn't matter how many times he tried to get them to stop addressing him in that way. No one listened. Chade glanced around and didn't see Ahmad and was confused. It wasn't like his friend to be late for anything.

"Don't ask. He's on his way," Malik said before Chade could ask about Ahmad's whereabouts.

"I hope he's not having cold feet. Even though I've tried talking him out of this whole marriage thing, but he insists on going through with it."

"Man, Chade, everybody isn't trying to play the field for the rest of their lives like you. Samir dealt with yo' bullshit until the day he said I do. Look at him three years later; still married with a beautiful baby girl and happy." Vincent sat in one of the chairs and crossed his leg over his knee. "Maybe if you got to know a woman on some shit other than sex, you may find your forever too."

"Look at the man that don't have a steady woman in his life. When you find someone that is willing to stay with you more than a month, holla at me," Chade smirked.

"I've found my forever. I just know not to bring her around yo' hoe ass."

"Ohhhhhhhh!" the group of men said in unison as they pointed at Chade with hands over their mouths.

"I'm gon' let you have that one."

"Can't take y'all nowhere! Always showing y'all ass in public," Ahmad said interrupting the back-and-forth banter between Chade and Vince as he walked into the room. "Since we are all here, let's get this shit over with."

The sales clerk brought out their suits and passed each one to their rightful owner. Chasity chose mahogany and black as the color scheme. The men's suits were black with mahogany vests, ties, and handkerchiefs, with white button-down shirts, and black Armani dress shoes. Once everyone was dressed, the seamstress went around the room, making sure everyone liked the fit of their suit.

Chade looked in the mirror and he liked what he saw reflecting back at him. In his mind, he was imagining all the women that were going to be throwing themselves at him. Chasity had a few friends he wanted to have a little fun with and he couldn't wait. Chade had already made the mistake of sleeping with her best friend Emery and had to block her from contacting him. He was the reason she declined the invitation to be Chasity's Maid of Honor. Hell, she came up with a logical reason why she couldn't attend the wedding at all. He knew it was a lie though.

"I've never seen a man lust over himself like this nigga," Malik said, causing another round of laughter towards Chade.

"Stop hating and get on my level, fool. Shid, I look better than all you muthafuckas; even the groom."

"We all clean up nicely," Ahmad said, standing next to Chade. "I'm nervous about this marriage shit, y'all."

"You won't be nervous when we hit Vegas. We sending you out of the single life in style." Samir patted Ahmad on his back. "What happens in Vegas—"

"Stays in Vegas," they all said together.

"Samir's lovestruck ass gon' be in the hotel room talking to Selena while we're partying hard. He's going to inform his wife about everything we do," Malik joked.

"I'm not telling her shit! You niggas grown. I'm only gon' tell her what I do. What happens to me in Vegas, going back to Cali. My wife will know about it. Fuck that; happy wife, happy life."

"And that's why I'm not trying to get caught in the web. I'm not explaining shit to no damn body. When you're single and make no commitments, you can do what the hell you want without anybody having a say about the matter. Can't no female question me about shit because that's grounds to get cut the fuck off. I tell them not to expect shit from me because their feelings are destined to get hurt."

"You a cold muthafucka, Chade," Vincent scoffed. "You're gonna meet your match, and the woman that grabs ahold of your heart is going to have you questioning your damn self. I'd advise you not to let your guard down because once you do, you won't know how to act. Believe me when I tell you, she may feed you a lot of your own medicine."

"That will never happen, Vince. My heart ain't set up like that anymore. But wishful thinking is good for you to do. Save that scenario for the mystery woman you're keeping at bay," Chade said, looking behind him.

The men finished up in the shop and confirmed with the clerk that their suits were good to go. Each of them collected their items after they were bagged and left. Outside, they talked for a bit before going their separate ways. Everyone was excited about the weekend they would spend in Vegas in two days for Ahmad's bachelor party. The trip was Chade's idea, and he had a lot lined up for them to do.

Chade had a VIP section reserved at the Hustler strip club. They would arrive by limo and have endless drinks on deck as they watched the women take off every piece of clothing on their bodies. Afterward, the guys would hop from club to club and whatever happened after that was on them. They would be staying at the Bellagio hotel and whatever happened behind closed doors was on them.

Stopping to grab dinner, Chade finally made it home. After placing his food on the island, he went into his room, placed the suit in the closet, and tossed the duffle bag on the floor. He would empty it before heading to bed. Chade had to go into the office to complete a few accounts before his vacation started. He would be off work for two weeks, and it was long overdue.

Chade sat down to enjoy the beef and broccoli, beef fried rice, and egg rolls he decided to get for dinner. He scrolled through his social media and found himself on LeiLeiBay's page. She posted a lot of inspirational quotes that he enjoyed reading. As he scrolled down her page, Chade came across a post from a couple days before that she had typed out.

"If you can't do anything about it, then let it go. Don't be a prisoner to things you can't change."

The message to Chade was encrypted in some sort of way because she ended it with a sad face emoji and it prompt him to go to her inbox. Chade read the message from earlier and decided to start where the brief conversation left off. He and LeiLeiBay didn't know anything about one another, so he didn't know how much she would disclose.

ChanceLover: Hello, Beautiful. I was sitting having dinner and remembered I told you I would hit you up when I made it home. How was your day?

Chade continued eating and scrolling while he waited for LeiLeiBay to respond. It didn't take long for his phone to chime with a return message. Chade opened the message and skimmed the message. She had responded to what he said and kept it simple.

LeiLeiBay: My day was just what it was; another day. I don't want to burden you with my drama. I'll talk to you later.

Chade wasn't trying to hear any of what she was saying. Obviously, something was bothering her and he wasn't going to say okay leaving it at that. Chade didn't know her well enough to actually care, but he wanted to make sure she was alright.

ChanceLover: Don't do that. Talk to me, Baby girl.

Chade continue to eat as he waited on LeiLeiBay to respond to his message. When she didn't reply, he went back to her page and she had posted a goodnight post and her light was no longer green; indicating she logged off. He went into her inbox and started typing, but stopped. If she wanted to tell him what was going on, he would allow her to do so when she was ready. Chade exited out of the app and finished eating.

Chapter 4

Baylei sat in her office, working hard to keep her mind busy. Noah had been calling and leaving text messages nonstop trying to apologize since the night of his parents' anniversary dinner. She refused to respond, but read every message that was sent to her phone. Baylei was battling with herself to determine her next move. Usually, she was able to confine in her two best friends about what was going on in her life. Not with this dilemma though. Toni and Jordyn, along with her mother, didn't approve of Baylei's relationship with Noah.

Their disapproval didn't have anything to do with the fact that Noah was Caucasian. It had everything to do with him not standing up to his parents. Baylei's mother felt if Noah didn't think there was anything wrong with the way his mother treated her daughter, he felt the shit was right. His learned behavior was showing more and more as the days went on.

If anyone ever found out he put his hands on her, Noah would be a dead man because Baylei's family didn't play that domestic shit. Since her father passed, her uncles stepped in to make sure their niece had male figures to come to for any and everything. At thirty years old, Baylei was still spoiled because she was the first child and grandchild born into the family. The village always looked out for her no matter what.

The first year she'd been with Noah, things were good for the most part. Other than his racist-ass family, the only problem they'd encountered was when Baylei came to his job and caught him kissing one of his female co-workers. Noah claimed nothing other than them kissing ever happened. She forgave him and took his word that he didn't have sex with the woman. Baylei hid it from everyone and never mentioned it. She stopped going to his job because she was too embarrassed to show her face after that day.

A knock on her office door brought Baylei out of her thoughts. "It's open," she called out as she sat up in the chair.

Wes, her boss, walked in with a bouquet of assorted colored roses and a blue Tiffany's bag in his hand. Baylei frowned because there was only one person that could've sent gifts to her job.

"Good afternoon, Baylei. Noah asked me to bring this in to you." Wes set the items on her desk and she didn't crack a smile. Hell, she didn't even seem excited about Noah bringing gifts. Noah was trying to make up for his bullshit and she wasn't falling for it.

"Here you go, Mr. King. I sent the contract to your email. These are the sketches that I finished and I need your approval on them. Be honest about them please. I put my all into them and I love everything about what I've done."

Wes accepted the sketches and tucked them under his arm. The expression on Baylei's face puzzled him because she and Noah seemed so happy whenever he saw them together. If he bought his wife flowers and something from Tiffany's, she would be beaming brighter than the sun from the sight of the gifts alone. Baylei couldn't have cared less from the looks of it.

"Uh oh, somebody's in the doghouse, because you haven't looked at your gifts yet."

"I'm going to look at them, but right now, Noah can kiss my ass. He knew better than to attempt bringing that shit back here himself. He would've gotten embarrassed. Thanks for taking the time to deliver them to me. I appreciate you." As Baylei finished speaking, her phone vibrated against the desk and she rolled her eyes to the top of her head. Wes laughed lowly as he turned to leave.

"Tell Noah to make whatever it is right," Wes said over his shoulder.

"Get out of my office, Mr. King. I don't think he can make it right this time. Enjoy the rest of your day. Don't work too hard."

Baylei sat staring at the flowers for a good ten minutes before she grabbed the Tiffany's bag and sighed. Reaching inside, she took the square box out and sat it in front of her on top of the desk. She lifted the lid and gasped loudly as she admired the platinum bracelet with round brilliant diamonds encased in it. Baylei had the bracelet taped inside of her scrapbook for a few months and knew it cost well over ten thousand dollars. Noah was really trying to show how sorry he was through his bank account.

Even though he was a high profile lawyer, he really didn't need to work because his grandparents came from old money and made sure he was set for life. Noah was really responsible when it came to money and didn't like to splurge just because he had it. Baylei looked inside the bag and pulled out a long white envelope and hesitated briefly before tearing it open. There were three round trip tickets to St. Thomas inside a handwritten letter.

Baylei,

I'm sorry for reacting the way I did earlier this week. I love you and will never raise my hand to strike you ever again. Please forgive me for the dumb mistake that I made. There's nothing I can say to take back my actions, but I want to make it up to you. Here's three tickets for you, Toni, and Jordyn to enjoy a vacation on me. I apologize from the bottom of my heart. Your vacation starts Tuesday and will last seven full days. The hotel is paid in full. Actually, it's all exclusive. I left my black card at your house for you to shop for whatever you may need.

You don't have to contact me to say thanks. I know you are appreciative and hopefully when you return, we would be able to talk about what transpired and move forward. Enjoy your trip, and have fun.

Love you, Noah.

Baylei blinked repeatedly because she couldn't believe Noah sponsored a trip and included her girls. She wanted to call and tell him to take the tickets back and shove them up his ass, but that would've been one of the stupidest things she'd ever done. Instead, she picked up the phone and texted Toni and Jordyn.

Baylei: Get ya passports ready bitches! I need y'all to put in for a week of vacation, starting Tuesday.

Waiting for both Toni and Jordyn to chime in on the text thread, Baylei thought about all the things she was going to buy with Noah's money. With the job she had, Baylei didn't need to spend any of his shit. Not to mention, with every dime he had deposited in her account for the past year and a half, she was good financially. On one hand she wanted to forgive him, but on the other, she felt he wasn't sorry at all.

Her phone chimed back-to-back letting her know her friends were all in.

Toni: Did I hear passport?

Jordyn inserted two eyeballs indicating she needed more information.

Baylei couldn't do anything but laugh as she prepared herself to respond. Thinking quickly, she arranged the tickets on her desk and snapped a picture. When she pressed send, Baylei picked up the desk phone and listened to it ring.

"Yes, Baylei?" Wes asked in his deep baritone voice.

"Bossman, Noah is pleading his case in a way I can't refuse. I need seven days off starting Tuesday of next week. I know it's short notice—"

"Don't worry about all that. Mr. Wright loved your sketches and approved them. The contract is underway. I can handle everything until you return. Enjoy, and don't come back pregnant because I need my top architect in the office. Let that man love you, Baylei. Whatever ever happened is a test of y'all relationship."

"Noah isn't going on the trip with me; my girlfriends are. If you knew the half of what's been going on, you wouldn't be advocating for Noah at all. I'm going on this trip to clear my mind and make the correct decision about our relationship. But thanks for the week off."

"Well, have fun anyway. Enjoy the rest of the day, I'm heading out of here. You should do the same. Take Monday off and get pampered for your trip, and bring something back for me. Don't ask what because I don't care."

30

"Thank you! Tell Justice I said hello. I'll see you when I get back, and I got you on the souvenir."

Hearing Wes tell her to take the rest of the day off was music to Baylei's ears. After powering off her computer, she gathered her briefcase as well as the gifts from Noah and damn near broke her neck leaving her office. She had to double back because she left her phone on the desk. There were several messages displayed on her screen, but she decided to give Toni and Jordyn a call once she was settled in the car.

When Baylei got to her car, she put everything in the backseat and climbed inside and started the ignition. Connecting her phone to the Bluetooth, she placed her phone in the holder on the dash and wasted no time Facetiming her best friends. Baylei backed her Nissan Rogue Sport, courtesy of Noah, out of the parking spot as both of her friends appeared on the screen of her phone.

"Bitch! What the hell were you talking about in the messages? Why do I need to pull out my passport?" Toni asked excitedly.

"Yeah, what she said," Jordyn chimed in as she sat in wait behind her desk. "Where are you going at two o'clock in the afternoon?"

Merging into the left lane on Jackson Boulevard, Baylei made her way to the expressway to head home. "Well, I'm on my way home. Wes let me have the rest of the day off so I can get ready for our trip. I have Monday off too." Baylei smiled. "Now, did y'all request the days off like I asked?"

"What trip?" Jordyn asked curiously. "The last message I received was you saying take a week off. You didn't say nothing about a trip. I have the time to take, but where the hell we going spur of the moment?"

"Y'all didn't get the picture I sent?" Baylei asked.

"No!" both of them shouted.

"Okay. Noah is sending us on a seven-day trip, all expenses paid, to St. Thomas!"

"Hold the fuck up. Noah don't fuck with us like that! Why would he include *us* on a trip to the Virgin Islands?"

Toni was always on guard when it came to Noah. She always thought he had an alternative motive behind his gifts. Even though she was correct with her intuition, Baylei found a way to ease her mind before it went too far left.

"He wanted to do something nice for me and included you guys to enjoy with me."

"Nah, I'm not buying that bullshit story, Lei. What is he trying to make up for?" Toni asked, digging deeper. "There's something you're not telling us and I'm not feeling that right now."

"Stop asking so many questions because as I've said, nothing has happened. You're looking into this too much. Noah wants to send me, us, on vacation and you're trying to figure out why. Fuck the why, are you rolling?" Baylei was trying not to show how frustrated she was at that point.

"If she's not, I am!" Jordyn danced in her seat as she typed away on her keyboard. "I just submitted my week. If they approve the days or not, I'm out of this bitch after today. St. Thomas, here we come!"

"Are you in, Toni?" Baylei all but pleaded.

"I put my days in already and I'm ready." Toni smiled. "Baylei, if I find out Noah has done you dirty, I'm beating his ass. The truth is going to come out one way or another. Anyway, we need to go shopping! Seven days in the sun, we have to slay bitches."

"That's what I'm talking about! We are going shopping tomorrow. Be at my house bright and early in the morning. We heading to the outlet mall in Michigan City."

It was important for Baylei to keep the situation she was having with Noah between the two of them. She would know what route she was going after she returned from St. Thomas. Depending on her decision, she might reveal what actually happened with her relationship. It would never happen if she decided to stay with Noah.

"Thank you so much, sis. We're going to have so much fun!" Jordyn exclaimed flaring her arms over her head.

"We are going to meet some men and do some hoe shit!"

Baylei and Jordyn laughed because Toni was the ratchet one of the group and they knew she was serious than a heart attack. There wasn't going to be a dull moment with Toni in tow. She was going to make sure they lived their best lives and she was glad Noah would be nowhere in sight.

Toni felt Baylei deserved someone better than Noah and she was going to make sure she got it.

Chapter 5

The guys stood in wait outside the rental car port as they waited for their car to arrive. They decided to get an SUV to accommodate all of them because they were going to turn the fuck up for Ahmad. Once they were comfortable in the truck, Malik drove through the streets of Vegas to the Bellagio hotel. The city that never sleeps was live and everybody was ready to have a good time.

When they checked into the hotel, Chade, Ahmad, Malik, Vincent, and Samir agreed to freshen up and meet back in the lobby in an hour. Chade enter his room and placed his luggage on the king-sized bed and started unpacking immediately. He placed a pair of jean shorts, a white T-shirt, along with his socks and underwear on the bed. Choosing a pair of white sneakers to go with his outfit, he sat on the edge of the bed and called his mom to let her know he made it to Vegas safely.

"Hey, baby," his mother sang into the phone.

"I wanted to let you know I landed safely and I'm in the hotel. I love you and will talk to you later."

"Chade, you ain't getting off this phone that fast. I know you're grown, but I want you to be careful out there. Don't be out there messing around with those funky-tailed women. There are all kinds of diseases that can't be cured. It's time for you to find a woman to settle down with. When I see you bouncing from woman to woman, it reminds me of the way your father was at your age. That's why his ass is still going to paternity courts and he's damn near sixty. I don't want that for you, son."

Every time Chade talked to his mother, he heard the same speech about how his father jumped from one woman to the next. He knew his mother was trying to stop him from making the same mistakes, but he wasn't ready to settle down with one woman. He'd tried that route and it didn't work. Now he was all about working and having fun. Chade didn't want children, so that wasn't a worry of his either.

"Ma, please stop saying the same thing over and over. Have you ever thought maybe me being with one woman is something I don't want to do? You said it yourself. I'm grown. I don't mean any disrespect, but let me live my life the way I choose to live it. I understand you want grandchildren; you just won't get them from me. I came to Vegas to have a good time and that's exactly what I'm going to do. I have a lot of condoms so I'll be safe as I can be. I love you and I'll talk to you when I get home. I'll also be coming to Chicago to see you soon."

"I guess you told me. Chade, I'll leave you alone about the matter. Just know, what happened with you and Sheena shouldn't determine how you view all women. I know she broke your heart, son. Let it go and allow yourself to love again."

Chade wasn't trying to hear what his mother was saying and wanted the call to end quickly. Instead of responding to what she said, he took a deep breath and said his goodbyes. Rubbing his hand down his face, he went to his social media and noticed a message in his inbox.

LeiLeiBay: Hey, sorry about the other day. I wasn't ready to talk about what was going on with me. Hopefully all is good with you.

LeiLei was in a relationship and Chade knew she had reached out as a friend. He wanted to get to know her, but it was on her to open that door. Chade didn't know what she looked like because she didn't post any pictures and Chade didn't either. To him it was a good thing because if she was beautiful, he would find a way to make her forget she was committed to someone.

ChanceLover: It's cool. I hope all is well with you. Our last interaction told me you weren't alright that day. To answer your question, I'm good. I'm in Vegas about to turn up for my best friend's bachelor party.

Waiting for LeiLei to respond, Chade went to the bathroom to take a much-needed dump. As soon as he sat down on the commode, a message came in. He took his shirt off so he could get comfortable and opened the message.

LeiLeiBay: I'm sorry for leaving the conversation so abruptly. I was going through something with my guy and I truly don't know why I reached out to you at that particular moment. We don't even know each other like that for me to even seek solace from you. Anyway, I'll let you get back to enjoying yourself in Vegas.

ChanceLover: I have time to talk. Don't run off so fast, Miss Lady. Tell me a little bit about yourself. Shit, you're here now and have my undivided attention.

She sent three laughing emojis and that made Chade laugh too. The three dots danced at the bottom of the screen and he waited patiently for her to send a response.

LeiLeiBay: Well, as you know, I'm in a relationship and I don't know where it's actually going at this time. I live in Chicago. I'm an architect and an only child. It's only me and my mama. She's all I got because my father passed away three years ago.

ChanceLover: An architect? I'm gonna have to see your skills one day. Chitown stand up! That's my hometown as well. I moved to Cali to attend college and never looked back. I still come home to see my mother and my sister, but Chicago isn't a place I would want to live ever again. I'll never forget where I came from though. I have a question for you. Why don't you have any pics of yourself on your page?

LeiLeiBay: I feel you about not wanting to come back to this city. It's not like it used to be back in the day. I guess that's why I live in the suburbs, but it doesn't make things better. Many of the people from the city have invaded the suburbs too. I've been thinking about relocating myself. But my mother doesn't want to leave and I can't have her here alone.

About pictures…I see you've been stalking my page lol. That's the reason I don't post pics of myself. Social media is a place for me to inspire and motivate people. It's not a social place for me on a personal basis. One day you may get the opportunity to see what I look like. For now, the conversation is good enough for me. I can ask you the same question. You don't have a pic either. A black Superman is not who you are in real life lol.

ChanceLover: I may be that superhero that can rescue you lol. Don't be over there judging me. Black Panther was put on the map. Don't count me out.

LeiLeiBay: True. What do you do for work and to pass time?

Chade sat thinking about her question for a minute. He wondered if he wanted to be blunt with her like he did many other females or just straight out answer the question as she had done. Chade wasn't used to having conversations with females at all. After hello, there were no words spoken because nine times out of ten, he was balls deep in their tunnels. The only sounds heard were grunts, moans, and cuss words for him to go deeper. Then he was out the door and the only time any of them heard from him again was when it was their turn to ride his dick again.

LeiLeiBay: Are you still there?

ChanceLover: Yeah, I'm here. I was brushing my teeth. I'm an accountant and in my free time I just chill with my homies most of the time.

What he said wasn't a total lie, Chade thought in his mind. He was confused as to why he was lying to a woman he didn't know and might never meet in person. That was new to him and he didn't quite understand why he'd said it.

LeiLeiBay: You mean to tell me you don't have a woman in your life? I find that hard to believe because I know you don't spend all your time around a bunch of men. Wait, are you gay?

ChanceLover: Hell nawl! Aight, you want to know the hardcore truth I see. I don't have a special woman in my life, but I do have a lot of women that I entertain to keep me busy. Is that what you wanted to hear, LeiLei? I didn't want to reveal that I'm somewhat of a male whore. You forced my hand.

LeiLeiBay: LOL whatever rocks your boat, homie. You have to be careful with these women out here though. Some want more than sex and turn into stalkers. Many try to get in good to see how much cash a brother is dishing out too. It seems like you got your side hustle under control though. I'm here for all the drama you have gone through and whatever there will be in the future LOL. You're definitely going to need somebody other than your boys to talk to about the bullshit that awaits. I'm quite sure they be roasting your ass about your shenanigans.

ChanceLover: Don't be wishing bad luck on me, Lei. That's not cool at all. Since you want to be my counselor, you got the position lol. I need an inside woman to tell me how to handle these women.

LeiLeiBay: I got you lol. Look, I'm going to let you go. You didn't go to Vegas to sit in your hotel room and talk to me. Have fun and make sure you strap up. There are diseases out there you won't be able to get rid of.

ChanceLover: You sound just like my mama. Y'all just fucked it up for a brother. I won't be seeking to fuck around on this damn trip. Both of y'all poured enough salt for me to keep my joint in my pants smh. I'll talk to you later. Enjoy the rest of your day, Beautiful.

LeiLeiBay: LOL talk to you later, Chance.

Chade smiled as he placed his phone on the sink. Wiping himself, he kicked off his joggers and stood from the toilet. After flushing, he washed his hands and sprayed some air freshener because it smelled like something crawled up his ass and died. He turned on the shower and hopped in and washed thoroughly.

Chade got out and moisturized his body, brushed his teeth, and applied his balm and oil to his beard. Once he was dressed, he looked at the time and realized he was ten minutes over the time he and his boys agreed on. As he put his shoes on, his phone rang.

"I'm coming down now," he said into the phone before hanging up on Vincent.

Taking five hundred dollars from his stash, he walked the rest to the safe in the closet. After setting a code, he put his money and phone in his pockets and grabbed the room key, putting it in his wallet as he left the room. Chade stepped off the elevator and everyone was standing off to the side of the lobby watching him make his way to them.

"You ain't ever on time, nigga. What we getting into today?" Malik asked.

"We in Vegas! Ain't no such thing as being late around this muthafucka. Don't shit close; ever! We about to hit the casinos first.

39

Then we can grab something to eat before we hit Fremont Street and get it crackin' later tonight. Ahmad, it's all about you tomorrow, bro."

"Sounds good to me. Let's get out of this lobby. I'm tired of these muthafuckas staring at us like we about to rob them or some shit." Ahmad walked toward the door and everyone else followed.

"Samir, did you check in with Selena before you left the room? The last thing we need is for you to lose your money because you're not back by curfew."

"Malik, did Ailani give you enough money to spend on this trip? Or do you need us to ante up to help you out? You know how she gives you an allowance out of your own muthafuckin' cash, nigga."

We all laughed because Malik couldn't say shit in return. Ailani had his ass on a strict spending limit and his boys couldn't understand how the fuck he let that ride. They'd been together for about four years and at first Malik had Ailani's ass in check. After a while he was coming to them with a story every time they linked up. Malik was miserable in his relationship, but didn't know how to get out.

"Fuck you, Samir. I handle my own money now. I changed my banking information because while she was dishing my shit out to me, she was spending most of the shit on herself. She wasn't buying a nigga a pair of socks!"

"That's your fault, fam. Never give a woman that much control over your paper. Are you bringing her to St. Thomas?" Chade asked.

"Nawl! I'm rolling solo to Ahmad's wedding. I wouldn't be able to do shit with her ass around. Ailani acts like she's my mama and I'm the child. Sometimes I regret the day I met her, Man. Straight up. I can't even go piss without her sticking her head in the door. A nigga ain't had no pussy in a month! That's when I changed my shit at the bank." Malik's guys couldn't stop laughing because he looked like he was ready to cry.

"Well, you better go in here and win some money so you can have a nice nest egg when you get back home. Make her ass shake a lil something for a little bit of change." Chade laughed as they walked into the Harrah's casino.

40

They walked right to the blackjack table and sat down. The dealer looked at them with a smirk on his face, but they were ready to make his ass pay up. Each of them put their money up in exchange for chips and waited as the dealer got them right. Chade started off betting twenty-five a hand. He was the only one that didn't mind gambling every now and then. Everybody else was playing ten dollars a hand and Chade laughed at them.

An hour later, Chade was up five hundred dollars, Malik quit after losing a hundred, Samir was up one hundred dollars, Vincent got up ten minutes into the game and went to the craps table, and Ahmad was up six hundred after raising his bet to fifty dollars a hand. They thanked the dealer and went to find Vincent.

The table he was playing at was lit. Vincent had the dice and he was killing 'em. There was a blond woman standing next to him with her breasts against his arm. She must've been his good luck charm because every time he threw the dice, he was hitting a seven or an eleven. His boys wasted no time making side bets to get in on the winnings.

Vincent made them all some money within an hour and Chade convinced him to leave the table after he crapped out three times. After the first time Vincent crapped, he was on his own because nobody made a side bet. They had won off him and weren't willing to lose their money because he was being greedy.

Once they left the crap table, they headed out and went to Caesar's Palace to play poker. Texas Hold 'Em was the game they all knew how to play expertly. Chade and Ahmad went to one table, and Vincent, Samir, and Malik went to another. There was big money at the table Chade chose and his eyes sparkled. He put his whole thousand on the table and Ahmad started out with six hundred.

Putting on their best poker faces, they sat and watched until the hand ended and were ready to do damage. The dealer dealt the cards and Chade peeked at his cards, which were a jack and eight of clubs. When it was his turn to bet, he called and sat back. Ahmad folded his cards and twirled his chips between his fingers as he watched on.

The pot stood at eight hundred dollars before the flop. When the flop was shown, there was a queen of clubs, a ten of clubs, and a nine of hearts on the table. Chade had a straight off top and waited to see how the other players were going to react. There were five players in the game once it got around to Chade. He studied his cards and called. The dealer revealed the turn card and it was a nine of clubs. Chade had a straight flush and there was no way he could lose the hand.

Three of the players folded and that left Chade and a fat white man going head-to-head. He kept trying to figure Chade out, but he didn't give the dude any signs. He raised the bet four hundred dollars and Chade called him. The river card was revealed and it was a two of hearts. The dude raised again, this time four hundred dollars, forcing Chade to go all in. Chade pretended to be defeated as he checked his cards. After a few minutes, he pushed his chips in and smiled. Chade revealed his cards and the guy turned red as hell as he watched Chade collected the twenty-one hundred dollars in chips.

By the time they got up, Chade was seventy-five hundred dollars richer and the players were mad as hell. Not all of the guys were winners, but they didn't lose a lot of money either. They made their way to the hotel to put up their money and hit Fremont Street.

It was well past five in the morning before they made their way back to the hotel to sleep. Chade couldn't wait for the festivities he had in store for Ahmad's bachelor party.

Chapter 6

Baylei was awakened by her alarm blaring throughout the room. She jumped out of bed after silencing the noise. She entered the bathroom and took care of her hygiene. Going to her closet, she grabbed a yellow maxi dress with a pair of white sandals. Slipping the dress over her head after moisturizing her body, she slipped her feet into her sandals and removed the scarf from her head. Baylei combed her wrap down and it framed her face perfectly.

She went downstairs and cooked a couple pieces of turkey bacon, two scrambled eggs, and a piece of toast. As she sat down to eat her breakfast, her phone rang on the counter. Knowing it was Jordyn or Toni calling, Baylei grabbed a piece of bacon and grabbed her device.

"Good morning, Suga."

"I wanted to make sure you were awake. We'll be there in about fifteen minutes," Jordyn said.

"Toni must've picked you up."

"Yeah, she didn't trust me to drive myself, I guess."

"Lei, you know we would've been leaving at noon had I not came to scoop her ass. You would've been good as left because I wasn't waiting," Toni said seriously.

"Get off my phone. I'm trying to eat," Baylei laughed. "I'll see y'all in a minute."

Baylei went back to eating as her mind reverted back to the conversation she had with Chance. She smiled every time she thought about it. Baylei thought he was cool, but she couldn't wait to hear about the mess he would share about all the females in his life. Her phone rang and she sighed heavily as she swiped to answer the call.

"Yeah."

"Baylei, I'm sorry—"

"Noah, I know you're sorry. Thank you for the gifts and the trip. I'm on my way to shop for the trip. I've decided not to use your card, but I appreciate the offer."

"Baylei, stop with the bullshit, okay? I left the card for you to spend as you choose. I want to show you how sorry I am, baby."

"Money won't change what you did, Noah. You can't buy anything to make me feel better after putting your hands on me. That's some domestic shit I want no parts of. That doesn't convince me that you won't smack me again somewhere down the line. I've never had a man raise his hand at me and I'm not going to sit back and sweep what happened under the rug."

"I was wrong, okay? I'm trying to apologize."

"No, you're trying to buy me to forget. It's not happening. Look, I have to go. Thanks again for the tickets."

Baylei hung up the phone and heard Toni's car pull in the driveway. She had "Gonna Love Me" by Teyana Taylor blasting. She grabbed her phone and clutch as she danced to the door. She opened the front door and stepped out before going back inside to get Noah's card. Just in case she changed her mind about using it. Snapping her fingers to the music, Baylei locked the door and bopped down the steps as she started singing along.

"I wanna spend my nights with you. My life with you, oh baby, babe. Please wait up for me til whenever I get home. I know that you're all alone, thinking about what I'm gon' do. I hope that you see it through. And oh, you're gonna love me. You're gonna wanna hug me, and squeeze me."

Baylei jumped in the back seat and kept grooving to the music as Toni backed her car out onto the street. All three ladies jammed for the next twenty minutes before Toni turned the music down. Jordyn stared at the side of her face, wondering why she interrupted their live concert.

"Baylei, how much are we spending off Noah's card?" Toni asked as she glanced quickly into the rearview mirror.

"I'm not spending anything off his card. We just argued about that very thing before y'all pulled up."

"Are you high, sis?" Jordyn asked turning around to face her friend. "Noah owes you everything he bought because I know he did some fuck shit. You just ain't saying nothing."

Baylei sat back in the seat and folded her arms over her chest. Jordyn watched her like a hawk and Toni glanced up into the rearview mirror periodically while keeping her eyes on the road. The silence was deafening and Baylei was thinking of a lie to tell her friends, but decided to give them a half-truth instead of nothing at all.

"Noah and I had an argument a few days ago because I purposely missed his parents' anniversary party. He said some things that angered me and I put him out and sent his ass home. Now, will y'all leave the shit alone?"

"Nope, because it's deeper than that. Lei, we know you better than you know yourself and you just tried to give us the watered-down version of what happened," Toni said as she drove like a NASCAR driver on the expressway. "It's cool because I have a feeling I know what set you off this time. When you're ready to talk, we're here to listen."

The subject was dropped and the three friends sang their hearts out all the way to the mall. When they pulled into the parking lot, Baylei looked around with a frown on her face. The outlet mall looked like a deserted western saloon. Where there were once many different stores to choose from, now there was barely twenty stores that were open for business. Jordyn was the first to speak her mind about the situation.

"What the fuck happened around here?" she asked as they all got out after Toni parked.

"I don't know. This used to be the spot to get any and everything at low rates. Ain't shit here no more," Baylei said disappointedly. "Come on, let's see what stores are still here.

Toni led the way to the Coach store. They browsed and didn't buy anything because they had enough purses to last a lifetime. Baylei went into the Sunglass Hut and bought a couple pairs of sunglasses. Other than that, they were mad for making the blank trip to the outlet mall.

"Man, we were better off going to the mall closer to home. Fuck this, that's exactly what we're about to do. There's no way Noah's card won't get used today."

The ladies piled back into the car and this time Baylei was behind the wheel. They chattered about the condition of the mall, then Jordyn went off subject about her nonexistent sex life. She was in a drought stage since the death of her long-time boyfriend Lamar. His passing was a shock to everyone that knew him because he was always in excellent health and stayed active in sports.

Three years prior, Lamar was playing in a basketball tournament for charity when he collapsed on the court. He was rushed to Northwestern Memorial Hospital, where he died. After the autopsy report came back, his mother learned her son had an enlarged heart and it failed while he was running up and down the court that day. Jordyn was devastated and hadn't dated since he left this earth.

"I think it's time for me to get back into the dating scene, y'all. I've bought every type of toy known to man and nothing gives me that Big O. I haven't had an orgasm in so long I can feel the buildup in my back!"

"Well damn! Where did that come from?" Toni laughed as she looked back at Jordyn.

"It's been three years too long and this trip got me thinking about taking you up on what you said yesterday. I want to do some hot girl, hoe shit in St. Thomas!"

"That's what the fuck I'm talking about! Now, if only Miss Faithful would hop on board, we won't feel bad about leaving her to get our asses wet in the islands."

"Toni, I will not have a rendezvous with a total stranger. You have never known me to be that type of woman. If that's what y'all want to do, go for that shit. I'm not judging, it's just not for me," Baylei said, pulling into the Orland Park Mall parking lot.

"We will make your ass come into the light soon as we step foot off the plane. Get out of my shit and let's go in here and run up this check on Noah's muthafuckin' dime. We about to wear the strip off his card." Toni laughed as she hopped out of the car leaving Baylei and Jordyn to catch up with her.

***

Baylei felt good as she entered her home after a day of shopping and getting pampered with her girls. Just like Toni said, they put a hurting on Noah's card and loved every minute of it. They got manicures, pedicures, went to the salon, and got full body massages. Baylei found all kinds of cute outfits and skimpy bikinis for her trip. Her hair was bone straight after the Brazilian silk press she decided to rock.

Baylei was excited about her upcoming trip. Noah hadn't tried to reach out to her and she was happy he didn't. She couldn't stand the pitifulness of his voice and Noah was the last thing she wanted to think about before she took flight to enjoy a much-needed vacation away from reality.

Baylei went straight up the stairs to her bedroom and started packing clothes into her brand-new Louis Vuitton luggage. She wanted to make sure she didn't forget anything.

It took almost an hour for Baylei to pack and take her bags downstairs to set them next to the front door. Going into the kitchen, she grabbed a couple bottles of water before making her way back to her bed. She wanted to take a shower, but she was tired as hell. Instead, she changed out of her clothes, slipped on a long T-shirt, and climbed into her bed after tying a scarf around her hair.

Turning the television on, she went to Hulu and started season eleven of *Married at First Sight*. Baylei took a liking to Woody and Amani off the bat. Woody looked like a darker version of the late Nipsey Hussle and he was so attentive to Amani's needs. The show always had Baylei wishing she could find a man to love her in such a manner. Some of the men were pure assholes and put zero effort into getting to know their new wives and a couple of the women as well didn't do right by their husbands.

At the sound of her phone chiming, Baylei groaned loudly because she left it on the dresser and didn't want to get up to retrieve it. That's how tired she was, but she got up anyway. Scooping the phone up, Baylei hopped right back in her bed and got comfortable against her fluffy pillows. There was a notification from her inbox and she smiled because she knew it was Chance.

ChanceLover: Hey, Beautiful. Just wanted to pop in to see how your weekend was going. I hope things are going better than the last time I talked to you. Remember to keep your head up and troubles don't last always. Don't give up on your relationship. If there's a way to rectify the situation, do everything you can to make that shit right. I'll talk to you soon. I'm about to take a nap before I go out to watch these naked bitches shake their asses in the strip club.

Baylei laughed at the message as she read it twice before responding.

LeiLeiBay: I'm trying not to think about my relationship right now. All I can do is keep things positive for my own sanity. I'll know in a week what I'd want to do as far as staying with the man that I'm with. Enough about me. How are you napping at six in the evening in Vegas? There's no sleeping in the city that never sleeps! You must've found a hot chick that dropped some good shit on you lol.

Baylei had tuned back in on her show when her phone rang. "Mommy" displayed on the screen and she pressed the button to answer quickly. "Hey, Slim," she sang.

"Hello, baby. How you doing over there?"

"I'm tired, but pretty good. Me, Toni, and Jordyn went shopping for the trip we're going on next week. Don't start talking crazy. I was going to tell you about it. I just found out yesterday and I wanted to wait until I came over to tell you. Speaking of, what are you cooking for Sunday dinner?"

"Nope, you will not change the subject. Where are you going and why did it come about in such of a spur of the moment?"

Baylei didn't want to tell her mother the truth. She had to dance around the issue the same way she held it back from her friends. With her not knowing which way she wanted to go with Noah, she didn't want to indulge in too much information. Anita Jefferson didn't play when it came to her one and only daughter.

The first time she revealed Noah's action towards his mother's disrespect, Anita wanted to go beat the fuck out of her. Baylei had to beg and plead for her mother to calm down. It took a lot out of her mother to turn a blind eye to the bullshit her daughter was dealing with. But Anita sat back and allowed her daughter to make her own decisions since she was a mature adult. It was Baylei's life and she had to live it the way she saw fit.

"Noah gifted the tickets for Toni, Jordyn, and I. An all-exclusive vacation and a beautiful bracelet from Tiffany's."

"I know there's more to the story, Baylei. Noah doesn't call me of all people out of the blue knowing I can't stand his ass."

"Wait, what do you mean Noah called you?" Baylei asked, shifting her weight on the bed.

"He called me earlier today and apologized for the way he ignored his mother's actions toward you. Noah was pretty much dancing around exactly why he was calling, so I decided to call you to see what's really going on between the two of you."

Baylei was pissed that Noah called her mother because it basically put her in the position to lie. He had no right to call her mother thinking that would help him get back good with her. It actually fucked it up for him because now Anita was all in their business, and that was the last thing Baylei wanted.

"Noah had no right calling you about what's going on in our relationship! Since he wanted to get sympathy from the one person that's always going to side with me, let me tell you what the disagreement was about. Noah lied to you. He isn't nowhere near sorry for how his mother talks to me. Noah and I had an argument because I purposely missed his parents' anniversary dinner Friday night." Baylei explained.

"First of all, he pissed me off by telling me to leave my ghetto mannerisms at work when he called to remind me of the dinner. Yes, I had forgotten about it, but I was going to make it my business to attend on account of him, until those words fell from his lips. I continued to work and said screw him, but when I got home, he was mad because I didn't go. He said something about my black ass and I put him out of my house."

Baylei left out a good portion of what happened and she hoped her mother was satisfied with what she'd shared. The silence on the other end of the line had Baylei holding her breath until her mother finally responded. She listened without interruption and now Baylei knew she was going to speak her peace and expected the same respect in return.

"As you know, I'm tired of every time something goes wrong between you and Noah, there's some racial shit spewing from his mouth. You are grown and I don't want to be in your shit, but what are your planning on doing from this day forward, Baylei? How many more times are you going to allow his ass to disrespect you? That's not love! If your father was alive and breathing, Noah would've disappeared a long time ago. You and the fact that he hasn't physically put his hands on you, is the reason I haven't mentioned anything to your uncles. This will be my last time saying this. Mental and verbal abuse is just as bad, Baylei."

Baylei was quiet as she let her mother's words marinate in her brain. She knew everything her mother said had truth behind it and she couldn't do anything but shake her head in agreement. The questions her mother asked, she didn't have an answer for at the moment.

"Ma, I understand your anger and you are right. It's not love. To be honest, I've been wondering about my next move since everything took place. I just want to relax in the Virgin Islands and enjoy my time away before I make a decision."

"I have a feeling there's something you're not revealing, but I'm quite sure you will tell me the whole truth someday. Until then, I want you to enjoy your trip. Do something wild and let your hair down. What time is your flight?" Anita asked.

"It's an early flight Tuesday. Six forty-five to be exact. I'll call you when I land. But I'll see you tomorrow when I come for dinner since you won't tell me what you're cooking."

"Make sure your stomach is empty and you're ready to eat when you come. I love you, Lei."

"I love you too, Slim."

Baylei ended the call and tossed it onto the bed. Sleep was calling her after the long day she had with her girls.

Baylei got comfortable and started watching the show she'd abandoned while talking to her mother. She didn't want to think about her relationship with Noah because she didn't know what she wanted to do about it at the time. She had time to give it some thought, but it damn sure wouldn't be while she was away on vacation.

Meesha

Chapter 7

Last night was one for the books. Ahmad had a good time getting his party on at Hustle's and his boys made sure it was epic. With all the pussy in his face, Chade wanted Ahmad to get his dick wet before he was tied down for what some would say the rest of his life. Chade, on the other hand, had placed a wager that his nuptials would last six months or less. Samir stopped Ahmad from going into the Champagne room with one of the strippers and Chade just sat back and shook his head.

The night came to a close about four in the morning as everyone climbed in the back of the limo to head back to the hotel. The guys were talking and laughing about the night they'd had; all except Samir. He was glaring at Chade as if he wanted to take his head off his body. Samir was still uptight about Chade suggesting Ahmad fuck the stripper back at the club.

"Hey, Chade. Why would you try to get Ahmad to sleep with that stripper bitch back there? He is getting married in a matter of days and you want to fuck shit up before he can even walk down the aisle."

Chade laughed at what Samir said, but everybody else was quieter than a church mouse.

"Leave that shit alone, Samir. We were all out to have a good time. What happens in Vegas, stays in Vegas. Remember?" Vincent cut in.

"Nah, he doesn't have to leave it alone, bro. Samir, were you singing that same tune at your bachelor party the night before you were getting married? If I remember correctly, you fucked two of the bitches that you were making it rain for in the club twenty minutes from yo' crib. Nigga, you only live once and you're still with your wife in spite of all the freaky shit you did that night."

"That was different—"

"How? Oh, wait. The only difference was you stopped Ahmad from going through with the deed. When it was your turn, you fought Vince tooth and nail to get back to that hotel so you could enjoy the threesome that took place. That shit never got back to your soon-to-be wife and we made sure of that shit."

Chade didn't understand why Samir was mad at him and frankly, he didn't really care. The shit didn't happen, but Samir was carrying on as if Chade had pushed the issue. Vincent sat up and held his hands out to stop things from escalating further.

"Y'all need to chill. Ahmad said he was cool, so drop this shit. We boys, man. We don't do shit like this. Samir, you know how Chade is. Hell, all of us know this nigga is the life of the party. He hasn't changed one bit, so why are you questioning something that he does all the damn time? If Ahmad had gone through with the shit, that would've been on him, not Chade. We not in college no more! We are capable of making decisions on our own regardless of who initiated the shit."

"You right. The shit was wrong regardless of how you look at it. But you got it, Chade. I'm gon' drop it as if it never happened," Samir said, throwing his hands in the air. "We cool?"

"Mir, ain't shit gon' ever have me at your throat. We family, muthafucka. I don't pay you an ounce of attention when you start going off while you're full of alcohol. Now, if you come back with this shit in the morning, we can hash it out then. To answer your question, we will always be cool."

The limo stopped in front of the Bellagio hotel and before long, the door opened for everyone to get out. It was still live in the streets of Vegas. Samir and Ahmad headed for the elevators while Chade, Vincent, and Malik hit the casino. All three men sat in the same section and played penny slots just because they weren't ready to go up to their rooms to sleep. Malik was acting like a baller, betting the max, and lo and behold, his ass hit the jackpot after hitting the button three times.

"Holy shit! I just won fifty grand! Ailani can't find out about this shit. Promise me y'all won't say shit about this win."

"Damn, nigga, I ain't gon' say shit. But what I want to know is, why the fuck you have to put such hard emphasis on it? What's going on with you and Ailani, brah?" Vincent asked seriously.

The slot attendant approached the machine Malik had won on and confirmed that he indeed won the jackpot. Malik had won fifty thousand smoothly and the machine was going off, drawing the attention of everyone around them. A few minutes later, the floor manager came to verify the win and produced a form for Malik to fill out. They asked for his identification then asked him if he would like the cash or a check. Malik told the floor manager to give him two thousand in cash and the rest in a check.

Vincent and Chade sat as Malik went through the process. Vincent started hitting the max button on his machine and lost fifty dollars, fast. He went to put another twenty in the machine and Chade laughed.

"Vince, you ain't winning no damn jackpot. Malik's ass got lucky in this muthafucka. I want to hear his answer to your question."

"There's been something going on between them for the longest time. It has to be serious if he's not bringing Ailani with him to Ahmad's wedding. I'm not going to speculate, but I'm curious as hell."

Malik walked over with a smile on his face as he rubbed his hands together. "Y'all just don't know. This just gave me the cushion I needed to put in my savings account."

"What do you mean?" Chade asked.

"Ailani's been fuckin' up with her shopping habit. She hid that shit when she was handling the money. I trusted her to make sure the bills were paid and never thought to check the account. One day I got hold of the mail before her and found out my mortgage was behind six months." Malik sat down and laid out everything that was going wrong in his relationship.

"I lied and said the reason I changed my banking information is because I wasn't getting sex. That had nothing to do with it at all. Ailani was milking me dry and the level of trust I had for her was abused. I had to use my savings to pay the past due amounts on the mortgage, utilities, car notes, and my fuckin' credit cards. She stopped fuckin' me when I cut off access to my money. The only thing that saved me from going bankrupt is the fact I have a good ass job and I had to rely on my 401k to get back afloat."

Chade and Vincent couldn't believe what they were hearing. They were jokingly talking about Malik's finances and all along, he was truly in debt and hadn't said a word about it. Ailani and Malik weren't even married and he was going through all of the trials and tribulations of being a husband. They didn't have any children, so it was a wonder why he stayed in the relationship.

"Damn, man. Why didn't you tell us about this shit? You know we would've had your back," Vincent spoke up.

"Fuck all that! He knows we would've been there for him. My question is, why is this bitch still in yo' shit?" Chade asked angrily.

"I am the only family Lani has. Putting her out will leave her with nowhere to go, and I can't have that. The love I have for her trumps the shit she has done. I've started dishing out money to her, but it's not enough. She leaves the house bright and early in the morning and don't come back until late at night. Don't ask what she's doing because I still don't know. It's been going on for about two months now."

The floor manager returned with two thousand in cash and a check. He handed both items to Malik. Chade rose from the chair he was sitting in, hit the cash out button, and snatched the ticket out of the machine. Leading the way to the elevators, he stopped at one of the kiosk stations and inserted the ticket as he waited for his money.

"It's time for you to let her go, Malik. She's draining your pockets and your energy. That shit isn't healthy for anybody. When we return from the wedding, I will come through and help you get the ball rolling."

"I'll be there too. I'm sorry you're going through this," Vincent said tapping Malik on the back. "This shit is heavy and I'll be there for you anyway I can. It's a good thing you hit on that machine, but don't hesitate to come to me if that's not enough to keep you afloat."

"Vince, I'm a damn doctor. I make more than enough money. I just have to figure out what I'm going to do with the dead weight I'm carrying on my back. This trip and the wedding are my temporary relief until I get back to reality. By the time I get back, I should have a game plan in place," Malik said as they entered the elevator. "Chade, don't think I'm ignoring what you said, but I have to end things the right way. To be honest though, I believe Ailani has already ended what we have. She's just waiting on me to tell her to get out."

The three friends exited the elevators and made plans to meet up the in a few hours for breakfast. Their flight back home was scheduled for five in the evening and they were going to check out some of the attractions before they left.

Malik entered his room and sat on the side of the bed and sighed. He felt ten times lighter after revealing the secret he'd been hiding to his friends.

There was a soft knock at the door and Malik got up to see which one of his boys wanted to talk at almost five in the morning. Samir stood in the hall with a frown on his face. Malik stepped to the side so he could enter. Samir and Malik were closer to one another, just as Chade and Ahmad were. That didn't matter to any of the guys because in their eyes, they were all brothers at the end of the day.

"What's going on, fam? I hope you didn't come to talk about that shit with Chade," Malik said, sitting on the foot of the bed while Samir plopped in a chair across from him.

"Nah, I'm over that. Chade is always going to be the man that he is. He isn't going to change until he meets a woman that's going to have his ass running around in love, and he's going to run to us for guidance."

Both men laughed because they knew it was true, but they weren't going to hold their breath waiting for it to happen.

"I came to talk to you, man. Selena sent me a text earlier and told me to call her when I got back to my room. When I did, she dropped a bomb on me." Samir was looking at the floor as he spoke to Malik and he ran his hand down his face before looking up. "She didn't want me to say anything about it and I couldn't stay mum about what she told me."

"Brah, spit it out. What are you trying to say?"

"Selena saw Ailani in the grocery store and she was hugged up shopping with a dude. She said Ailani ducked off into another aisle and left the store quickly when she saw her."

Malik smirked and let out a wicked laugh. Samir looked at him and waited for Malik to say something. "Now I know why she's never home anymore," he said lowly. "Ailani and I haven't been in a good place for several months. In the back of my mind, I knew there was someone else in her life."

Malik went ahead and told Samir the story he'd told Chade and Vincent in the casino. Samir sat back in the chair shocked as he listened to his friend tell him what he had been enduring with Ailani. He would've never thought they were going through anything so extreme. The way Ailani dished his money out to him, one would think their finances were in tip top shape.

"How did you allow this to go on for so long? This shit didn't just start months ago," Samir said, sitting up.

"I trusted her, Samir. There was no reason for me to check behind her to make sure shit was getting handled accordingly. With the hours I work, Ailani had more than enough time to fuck around. I don't even know how she pulled off not paying the bills, but nothing was shut off or repossessed. When I cut her off financially and started giving her, shall I say, an allowance, her true colors started to show."

"I mean, you did save her from the streets and provided a lifestyle that had her living very well. Ailani has never seemed like the type who was all about money. She had all of us fooled to some degree and hid that shit for four fuckin' years, my nigga. Now she's back in Cali parading around with another muthafucka while you're out of town. That's fucked up on all levels." Samir was pissed and Malik didn't seem like there was anything going wrong in his life. "What are you going to do?"

"I'm going to deal with everything after we come back from the wedding. At first, I was going to sit her down and have a deep conversation about the whole situation. Now that I know she's out entertaining another nigga, Ailani can have all the fun she wants. I don't care. Hopefully, the nigga has a place for her to lay her head when I kick her ass out."

"Well, I couldn't keep that shit to myself and I'm glad I followed my first mind. If you need me when we get back to Cali, I'm there. We will be leaving to head for the Islands bright and early Tuesday morning and if you want, you can crash at my crib for the night."

"That would be cool. Not because I'm trying to stay away from Ailani though. Your house is closer to the damn airport." Malik laughed. "Thanks for letting me know. I'm about to get in this bed. I'm tired as hell."

Samir got up and gave Malik a brotherly hug then left to return to his room. Malik got into bed and stared at the ceiling for about an hour before he finally closed his eyes and went to sleep.

Meesha

Chapter 8

The day finally arrived for Baylei and her friends to leave Chicago and fly the friendly skies to St. Thomas. Anita wanted to see her daughter off, so she volunteered to be the designated driver to pick everyone up and get them to the airport. After hugging her mother, Baylei, Toni, and Jordyn collected their luggage and made their way inside.

"Bye bye, Chicago! It's about to be a hot girl vacay," Toni sang, swinging her hips as they found their way to the security check-point. "St. Thomas is about to be lit as fuck! Watch out, boys, a trio of beauties is on the way to invade ya land."

Baylei and Jordyn laughed at Toni's excitement. It had been a while since the three of them had taken a trip together and it was long overdue. Work was their primary focus, plus Baylei spent majority of her time with her mother and Noah, leaving little to no room for traveling.

It didn't take long to get through TSA security, but Jordyn's luggage was set to the side for a thorough search because of her dildo and toy cleaner. The guard smiled at her as if he wanted to dip off to the bathroom for a quickie. Instead of being embarrassed, Jordyn held her head high and sashayed away with an extra swing in her hips after he was finished. She sat in a chair across from us and slipped her feet back in her shoes.

"Jordyn, what the hell you doing with that shit in your bag?" Toni laughed.

"Fuck what you talking about, bitch. I'm about to be away from home seven whole days. My dick goes where I go."

"I'm with you on that, because my bullet is safely stored in my purse," Baylei cosigned. "I'm not trying to fuck random ass men in another country."

Toni rolled her eyes and stood from her seat. They went to McDonald's and grabbed breakfast since they had time to waste. Baylei's phone chimed soon as they sat at an empty table. There was a message from ChanceLover in her inbox and she smiled.

ChanceLover: Good morning, Beautiful. I hope all is well.

LeiLeiBay: Hey, you! Everything is good on my end. How was Vegas? Hopefully you didn't take bugs back home with you. LOL

ChanceLover: Nawl, I told you I wasn't on that. You and my mama told me to strap up. After that, I wasn't interested in meeting any women. That may change once I get to my next destination though. I'm actually on the plane as we speak. I have seven hours to be on this muthafucka, so I decided to hit you up before you got to work.

LeiLeiBay: Damn, you're getting your frequent flyers miles in, aren't you? Remember, you can still catch cooties this time around just the same. Far as work, I'm off for the week and getting away myself. I'm at the airport waiting to board my flight.

ChanceLover: If you don't mind me asking, where are you headed?

LeiLeiBay: You so nosy! Just know that my flight will be just as long as yours. Looks like we will be keeping each other company on these flights. I will buy a one-day pass for internet just for you.

ChanceLover: You will do that for me? That's so sweet of you. Since you don't want to tell me where you're headed, I'll take the fact that you will communicate with me until you reach your destination. Get yourself settled and I'll be here when you're on the flight.

LeiLeiBay: Sounds good. Talk to you later.

The feeling of being watched came over her. Slowly lifting her head, she saw that all eyes were on her. Baylei was so engulfed in the conversation with ChanceLover that she forgot she was sitting with her friends. Toni was chewing slowly and Jordyn had a devilish smirk on her face as they waited for Baylei to say something. When she picked up her fork and shoved pancakes into her mouth, the craziness started.

"Oh no the hell you won't! Who got you over there cheesing from ear to ear? I know damn well it's not Noah's pale ass, because you have never looked as happy like you are now." Toni popped a piece of hash brown in her mouth waiting for Baylei to fill her in on the secret she had been withholding from them.

"I wasn't even smiling." Baylei blushed.

"Um, Lei, yeah you were," Jordyn confirmed. "Spill it, bitch. Who is he?"

Placing her phone on the table, Baylei picked up her fork and stuffed her mouth with food. She watched as people swiftly moved through the airport while she kept her friends in wait of her response. Baylei knew there was nothing to tell, but they didn't, and that was the fun part about it.

"Since I can't text on my phone in peace, I'll tell you two heffas," Baylei laughed. "I've been talking to someone online for a few months. We are just social media friends that's getting to know one another, nothing serious."

"Well, what's his name?" Jordyn shrieked. "And is he fine?"

"To be honest, I don't know what he looks like. He uses the username ChanceLover on social media. All I know about him is that he keeps me smiling and laughing. He's a man whore and has no problem talking to me about any and everything. One thing I can say, he keeps my mind off Noah and the bullshit."

"If he's a man whore, what's the point in wasting your time talking to him?" Toni asked.

"It's just something to do. I'm never going to meet him in real life. He's from Chicago, but no longer resides here. I like his honesty and conversation. I'm not expecting anything else to come from any of this."

"Mr. Lover Man is gonna shoot his shot sooner or later. You and him are one and the same because it seems neither one of you know what the other looks like. I think that's the best way to start a relationship to be honest. It gives you the opportunity to get to know each other on another level. Build on conversation and personality instead of appearance. I say go for it and see where it goes."

"I doubt that." Baylei laughed.

Jordyn was digging into Baylei and ChanceLover's relationship a little too much, but Baylei wasn't going to argue the fact that there was nothing between them other than friendship. They finished eating in silence until Jordyn checked the time on her Apple watch.

"We board in ten minutes. I think it's time to go. We are in the A Group and I want to be there to get on this plane. I don't know about y'all, but this girl right here is sleeping the entire flight. I want to be well rested when we touch down. There's no sleep once we get to St. Thomas."

"Hell, me too," Toni said, gathering her garbage. "It feels good not to be heading to work at the crack of dawn."

Baylei didn't say a word as she finished her food and tossed the remainder in the trash. She grabbed the handle of her luggage and rolled it behind her as they made their way to the gate. As soon as they arrived, the attendant was announcing the boarding of their flight. The flight wasn't too full, but they didn't have to wait.

Once they were settled in on the plane, Baylei had the window seat, Jordyn was in the middle so she could have multiple shoulders to choose from when she fell asleep, and Toni was sitting on the outside. Baylei got comfortable and automatically paid for the Wi-Fi service. The flight attendant was going through the safety procedures and Baylei tuned everything out and went straight to her inbox.

"Have you heard from Noah?" Toni asked out of the blue.

"No, he hasn't called. I'm not thinking about his ass at this point. Whatever he's doing, he can keep that same energy throughout the week."

"That's what I wanted to hear. Hopefully by the end of this week, you will be leaving him for good. There's someone out here that will treat you way better than his racist ass."

As soon as Toni finished what she said, Baylei's phone pinged and lo and behold, Noah had sent a message. "You talked his ass up, Tone!" she said, opening the message.

Noah: Enjoy your trip, baby. Have fun, but not too much. I'll see you once you return. Love you.

Baylei didn't bother responding because he could see she read the message.

The plane started making its way down the runway and that prompted her to put her Airpods in. Baylei put her phone in airplane mode and let H.E.R. fill her eardrums while glancing out the window as she watched the plane lift off. The higher the plane rose into the clouds, the calmer Baylei became.

Jordyn was already snoring lightly with her head on Toni's shoulder and her mouth was partly opened. Toni was reading silently on her Kindle while Baylei was tapping away on her phone, responding to the last message from ChanceLover. The music in her ears kept Baylei busy until she, too, found herself drifting off to sleep.

***

Five hours into the flight, Baylei woke up and dug around in her purse for a stick of gum. Her mouth felt like a cotton ball was sitting on her tongue and she didn't like the feeling. Toni and Jordyn were still sleeping, so Baylei picked up her phone to see if she had any messages in her inbox.

ChanceLover: I haven't been back to Chicago in a few months, but I'm going to plan a trip to see my mother at some point or another. How's everything with you and your man? I'll understand if you don't want to tell me. I've been wondering since the night you hit me up when you were upset.

Baylei contemplated if she wanted to tell him about her relationship with Noah. Baylei didn't know this man very well and she was conflicted at the moment. What happened between the night of the anniversary dinner was still heavy on her mind and she hadn't been able to talk to anyone about it. Baylei chose that time to get everything off her chest by disclosing the situation with Chance-Lover.

LeiLeiBay: I don't know where my relationship is right now. This trip will give me time to think things through thoroughly before I make a decision while I'm still angry. My emotions may have me making the wrong choice and I don't want to do that.

ChanceLover: You are making the right decision. Acting on something while in your feelings can be bad. I'm quite sure whatever the problem is, can be worked out with communication. All you have to do is hear him out and make sure the two of you are on the same page about moving forward with the relationship.

LeiLeiBay: That sounds good coming from someone that doesn't know why things are the way they are in my relationship. Feel free to give your honest feedback once I'm finished. I've been with this man for the past two years and everything was great for the first seven to eight months. I got along with his parents very well. His mother would call almost every day to see how I was do- ing.

The minute he took me to meet his parents, everything changed. I noticed right away how his mother looked down her nose at me as if I wasn't good enough for her son. Then the snide racist remarks started whenever I was around his mother. When I brought the dis- respect up to him, he blew it off like it was nothing. He would get upset and say things to me that I harbored inside for the longest time. Don't get me wrong, I defended myself and told him I wasn't going to tolerate the way he talked to me.

A few weeks ago, I forgot about his parents' anniversary dinner until he called to see if I would be off work on time. After assuring him that I would be there, he kept pushing the issue and I kind of snapped on him. When he told me to leave my ghetto mannerisms at my job, I decided then I wasn't going to the dinner. I stayed at work and didn't think about it anymore until I got home and he was stand- ing in my doorway.

We argued, and of course he had something to say about my "black ass". I told him to leave and he put his hands on me that night. I put up with a lot of things, but domestic violence isn't one of them. He has been trying to apologize, and I've refused to talk to him. Buying gifts, giving me a credit card to shop, and sending me on a trip with my girls is not going to make me forget about what he has done.

While waiting for a reply from ChanceLover, Baylei summoned one of the attendants and ordered a turkey sandwich, a bag of chips, and a can of cranberry juice. She didn't care about the cost because she used Noah's card to complete the purchase. Reaching into her purse, Baylei pulled out the travel-sized sanitizer she kept with her and a few napkins. She wiped down the tray after letting it down and started scrolling social media. She decided to make an inspirational good morning post for her friends.

"Sometimes you need bad things to happen to inspire you to change and grow. Good morning all."

At that moment, her food arrived and Baylei was ready to stuff her face. She did just that after sanitizing her hands. Baylei went back to scrolling social media when she got a notification on her post. Someone that didn't have a profile picture had inserted a laughing emoji and the word stupid in the comments. Baylei shook her head, not paying attention to the ignorance. Her phone vibrated, letting her know she had a message in her inbox.

ChanceLover: First of all, I don't want to sound disrespectful, but what the fuck you doing with a white boy? They; white men, don't really like our black women. It's the thought of having a chocolate beauty on their arm that arouses them. You would never be accepted by his family. So tell me, what is there to think about while you're away? Secondly, the muthafucka don't respect you at all if he's comfortable calling you black anything! Thirdly, he put his fuckin' hands on you! Leave his ass alone, Beautiful. You don't need that type of shit in your life. I don't give a fuck what he buys you. Return that shit!

ChanceLover was pissed about the situation and he didn't even know Baylei well enough to be upset. Baylei read his response as she chewed the side of her bottom lip. She wondered if she'd made a mistake by telling him what Noah had done to her. He had responded the same way her mama and friends did, minus the part about Noah slapping her. Before she could finish reading, another message followed.

ChanceLover: I'm sorry for going off, but that type of shit burns me up inside. If a muthafucka ever put his hands on my sister, he wouldn't live to try that shit again. Where is your people, baby girl? Ain't no way that punk should be able to send gifts and shit after everything he has put you through. I'm seething right now.

LeiLeiBay: No one knows he put his hands on me. You are the only person that knows that tad bit of information other than me and him. My uncles would make him disappear if they knew, and I don't want anyone going to jail on the account of me. The reason I told you is because I've been holding all of this in because I didn't want to tell anyone the whole truth about it. My circle protects me by all means and it would be a lot of bloodshed behind this.

ChanceLover: So what! His ass wouldn't raise his hands to a man like he did when he hit you! Why are you protecting this mutha-fucka?

LeiLeiBay: I'm not protecting him. Truthfully, I'm over all of this shit. I've ignored every attempt he has made to talk to me. I just want to enjoy my time away from him. Can we drop the subject please?

Baylei waited on a response after she saw that ChanceLover read her last message, but a reply never came. After ten minutes she logged out of her social media account, turned her phone off, and rested her head against the window. The conversation between her and ChanceLover replayed in her mind until she blocked it out and let sleep take over her body.

"Lei, wake up. We're landing." Jordyn elbowed Baylei until she opened her eyes.

"Okay, I'm awake."

As soon as the plane landed, the trio gathered their luggage and were off the plane the minute the door opened. Making their way to the car rental booth, Jordyn stopped in her tracks when they came off the escalator, causing Toni to shove her slightly in the back. Baylei looked around trying to figure out what was wrong.

"Why do that man have a sign with your name on it, Lei?" Jordyn finally asked, pointing in the direction of the automatic doors.

"I don't know. Let's go find out," Baylei said as she walked off to see what was going on. "Excuse me, I'm Baylei Jefferson. How did you know my name?" she asked the gentleman that held the sign.

"Hello, Mrs. Jefferson. I am Mark, and I will be your driver for the duration of your stay here in St. Thomas. Follow me."

Baylei looked at Toni and she hunched her shoulders and did what Mark suggested. They followed him out of the airport into the smoldering heat. Mark helped the ladies with their bags and opened the door to the limo so they could get inside. Before closing the door, Mark stuck his head in with a smile.

"There's champagne in the mini fridge; help yourselves. We have about a thirty-minute drive to the Margaritaville Vacation Club. You ladies chose one of the best places to spend your vacation. You will really enjoy your stay."

The scenery was beautiful as Baylei watched from the window with a smile. She got comfortable because the resort mentioned was the one on her itinerary. Toni wasted no time popping the cork on the champagne bottle and poured up the drinks. Baylei's phone chimed as she took the flute from her friend. Reaching into her purse, Baylei looked at the notification and saw Noah's name. Instead of opening the message, she immediately tossed the device back where it belonged; in her bag.

"To friendship, the turn up, and Lei having the freedom to fuck a nigga at least once on this trip!" Toni held up her glass and Jordyn joined in ready to toast it up. Baylei on the other hand, wasn't feeling that shit.

"I'm not toasting to that! You said that shit as if Noah controls me or something. I don't like the way you threw shade my way, Toni."

Toni scrunched up her face in confusion because she didn't know what Baylei was so upset about. In no way, shape, or form was she trying to throw shade or shots at her friend. Baylei rolled her eyes while sipping her champagne, but her eyes never left Toni's.

"Lei, what the hell you all bent out of shape about? You know we joke around all the time. Today of all days you're catching an attitude? What the fuck did Noah really do to you?"

"Nothing, okay? We are here to enjoy ourselves and that's what we're going to do." Baylei smiled and raised her glass. "To us! As well as you two hoes getting fucked every which way but up!"

All three of them drank to what Baylei said, but the tension in the limo was thick. Toni wanted to dig deeper into why her girl went off like she did, but decided to leave well enough alone. Both she and Jordyn had a silent conversation without opening their mouths. The two of them knew there was something Baylei hadn't told them about her relationship with Noah.

Jordyn broke the silence by connecting her phone to the iHome speaker. "B.S." by Jhené Aiko blared throughout the limo. Baylei started singing her heart out with her eyes closed.

Back up on my bullshit
Back up on the move
Touchdown in my hometown
Got nothing to lose
I am on my own now
I am in control now
I need you to go now
I can fix my own crown

Enjoying drinks and music, Baylei felt her purse vibrating, but she never went inside to take a look at her phone. She felt bad about jumping off the deep end with Toni. If it was easy for her to share everything with her friends, then the comment would've never been made. Baylei knew it was her fault and could admit she was wrong in every way. There was little conversation between any of them on the ride to the hotel and it was all because of the way Baylei reacted.

The thought of revealing the truth during the trip was strongly on Baylei's mind. She'd never held anything back from her loved ones before, so it would be hard sharing the secrets she held inside. Baylei wanted to be sure she would be ready for all the consequences that was bound to come after she told them Noah put his hands on her.

Mark turned into the resort and all eyes were on the scene before them. Entering the stoned wall, the palm trees waved hello as the limo cruised along the pavement. Baylei admired the fine white sand, the crystal-clear waters, and the island in the distance.

"Damn, this is beautiful!" Jordyn exclaimed. "I hope our suite is just as nice."

"This is bomb! I've never been here before and I know we won't be disappointed. We're about to have the time of our lives." Toni danced in the seat as the limo came to a complete stop.

After a few minutes, the door opened and Mark stepped to the side, allowing the ladies to exit. A fine man came out of the front lobby to help with their bags. Baylei went into her purse to get the itinerary when Mark turned to speak with the hotel employee.

"Hey, Pete! How you been?"

"Mark, my man. I'm good as can be. Who are these beautiful ladies?"

"These are my people."

Toni quizzingly looked at Baylei, who in turn hunched her shoulders in return.

"They are staying in building eight. If I'm not mistaken, that is a two-bedroom suite. I want them moved to a three bedroom because they deserve to have their own space while they are here."

"Believe me, Mark, they are in good hands. I'll make sure the staff knows we have V.I.P. guests in the house. They will get top notch treatment," Pete said with a smile.

"Sounds like a plan. Call me if anything is needed." Mark shook Pete's hand before turning to Baylei. "There are plenty of places within walking distance, but my services are exclusive to you for the duration of your stay. It was paid for in advance already."

Baylei didn't understand how they were given special treatment. She had never been on vacation and was treated as if she was a celebrity. "Why are you making these extra requests for us, Mark?"

"This is my establishment and I came here as a favor to Noah. He's a good friend of mine. Anyone that's special to him is alright with me. Don't worry, I'm here to make sure your vacation will be one to remember."

Baylei scowled, but replaced it with a smile quickly and thanked Mark for his hospitality. She wasn't happy about the fact that Noah had his rich friends keeping an eye on her while she was away. It pissed her off because she was a grown ass woman and didn't need a babysitter. Baylei was fuming on the inside, but she kept it to herself.

Pete finished loading the cart and led the way into the lobby so they could check in. Pete explained the upgrade given by Mark and the original reservations were changed without question.

It was officially vacation time and Baylei was ready to let her hair down.

Passing through the club, the property was gorgeous. There was a huge swimming pool in the middle of the resort and a bar off to the side. With it being early in the morning, there were little to no people out and about. Jordyn spotted a Jacuzzi in the far corner of the area and she was ready to relax the muscles in her body.

"Pete, is there a fitness center on the resort?" Jordyn asked as they entered the building they would be staying.

"Yes, there is a fitness room as well as a business center where you can access the internet if any of you need to complete any work from your workplace."

"Who the hell goes on vacation to work?" Toni scoffed. "I'm here to throw my ass in a circle and get drunk!"

"Toni!" Baylei laughed, pushing her in the back.

"Hell, I'm just telling it like it is. I'm not trying to check in with nobody back in Chicago. I have international calling on my phone, and that shit won't be getting any play for the next seven days. That whole work thing is dead with me."

Going to the elevator, they rode up to the fourth floor as soft music played in the car. There were only two rooms on the floor. Their suite number was 425 and Pete allowed Toni to insert her key card into the slot to unlock the door. The group entered the suite and was wowed with every step they took. There was a kitchenette off to the left and it was fully stocked with a microwave, refrigerator, and kitchenware. The sitting area was to the right and the view of the ocean was fabulous.

"Come look at this view!" Jordyn waved them over as she stood on the balcony.

"You ladies get settled in," Pete said from the doorway. "You can reach me at any time by dialing 1113 on the phone, no matter the time. I'm going to leave now, but welcome to Margaritaville Vacation Club."

"Thank you!" the friends sang as they waved goodbye. Pete blew a kiss in the air and let himself out.

Baylei and Toni joined Jordyn on the balcony. The view was gorgeous and the group of women were mesmerized. Baylei's phone vibrated for the third time since leaving the airport. She dug around in her purse until she found her device. Finally deciding to check the many messages from Noah, she opened them one by one.

Noah: I hope you made it to the airport safely. Have a good time and clear your head because I want to work on us when you return. The owner of the resort is going to look out for you. His name is Mark and he will be at the airport to pick you up.

Baylei rolled her eyes because she found out that information already without his help. Going to the next message, her heart fell to the floor. The text came from Noah's phone, but the picture message that was sent was not. Baylei stared at the photo and tears instantly filled her eyes. Turning abruptly, she rushed back into the suite and went into what she assumed was the master bedroom and closed the door. Sitting on the king-sized bed, Baylei continued to stare at the image before her.

The longer she stared at the image, the faster the tears rolled down her face. What she was looking at was a picture of the woman Noah was caught cheating with, lying next to him in his bed. They were both naked and she captioned it with: *This is the reason he sent you to St. Thomas. Have fun, bitch.*

Baylei was hurt, but it didn't stop her from opening the last message she had received. When she started reading the content, her tears stopped immediately and turned into pure anger. Baylei read the message three times and her blood boiled with every word she read. It was a few screenshots of a conversation between Ashley, who she now knew as the other woman, and Noah's mother.

Ashley: Good morning, Elizabeth. How are you doing?

Elizabeth: Hello, my future daughter-in-law. I'm doing well. I never got the chance to thank you for coming to John and I's anniversary dinner. I really appreciate you coming out for our day. That's more than I can say about the black child.

Ashley: LOL now you know I will always be there to celebrate with you guys. We all know that Noah's flavor of the last couple of years has always been a disappointment to us all. I don't see why he is hanging on to her when he it's obvious I'm the one he loves.

Elizabeth: The hold that tar baby has on my son is one I will never understand. I talked to him until I was blue in the face the other day and he refused to tell me why he keeps her around. I figured by now, she would've run for the hills instead of staying by my son's side. Lord knows, I disrespect her every chance I get. It doesn't matter what I say, she won't go away.

Ashley: His money is why she won't turn him loose. That's what black people worry about when they don't have anything of their own to fall back on. Noah foots all of her bills and she needs him. Don't worry though. Noah sent her to St. Thomas for the week with her ghetto ass friends. When she returns, Noah isn't going to want anything more to do with her. I'm going to work my magic to make sure of it.

Baylei couldn't believe the things Ashley and especially Elizabeth said about her. Then again, yes, she could. Elizabeth's racist ass never hid the fact that she didn't like Baylei dating her son. They didn't have to worry about her anymore though. Noah wanted out, then that's exactly what he would get.

Noah had been dealing with Ashley behind Baylei's back from the time she caught him with the tramp at his job. Not going back to his workplace gave him the freedom to do whatever he wanted with the bitch because he didn't have to worry about Baylei popping up unexpectedly.

A knock on the door interrupted her alone time. Baylei didn't have a chance to clean her face before the door to the room opened.

"Lei, are you okay?" Toni asked, stepping inside the room with Jordyn on her heels.

Baylei didn't lift her head as she felt the bed dip a little as both of her friends sat on each side of her. When she raised her head, Toni knew automatically Bailey had been crying.

"What's the matter, boo?" she asked.

Baylei was silent for a little bit, but she knew it was time to fill them in on what was going on with her and Noah. Taking a deep breath, she passed her phone to Toni as she started from the beginning and told them everything.

Meesha

Chapter 9

Noah turned over after waking up from the euphoric coma Ashley put him in and stared at the woman that was fast asleep in her naked glory. Guilt ate at him because he loved Baylei, but he loved Ashley too. His mother was breathing down his neck about making things exclusive with Ashley, but he didn't want to take that step with her.

Ashley was born with a silver spoon in her mouth and was spoiled as fuck. Both of their families were close and were pushing them to be together out of familiarity. Noah didn't want to have to cater to any woman, and that was exactly what Ashley would want him to do. If he did anything for a woman, it was a choice he made and not one that would be forced upon him. Ashley was what some would call a trust fund baby. She was set for life without having to lift a finger. Her father had stipulations on the money he had in the bank for her. Ashley could only spend so much of the money a month.

Baylei was a problem to Ashley because in her mind, Baylei was using Noah for money. Little did she know, Baylei didn't ask him for anything. Unlike Ashley, Noah did any and everything for Baylei for that reason alone. Baylei had a career and was a damn good architect. Ashley only knew how to shop, go to tea parties and brunch. An exhausting day for Ashley would be going to the spa for a manicure, pedicure, and getting her hair done at the salon.

Ashley's eyes opened slowly and found Noah in deep thought. "What's on your mind, babe?"

"Nothing really," was Noah's reply before he fell on his back as he glanced at the ceiling with his arm over his face.

"Noah, I know you not over there thinking about Baylei!" Ashley screamed, sitting up in the bed.

Before Noah could respond to Ashley, his phone started ringing. He reached over and grabbed it from the nightstand. Seeing Baylei's name caused Noah to spring from the bed and grab the shirt and shorts that were on the floor before making his way out of his bedroom.

"Noah!" Ashley called out as he crossed the threshold.

"Ashley, stay in your lane. You of all people knows you are not my bitch."

"And she won't be your bitch when you come back either," she smirked.

Noah didn't bother addressing what Ashley said. "Hey, baby—" he said, putting his clothes on as he listened.

"Don't hey baby me! What the fuck you doing, Noah? Is this the shit you doing now?" Baylei screamed at the top of her lungs. "You know what? It doesn't matter about the bitch in your bed. Let's talk about your mother! All the shit she said in the messages that were sent to me. I'm good on you and your racist ass family. Stay with the bitch, Noah. When I get back to Chicago, don't contact me at all!"

"Lei, what are you talking about? I messaged you to say have a good time. How did my mother become a topic of discussion and what bitch are you referring to?"

"Your *mother* and Ashley have been having conversations about my black ass! I've dealt with this bullshit long enough, Noah. I'm done with trying to prove that the color of my skin does not define who I am. What I refuse to do is accept the racist shit you don't see when it comes to your family. Be with Ashley, since that's what you want to do in your spare time. Fuck you!"

"Baylei—"

The line went dead and Noah looked at the phone to see if Baylei had actually hung up on him. Going through his text messages, Noah saw the last one he'd sent to Baylei and was more confused than when he was listening to Baylei's rant. Noah walked slowly back and forth across the living room floor when Ashley came up behind him.

"Are you coming back to bed?"

It doesn't matter about the bitch in your bed. Baylei's words rang in his ears and he knew right away that Ashley was behind the information Baylei had received. Noah turned with fire in his eyes as he faced Ashley.

"What the hell did you do?" Noah barked at Ashley.

"I didn't do anything. What did your little black girl tell you?"

"Don't refer to her in that manner ever again! Tell me what were you doing in my phone while I was sleeping!"

"I wasn't in—"

"Think about the lie before telling it, Ash. I know for a fact you sent something to Baylei because how would she know you were lying in my bed? I do not like playing childish games!"

"Oh, so you are mad at me because your bitch chewed you out about a text! Yeah, I sent her a picture showing her the reason she's in St. Thomas. You wanted to spend more time with me without worrying about her being suspicious, correct? So, I let her know." Ashley stood with her arms crossed over her chest without any remorse. "We've been creeping around for years since you've been with her, Noah. She's not who you want to be with. I'm tired of being the stand-in girlfriend when it benefits you! Even your mother doesn't want you with her! Everyone knows we belong together."

"You told Baylei what my mother truly thought of her? Ashley, you know how I feel about Baylei and you destroyed what I had with her by running your mouth. What did you tell her about my mother?"

Noah wanted to know honestly what type of damage he was facing with Baylei. From the sound of things, she was livid about whatever was revealed to her. Ashley was fidgeting nervously as her arms fell to her sides. Inching away from Noah, he noticed and was in her face in a flash.

"Answer me, dammit! What the fuck did you say to her?" Noah grabbed Ashley by the shoulders and shook her firmly.

"I—I sent a screenshot of a message Elizabeth and I had the other day."

Dragging Ashley back to his bedroom, Noah pushed her toward her phone and she stumbled on her feet. "Pull that shit up so I can see it!"

Ashley's hands shook vigorously as she scrolled through her phone. Hesitating as if she couldn't find what Noah asked for, Ashley finally passed the phone to him. Noah read the entire thread and threw the phone against the wall after he finish reading. He paused and glared at her momentarily before grabbing her around the neck and slammed her head against the wall.

"You have ruined my relationship, Ashley! Why would you do that? You and I have something special between the two of us. Baylei had nothing to do with any of it. We were fine the way we were and you just had to go a step further and let it be known what we have going on!"

"I'm not cool with being your side chick, Noah. You were just professing your love for me mere hours ago. Make a decision now! I'm not doing this shit with you another day. That black bitch doesn't deserve you anyway! I'm the woman for you! We were born to be together, Noah."

"Get your clothes on, Ashley, and get out of my fucking house! I don't want to discuss this with you right now."

Noah went into the bathroom and slammed the door. He called Baylei's phone numerous times, getting the same result; the voicemail. Baylei probably blocked him from contacting her and Noah was going to allow her to enjoy her vacation. They had a lot to discuss once she returned to Chicago. In the meantime, he had to figure out how he was going to rectify the problem Ashley caused. The bathroom door crept open and Noah stared at Ashley through the mirror.

"I can't believe you're putting me out for that nigger! I won't come second to someone that's beneath me!"

Noah turned around and before Ashley could blink, he back-handed her across the face. She fell into the wall and slid slowly to the floor. Ashley palmed her cheek as the tears cascaded down her face.

"The disrespect stops here! Don't ever refer to my woman as a nigger! I've stood back too long allowing this shit to take place right in front of me, but not anymore! Get out, Ashley, and don't return until I call for you to do so. In other words, don't call me. I'll call you."

Ashley scrambled to her feet and rushed out of Noah's sight. He calmly walked to the shower, turning on the water. Hurriedly, Noah undressed and stepped under the stream of water. He knew he had to go to his mom's so he could set her straight just like he'd done with Ashley.

***

It didn't take long for Noah to get dressed. He called into the office and informed his secretary that he would be in later in the day. Noah wanted to address the issue between his mother and Baylei once and for all. Technically, he was upset that everything unfolded the way it did because he could've put a stop to it all before it escalated to the level it had.

The drive to his parents' home took longer than usual since Noah was barely doing the speed limit. He had tried calling Baylei several times since leaving his house, but received the same results. As Noah pulled into the driveway, his mother pulled the front door open as he stepped from his car.

"Noah Connery, get your ass in this house!" Elizabeth yelled as she stood on the porch. "Ashley already called and told me you put your hands on her over that black girl."

"Mom, I'm not here to talk about Ashley. I want to speak with you respectively about my woman." Noah walked up the steps and went into the house, moving past his mother.

As Noah entered the family room of his parents' home, he saw his father sitting on sofa with his glass of bourbon. It was ten o'clock in the morning and John was drinking alcohol. That was one of the issues Noah had with him. John drank no matter what time of day it was, and that bothered his son to the fullest. Elizabeth sat beside her husband and Noah sat across from them on the loveseat. The room was quiet until Noah broke the silence by clearing his throat.

"So, Noah, what brings you to my humble abode?" Elizabeth asked with a small grin.

Noah chuckled. "Mom, like I told you when I arrived, I want to know why are you speaking badly about Baylei."

Elizabeth squinted at her son with a scowl. His father looked back and forth between the two of them, but didn't speak a word.

John crossed his ankles and sipped his bourbon as if he was waiting for the tea to be spilled.

"I know you're not coming in my house to talk about that black bitch! What I discuss with Ashley is between the two of us and isn't any of your concern. By the way, nothing I said was a lie. She doesn't deserve you,"

"Mother, you will respect Baylei! I've sat back for years listening to you belittle her, call her everything except a Child of God. It stops now! I will not tolerate the disrespect another day!"

John slammed his glass onto the coffee table and stood to his feet. "Who do you think you are talking to my wife like that?" He stalked over to his son and pointed his finger in his face. "Noah, I didn't raise you to date anyone outside of our race. It has been forbidden since the day you were born. I've sat back long enough while you parade around with that nigger and never opened my mouth when you brought her around." John was red-faced and breathed like a raging bull.

"Get rid of the jigaboo or you will be cut off permanently. It's time for you to realize Ashley is the woman for you. The black bitch is no longer allowed anywhere near this family. So, what is it going to be, Son?"

Noah was seething from the words his father spewed. Elizabeth sat back, enjoying the show that played before her. He loved his parents, but it was time for him to sever ties and live life the way he saw fit. Noah stood to his feet and moved his father's finger from his face. John grabbed him by the collar of his shirt and he pushed his father hard in the chest.

"I've done everything asked of me since I was a young boy. I finished my schooling from elementary through college with honors! I aced law school and passed the bar with my eyes closed and made both of you proud. Your words, not mine. Never been in any trouble, take care of my own bills, but I can't date who the fuck I want because my parents are racist bigots that judge a person by the color of her skin. You both disgust me! Fuck this family! I choose Baylei."

82

Noah stepped around his father and stomped to the door. His mother's voice halted his movements. "If you leave this house and continue frolicking around with that whore, the minute I find out, your trust fund will be no more!"

Noah left his parents' home in a huff. The whole house shook when he slammed the door behind him. Elizabeth started crying because her only son chose a black woman over her. She knew Noah didn't care about the money. So when he left, she knew her son wasn't coming back unless they accepted the woman he wanted to be with.

Meesha

Chapter 10

Baylei left the suite to call Noah about the messages she received. She had been walking for miles with no destination in mind because she knew nothing about St. Thomas. The tears that streamed from her eyes weren't from hurt, but more so from the anger that built up over time. Wiping her face, Baylei looked out into the ocean and decided to sit and reflect on the last couple of years.

Taking her shoes off, Baylei walked across the sand to a lounge chair closer to the water's edge. She sat down and relaxed her back against the cushion and closed her eyes. A vision of Noah and Ashley making love played behind her lids. The waterworks started again and ran into her ears.

"Are you okay?" Baylei looked up through the tears that continued to fall from her eyes. "This is a private beach. Are you staying at the Ritz Carlton?" He had on a white polo shirt with the hotel's logo on the right side of his chest with tan cargo pants. The word Patrol was stitched on his left sleeve.

"No," Baylei responded sitting upright. "I'm actually staying at the Margaritaville resort. I apologize for trespassing," she said, rising to her feet to leave the premises. "I was waiting on a friend."

At that moment, a dark-skinned muscular guy made his way toward Baylei and the patrol dude. He stood over six feet tall and was very handsome. Baylei forgot all about her relationship problems once she laid eyes on him. The black tank he wore had his muscles on display and the baller shorts left nothing to imagine about the log that was hidden in plain sight.

"Hey, babe. Sorry I took so long. I didn't expect you to get here so fast."

Baylei was perplexed because she had no idea what he was talking about. She didn't know who the sexy Adonis was or what his plans were, but she was glad he interceded in what was going on. The patrol guy had his hand on his walkie talkie and it all made sense. Mr. Fine was saving Baylei from getting in trouble for being on the beach. She jumped right into character once she caught on.

"I haven't been here too long." Baylei walked into his arms and hugged the stranger tight.

"Ahem." The patrol dude cleared his throat to get their attention. "Are you staying here at the Ritz?"

"As a matter of fact, I am. You are taking your job a little too seriously, man. Move the fuck around and stop harassing people. Go make your rounds and leave folks alone."

"I need to make sure only guest of the hotel is on the premises. I will need proof that you are staying here."

"I'm staying in the Presidential Suite, room 6509. There's your proof. Come see me."

The stranger grilled the patrol guy until he took the hint and walked away. He looked down at Baylei and took in all the beauty standing before him. He'd seen her the moment she took her shoes off and followed her every move until that rent-a-cop started hounding her. There was no way he was going to let her get away without approaching her.

"Are you alright?" he asked, glancing into her chestnut brown eyes. They were red and so was her nose. She looked like she'd been crying.

"I will be. Thank you for coming to my rescue. I wasn't thinking when I stopped here without checking for signs. If I'd known this was a private beach, I would've kept going," she said, looking everywhere but at him. "I'll let you go about your day. I've taken up enough of your time. Thanks again." Baylei forced a smile, turning to walk away.

"Whoa, I'm not letting you go that easily. Allow me to introduce myself at least," he said, blocking her from going any further. "Hello, Beautiful, my name is Chade. And you are?"

Baylei was mesmerized as she watched his lips move, and didn't hear one word that came out of his mouth. The way his lips parted had her lady parts pulsating like the beat of her heart. Any thoughts of Noah were out the window. The tall glass of water standing in front of her was the only thing on her mind. His beard framed his lips and it was very appealing to Baylei. The thought of gliding her kitty along it was on the forefront of her mind.

"Are you still with me?" he asked, snapping his fingers in front of her face.

"Uh, sorry. What were you saying?"

"I asked what your name is." Chade laughed.

"Baylei. Yeah, Baylei. My name is Baylei," she said, sounding like a parrot that learned its first word. "I didn't catch your name, Mr.—"

"Chade," he replied, fighting the urge to move the hair that was blowing in the warm breeze from her face. The small movement was irritating him because he wanted to see all of her beauty.

"Nice to meet you, Chade. How tall are you? Don't answer that. I didn't mean to say it out loud."

Chade smiled and licked his lips. He gave Baylei's body a once over, liking what he saw. "To answer the question you didn't mean to ask, I'm six foot four, two hundred thirty pounds, thirty-two, no children, single, and would love to get to know you, Miss Baylei."

Baylei blushed and turned her head so Chade couldn't see the effect his words had on her.

"Have you eaten? How about joining me for lunch?"

"Lunch? Oh my God, I have to get back to the resort. My friends may be worried sick because I've been gone longer than anticipated."

"Where are you staying? I'll have my car service take you back."

"No, no. I have a car service I can call. I'll see you around sometime. It was nice meeting you, Chade." Baylei put her shoes on and her phone rang. Glancing down, she saw Jordyn's name on display and answered quickly.

"Lei, where are you? Me and Toni walked the entire resort looking for you and was about to call the authorities."

"You don't have to do that. I'm on my way back. I had to clear my head. We can talk over lunch when I get back to the resort."

"Don't ever do that shit again. All the damn women coming up missing in these damn countries and you wandering around. Hurry back so I can whoop your ass!"

Jordyn hung up and the anger was evident in her tone and words. Baylei immediately dialed Mark's number and he told her he would be there in five minutes. While she waited, Chade never left her side. The limo pulled up and Chade opened the door before Mark could even get out to do so. When she was comfortably inside, he leaned down and smiled.

"Me and a couple of friends are going to check out one of the parties on the beach tonight. You and your friends should come out with us. What do you say?"

"I'm staying at the Margaritaville resort. Give me a call. Ask for Baylei Jefferson's room. See you later, Chade." Baylei smiled.

"Indeed, Beautiful," he said, closing the door.

Mark pulled away from the curb slowly. The way Chade called Baylei beautiful reminded her of ChanceLover. It always made Baylei smile when she read the messages he sent and it was no different with Chade. Baylei was caught up in her own world until the partition lowered.

"Be careful out here, Baylei. You can't trust everyone that appears to be nice to you. Besides, how would Noah feel about you talking to other men?"

"Stay out of my business, Mark. What I do on this trip has nothing to do with Noah. If I'm not mistaken, you signed up to drive me around, not monitor my movements. Now raise the partition and get me back to the resort, please."

Mark did what Baylei asked and pressed the gas to get her back to the resort safely. Baylei didn't wait for him to open the door. She got out and went inside to tell her friends about the fine man she'd met. Mark, on the other hand, sent Noah a text filling him in on what he had witnessed.

*****

"Lei, who the hell is this nigga and where are we going?" Toni yelled from her room.

"I don't know who he is, but his ass is fine! Wait 'til you see him. All I know about him is, his name is Chade."

"You mean like Chad with an E?" Jordyn asked. "Sounds like a white man to me."

"For your information, Smart Ass, he's filled with melanin. My days of dating outside my race are over. I won't put up with the bullshit I just went through ever again. On my daddy, the next muthafucka would die behind that shit."

Toni loved the way Baylei was letting her old self out of the box she'd been in. The ghetto swang was flowing without force and she was smiling more than ever. Noah hit a nerve playing with Baylei's intelligence. Toni believed she downgraded herself in a sense to please him.

Noah had underestimated Baylei and she was about to capitalize off his ass. When Baylei revealed how much money she saved every month from what she called her "Noah fund", the trio danced around the suite while unpacking.

Baylei stepped out of her room wearing a green and white striped crop top with the matching shorts. Her cheeks peeked out of the bottom, but they were sitting up just right. The roped choker around her neck set off her caramel skin tone along with the bracelet of the same material. Baylei's hair was pulled into a messy bun with curly tresses flowing on each side. The green strappy stilettos made her legs appear longer than they actually were.

"Damn, bitch! You not playin' wit 'em! I haven't seen you in your element in quite some time. It's about to go down in St. Thomas."

"Shut up, Jordyn! You act like I've been wearing moo-moos and shit." Baylei laughed.

"May as well. Your ass was walking around looking like Princess Diana every damn day. It's been forever since I've actually seen you in a pair of jeans or in an outfit like that."

"Don't do me." Baylei rolled her eyes playfully. "I started wearing shit that goes well with the atmosphere of the other side."

"That shit is dead because you about to have heads turning, tongues wagging, and muthafuckas fighting for *all* of your attention tonight. Hell, I think I need to change my outfit."

"No, you don't. What you have on is cute and you know it."

The phone across the room started ringing. Jordyn walked across the room and Toni entered looking just as good. Baylei touched up her makeup in the mirror on the wall.

"Damn, friend. Chade is on the phone and his voice just made my yoni twitch. Where are his homeboys?"

"They will be there tonight. I don't know how many, but we'll see."

Baylei had a walk as if she was on the runway whenever she wore stilettos. Picking up the receiver, she cleared her throat while glancing in the direction of Toni and Jordyn as they shuffled around pretending, they weren't eavesdropping on her call.

"Hey, Chade. Where's the party?"

"We're going to the Sapphire Beach Bar. Your resort is on the way to the beach. I don't mind stopping to pick you ladies up."

Baylei whispered to her friends and Chade listened while they decided what to do. He heard two other voices outside of Baylei's and knew right away he would be letting Malik and Vincent know what was up. Samir's ass was bringing Selena along, so he was going to be caked up for the night. Ahmad, of course, would be with his soon-to-be wife. Whatever the case, Chade knew he had Baylei on lock.

"Okay, sorry about that. Just so you know, there's three of us."

"No problem. The limo has more than enough space. I'll see you in about ten minutes, Beautiful."

Chade ended the call and Baylei stood with the phone to her ear. The butterflies in her stomach were fluttering a mile a minute because she was afraid of the thoughts that were dancing in her head. Baylei looked down at her heels and knew they were not a good choice for the beach.

"Lei, what did he say?" Toni asked.

"We are going to a beach party. Good thing I love the color green. I have the perfect pair of sandals to wear with this outfit," she said putting the receiver back on the base.

"Fuck all that. Will his friends be there?" Toni asked seriously.

"I believe so. He didn't say anything about his friends though. He will be here shortly so I have to change my shoes."

"No, put the sandals in your purse. Change them once we get to the beach. You are wearing the fuck out of those and your strut will get you the dick for sure," Toni chuckled.

Baylei crossed the room and pushed Toni's head back as she passed her. "I've told you; I'm not fucking anyone on this trip. If that's what you decide to do, have at it," she said as she disappeared into her room.

"That's what your mouth say. I can't wait to sing 'I told you so' in a few days!" Toni yelled while laughing loudly.

Toni stood at the door and Jordyn applied another coat of lip gloss to her lips as Baylei emerged with a medium-sized green Chanel bag that went perfectly with her outfit. She had added large hoop earrings and they were ready to hit the beach. Toni led the way out of the room and Baylei checked to see if she had her key card. Once she determined she had it, they took the elevator down to the ground floor.

"Girl, I hope this party is live," Toni said, pushing the exit door open. "I'm ready to twerk—" She stopped mid-sentence when she saw the stretch limo parked out front. It wasn't the vehicle that made her breath get caught in her throat. It was the fine specimen that stood outside of it. "Whew, chile. I know damn well that's not our ride for the evening. Just looking at all this chocolate is giving me a sweet tooth."

"Which one is Mr. Chade?" Jordyn asked. "I don't want to step on your shoes, sis."

"He's the one in the middle. But his friends are just as fine."

Chade moved forward as if he could hear his name. Baylei led the pack down the walkway and was greeted with a loving hug. She stepped back, but Chade didn't let her hands go.

"You look nice, Beautiful."

"Thank you." She smiled. "These are my friends, Toni and Jordyn." Baylei eased her right hand out of his grasp and turned to her girls.

"Hello," they both said in unison.

"Nice to meet you both. These are my guys Malik, Vincent, Ahmad and his soon-to-be wife Chasity, and Samir and his wife Selena."

Malik eyed Toni and she was thinking about all the things she could do with his lean body. His milk chocolate complexion was smooth and his goatee was crisp around his mouth just like the lining of his fade. He stood with his legs spread apart and the white linen pants were loose, making it hard for Toni to determine if his man parts were worth entertaining.

Vincent waved and stepped into the awaiting door of the limo. Chade thought he would be excited to have women in his presence, but the woman he claimed to have may have played a part in his demeanor. Samir said hello and his wife glared at the trio with a scowl. Toni laughed because neither one of them were going to attempt to get at her man.

"Okay, ladies. Let's go have fun." Chade motioned for them to climb into the limo.

There was more than enough room, just as Chade mentioned. Baylei and her friends sat side by side and it was quieter than a church service during prayer. Selena and Chasity were holding on to their men for dear life and Toni's petty ass was trying hard not to laugh again. Chade got in and sat in the empty seat next to Baylei and the driver pulled away from the resort.

"Come sit by me, sexy." Malik patted the seat next to him while looking at Toni. When she didn't move, he pointed right at her. "I'm talking to you." Malik held his hand out to assist her.

"My name is Toni. I don't mind sitting next to you." Toni moved slowly, taking his hand.

"Um, Malik, how is Ailani?"

"Selena, mind your muthafuckin' business. What that man does has nothing to do with you," Samir said, chastising his wife. She glared at him but didn't open her mouth again.

Nipsey Hussle's "Victory Lap" blared through the speakers. The awkwardness in the limo had dissipated for the most part. It didn't take long to arrive at the beach. The entire ride, Selena rolled her eyes at the ladies she felt invaded their space. The limo came to a complete stop and the driver opened the door. Everyone filed out and the party on the beach was in full swing.

Baylei swung her hips from side to side while snapping her fingers to the beat of "Action" by Terror Fabulous. The reggae music was flowing through her body and she loosened up with every twist of her hips. It was their first night in St. Thomas and she was ready to turn up. Feeling a pair of hands on her waist, Baylei looked over her shoulder and glanced up. Chade was moving in sync with her and after a moment, they were putting on a show with their sexual movements.

After the song ended, another jam followed suit and Chade held Baylei's hand and led her onto the sand. Her stilettos sunk down deep. Stumbling, she squeezed Chade's hand and pulled back gently. He stopped and caught her before she could fall.

"I think those are the wrong shoes for the beach, Beautiful. I love how they look on your pretty feet, but they must come off before you break your neck. Hold me around my neck so I can help you."

"Chade, I can manage. I brought a pair of sandals with me. They're in my bag."

Baylei reached into her purse and removed the sandals. Chade held Baylei up while she took the heels off her feet. She put her foot down and her toes sank down into the warm sand. Taking the other stiletto off, she placed them in her bag before placing her feet into the sandals.

"Okay, I'm ready. Sorry about that mishap."

"Now let's have some fun around this place. Would you like something to drink?" Chade asked, walking through the crowd of people that were partying.

Baylei glanced around, looking for her friends, and spotted Toni dancing with Malik, but Jordyn was nowhere in sight. She saw Chade's other friends standing by the bar where they were headed. Getting closer to their destination, Jordyn came into view with a frozen drink in her hand. Baylei let out a sigh of relief because she was ready to call a search party until her friend was found.

Chade ordered himself a rum punch as Baylei talked to Jordyn. He took it upon himself to order for her and chose a drink called the Bushwacker. It contained chocolate piña colada, coffee liqueur, cream of coconut, dark rum, and vodka. The hurricane glass was beautiful, just like the woman that would be drinking the content from a straw.

"Mister Lover Man!"

"Shaba!" all of Chade friends said loudly over the music. He turned his attention to the voice and smiled from ear to ear.

"Sanji, my nigga! The homie said you wasn't going to make it." Chade gave his college friend a brotherly hug.

"I wasn't because I had a couple of training sessions set up, but I knew being here for my boy would be so important to him. After moving shit around last week, I had Ahmad ship my fit to me and told him to keep it to himself. Sneaking up on you niggas and seeing the look on your face was priceless."

Sanji was the sixth link to the brotherhood. He had graduated college and moved back home to New York. He wanted to be closer to his mom because she fell ill and he had to be there for her every step of the way. Sanji became a firefighter, putting in work and climbed the ladder fairly quickly. When he left Cali, Sanji was a lanky-ass dude, but he wasn't the same person standing in front of Chade in St. Thomas.

"What the hell you been doing? I know being a firefighter didn't buff you up like that," Chade said, talking about the muscles that protruded from the short-sleeved button-down shirt Sanji wore.

"Man, we have to do better with communication. We're all doing our thang out here, but just a phone call away. I've been personal training for about three years now. It started at the firehouse. Fucking with the hoses and slinging axes and shit during calls. I kind of turned into a fitness junkie and decided to help others get in shape while getting paid for it. I have my own personal trainer gym and everything."

"Damn, fam. That's what's up. I'm proud of your accomplishments."

Baylei walked over and Chade handed the Bushwacker to her and she took a sip. Smacking her lips, she took another sip and nodded her head indicating she liked it. Chade winked at her and smiled. Sanji saw the exchange and his eyebrow rose in surprise. He never thought he'd see the day Chade gave a female any type of affection, but this woman had his boy smitten and Chade was clueless. Sanji wanted to see just how deep his friend was with the beauty, he decided to test his theory to see if he was correct.

"How you doing, Miss Lady? I'm Sanji; and you are?"

"She's mine, nigga." Chade laughed, wrapping his arm around Baylei's shoulder. "Her name is Baylei, by the way. This is her friend Jordyn."

Chade diverted Sanji's attention away from Baylei and the shit was funny to his friend. Just as he thought, Chade was going to fall in love with the woman he was holding on to tightly. Sanji didn't know how long they'd been together, but there was definitely chemistry between the two of them.

Chade was a playboy and would never be seen hugged up on a woman, handing her drinks and claiming her as his own. That had never happened in the past. It was a sight to see for Sanji but he loved it because it was about time for his brother to stop playing the field and settle down.

Sanji stepped over to Jordyn with his hand held out and introduced himself. "How you doing, Jordyn. Damn, you're beautiful."

The yellow sheer pantsuit that adorned her body complemented her radiant bronze skin to a tee. The long faux locs she wore in her head flowed down her back and were pulled from her face, showing all of her features. Jordyn's cheekbones were high, her full lips glazed in the light that beamed down on her. The sheerness of her outfit left nothing to imagine. She was toned in all the right places, but it was evident that she was self-conscious about her midsection. It wasn't too big, but there was a little fluff there. Sanji had no problem with fluff.

"Thank you," Jordyn said, placing her hand in his.

Sanji raised her hand to his lips and kissed the back of it. The way her fingertips grazed his thin beard sent shivers down her spine.

Immediately, the thought of raining her juice down his chin to give the hair a bit of moisturizer plagued Jordyn's mind. She looked up at him and automatically wanted to run her fingers through his long locs while riding his luscious pink lips. Usually, Jordyn would shy away from the pretty boy type of men because they weren't attracted to women as dark as herself, but Sanji seemed to be admiring everything about her, and the sparkle in his eye told her everything she needed to know.

"Walk with me so I can drink with ya and get to know you."

"You were just lusting over my friend though. I'm not an afterthought type of woman, Sanji." Jordyn didn't move when Sanji walked toward the bar and stopped when he heard her words.

"Nah, Sweetie, I never had my eye on your girl. I knew the way Chade was looking at her would make him react. It's the way I can tell if he's really feeling a female. Now, are you going to head to the other side of this bar with me?"

Jordyn looked over at Baylei and she nodded her head for her friend to go with Sanji. "No Guidance" by Chris Brown started playing and Sanji grabbed Jordyn and started dancing with her. He sang in her ear along with the song and Jordyn had the biggest smile on her face. The lyrics sounded good coming from his mouth, but she wasn't taking it seriously because she had just met him two minutes prior.

She got lost in the scent of his Tom Ford Black Orchid cologne. Jordyn could tell what a man was wearing without seeing the bottle. She was obsessed with following the new fragrances that premiered because one day she would have a man to buy some for. Sanji didn't disappoint because he smelled divine and she buried her face into his chest. It was rock hard and his pecs were strong. Curiosity may have killed the cat, but that didn't stop Jordyn from running her hands down his abs. Fuck a six pack; Sanji had an eight pack, if that was even a thing.

A group of females stepped onto the sand and their loud 'ayes' and 'heys' got everyone's attention. Ahmad's fiancée Chasity got excited and ran through the sand, dodging people to get closer to them. Hugs were given all around and they started dancing in a huddle. Baylei looked at Chade and smiled nervously.

"Everything will be alright. I know Chasity and Selena didn't give a warm feeling when we picked you and your girls up, but Selena has to scope you out before she can let her guard down and accept you in our circle. I don't know much about Chasity so I really can't speak for her."

"I don't need anyone to accept me. I don't know any of you and after tonight, I may never see any of you again, so I don't care how anyone looks at me. I'm here with you because you asked and to have a good time. Nothing more, nothing less."

"You will definitely see me again. I don't know about any of them, but yeah, me for sure."

Baylei smiled because she really did want to spend more time with Chade. He was cool and she enjoyed his company.

Toni finally made her way to the bar after she and Malik danced all over the sandy beach. They were really feeling one another and Toni didn't have a problem with Selena's messiness back in the limo when she mentioned Malik's girlfriend. Hell, she wasn't trying to take him home with her. All she wanted was a fuck buddy for her duration in St. Thomas. It was going to be his problem when he explained to his bitch about what happened while he was on vacation.

Mulatto's "Muwop" came on. Jordyn ran over from the bar and on cue, the trio started twerking like no one's business. Asses bouncing to the beat had every man on the beach mesmerized and that only made them go harder with their moves.

'Cause I'm a freaky girl
Get it from my mama
I'm not with the games
I'm with all the drama
Make 'em give me brain in the front seat of the Hummer
Make 'em give me brain in the front seat of the Hummer

The lyrics to the song didn't define the women, but the looks on the faces of Chasity and her girls couldn't tell them different. They made it a competition thing by twerking themselves and felt like shit because the ripple of Baylei's, Jordyn's, and Toni's asses had the men in a trance. The animosity was on high and when the song ended, the daggers could cut through the air as if it was meant to be war. One of the girls in Chasity's crew stormed over and stood in Chade's face. He frowned upon her and crossed his arms over his chest.

"What's up, Chade? This how we doing it now? You knew I was coming, but you're in the next bitch's face," she said with an attitude.

Baylei knew that was her cue to allow Chade to handle whatever issue ole girl had with him. It had been a long time since she was in any type of altercation with a female about a nigga. He wasn't hers to argue and fight over, so Baylei wanted to eliminate herself from the equation before shit got ugly.

Chapter 11

Chade watched Baylei dance and knew she was letting her hair down to enjoy herself to the fullest. He enjoyed the performance she and her friends put on and nodded his head in approval. His dick rocked up as the vision of standing behind her, buried deep in her pussy while she moved on his joint just like she was dancing. He felt that shit and gripped his pipe to calm it down. With his lip tucked between his teeth, Chade looked up and his python deflated instantly when he saw Sakeenya walking in his direction.

Sakeenya's approach on Chade pissed him off. Baylei walked away and left Chade to handle whatever issue he had with the envious female. There wasn't anything between the two of them other than Chade using her tonsils to toggle the tip of his dick a time or two. Sakeenya hadn't been around in months and wanted to use her position as Chasity's bridesmaid to call herself confronting him.

"What you doing, shawty?"

"You knew I was going to be here! How are you in another bitch's face disrespecting me like that?" Sakeenya rolled her neck with every word, embarrassing herself in front of everyone. Chasity walked over and tried to pull her friend away, but she snatched out of her grasp. "No, Chas. This motherfucker is going to answer me!"

Chade rubbed his hand down his face and attempted to walk away. He hated any type of confrontation with a woman, especially in public. It was distasteful and looked bad for both parties. Sakeenya pushed him in his back and Chade paused, but continued moving. This was the reason he didn't want to be in a committed relationship. Chade didn't have the patience to deal with the nagging, jealousy, and having someone questioning him about what he was doing within his life.

As bad as he wanted to go back to Baylei, he had to take the drama away from her. It wasn't a good look for anyone when they were trying to get to know a person. Even if it was for a week. Chade walked until he was far away from the partygoers and Sakeenya was right on his heels. When they were out of earshot, he turned abruptly with fire in his eyes.

"The fuck is wrong with you, Keenya?" Chade asked angrily.

"No, what the fuck is wrong with you? I haven't heard from you in months, then I pull up in another country to you all in the next bitch's face!"

"Don't raise your voice at me. We have never been a couple and I've never given you the impression that we would ever be one either. You made yourself look like a fool in front of your friends and many strangers." Chade paused to give her the opportunity to speak, and when she didn't say anything, he continued.

"I don't like to air my business out for everyone to hear. It doesn't take a rocket scientist to know I've had some type of involvement with yo' ass. Any plans of doing it again has been cancelled by the way you acted back there. It would be in your best interest not to say anything else to me during the rest of this trip."

"That black Barbie got your nose wide open. She would never suck your dick the way I do, Chade. You will be knocking on my hotel room door in no time. I'm going to let you think you're done with me, but we both know that's never going to happen."

"Did it ever occurred to you that maybe I didn't enjoy the fellatio you gave me?

"I've never given you that!" she shrieked.

Chade smirked and shook his head. "Keenya, you just popped off about sucking my dick. You may want to broaden your vocabulary a little bit. That's another reason I couldn't be serious about you."

"What do you mean? There are no reasons other than that bitch back there!"

"That's where you're wrong. You have nothing going for yourself. From what you told me; you're living your life by the wish creed. Wishing you had money to do everything you want to accomplish without getting your ass up to work for it. I guess you thought you hit the jackpot when Chasity brought you around her man's people. Well, I have news for you. I like my women with ambition, and if she doesn't fit the criteria, sucking dick is all she can do for me. That's the category you were placed in, sweetheart."

"You ain't shit! For your information, I've never asked you for anything. Fuck you, Chade. You won't get the chance to disrespect me ever again. Do what you want to do. You're not the only nigga in St, Thomas. I'll have someone in my bed before the end of the night."

"Keenya, I haven't disrespected you at all. You're doing a good job of that yourself. Good luck finding someone to keep you company, because it won't be me. I'm going back to the party. Be careful out here though."

Chade walked around Sakeenya and headed back to the party. His mind replayed the little argument and it made him question Chasity's loyalty to his boy even more. Birds of a feather flocked together. If Sakeenya had the mindset of getting money, he was quite sure her girl was on the same shit. It also had him thinking about stepping back a little from pursuing Baylei so strongly. She might be out to find a nigga to finance her ass too.

The party was in full swing by the time he made his way back and Baylei and her girls were fucking the sand up to the tunes of Megan Thee Stallion's "Body". Chade went straight to the bar. Sanji handed him a double shot of Hennessy soon as he propped his back against the bar.

"Ya girl bought this for you. She said you would need it." Sanji laughed. "What the fuck was that about, bro?"

Chade threw the shot back and place the glass behind him on the bar before responding. "Me letting a birdbrain top me off. Nothing major. Shawty in her feelings because she thought coming here gave her easy access to a nigga. I haven't talked to her in months. Any other female would've taken that as a sign to leave me alone. Not Sakeenya. I'm glad she never let me fuck, because she would be acting ten times worse than she just did."

"Where the hell you meet her? She got a body on her."

"She's one of Chasity's friends."

Chade's eyes were on Baylei as she twined her hips to the beat. Her movements alone let him know she could ride the fuck out of his joint if given the opportunity. He shook the thought from his head because he was going to take a different approach with Baylei.

His dick wasn't going to like it, but he would understand in the long run.

"Is Chasity a good girl? What's her story?" Sanji asked.

"I personally don't think she's marrying for love. I've voiced that to Ahmad, but he's in too deep to hear me out. All we can do is wait for shit to unfold. Maybe I'm wrong, but I don't think so. Chasity is one of those Instagram models types."

"Me and Ahmad talk, but we've never discussed his relationship," Sanji said looking out at the partygoers. "Man, who is Jordyn? She is fine as hell!"

"I don't know. I just met Baylei earlier today, actually."

"Hold up you met her here? So, ole girl spazzed out over a vacation fling?" He laughed.

"Yeah, man. That stupid shit would have a female on all kinds of bullshit. She doesn't know the dynamics of what's going on with me and Baylei anyway."

"Shawty needs to chill the fuck out. Enough about that shit. I may as well fill you in on what's been going on with me." Sanji took a sip of his beer. "I am transferring to the Los Angeles Fire Department as a sergeant."

"Get the hell outta here! Congratulations, bro. I'm proud of you." Chade gave Sanji a brotherly hug and pulled back. "What about Moms?"

"Thanks. I appreciate that. Mom is coming with me. She's tired of all the violence in Harlem and is ready to relocate. Los Angeles isn't much better, but the change of scenery would be good for her. After Pops passing, she hasn't been the same. It would brighten her up to see all of you guys all the time. I found a nice house not too far from Vincent."

"The crew is back together once again! You know we love Moms like our own and we got her. Welcome back to Cali, Man. It's time to celebrate your promotion. Aye, let me get six shots of Henny, baby girl," Chade called out to the bartender.

Waving the other guys over, Sanji shared his news and they were just as excited as Chade. Baylei, Toni, and Jordyn came over and Chade appeared nervous for a second. He didn't know what type of mindset Baylei would have after Sakeenya's shenanigans.

"Everything okay?" she whispered in his ear as she stood beside him.

"Yeah, I'm sorry 'bout that—"

"You don't have to explain anything to me, Chade. Whatever you and that woman has going on is between the two of you. I just met you a few hours ago. To be honest, you were wrong to invite me out knowing another woman would eventually show up under the impression she would be hanging with you for the duration of this trip."

Chade held his head down as he listened to what Baylei was saying. Even though her assumption didn't hit the mark at all, he understood where she was coming from. The way things occurred, it would look as if he invited Sakeenya to kick it with him. But that was far from the truth. Chade made eye contact with Baylei and grabbed her hand. She tried to pull away, but his grip was solid.

"You're right, I don't have to explain anything to you, but I will. Sakeenya isn't, nor has she ever been, my woman. I'm single as a piece of bread, Beautiful." Chade's gaze never wavered and Baylei didn't see any signs of deception. Then again, women never could see right away if a man was lying. Something had gone on between them for the woman to act the way she had.

"There is history, but nothing serious. I set the record straight when I led her away. She won't be a problem. I want to get to know you."

Baylei looked to her right and laughed. "Is that the reason she's shooting daggers over here along with her entourage?"

Instead of giving Sakeenya the satisfaction of knowing she was watching, Chade decided to pull Baylei into his arms without thought. "You don't have to worry about her."

"Do I look worried?" Baylei asked, looking up at him. "I'm not the one she should have a problem with. That's all you. I don't do drama, Chade. I can be the pettiest female if need be, though. I'll have her ass running to the car crying every time she sees us together."

Baylei had a twinkle in her eye and Chade knew she was up to no good. "As a matter of fact, you're my man for the week. Let's have some fun."

Baylei stood on her toes and kissed Chade's chin. She couldn't reach his lips because she was too short to reach them. He didn't miss a beat when he lowered his head and stole a little bit of her soul as he kissed her.

***

The night ended with plenty of drinks and dancing. Instead of getting back in the limo with Chade, Baylei and her friends called for Mark to pick them up. They had a lot of fun on their first night in St. Thomas and couldn't wait to see what the days ahead would be like. Once they entered the suite, all three of them fell onto a piece of furniture in the sitting room.

"Girl, Malik is so fine!" Toni hooted as she kicked her feet back and forth. "I almost left y'all asses at the beach when he asked if I wanted to get out of there. The only thing that stopped me was the fact the chick that made a scene with Chade was giving me a vibe. I had to stay put in case she needed a dose of an ass whooping."

"You peeped that shit too! I was watching her ass like a hawk because obviously, my girl over there was too busy trying to touch Chade's tonsils with her tongue to notice." Jordyn smirked.

"Oh, no, boo. I knew she was watching. That's why I gave her ass something to look at. Chade and I had a conversation about why she approached him the way she did. He claimed they have history, but there's nothing to it. I know there's more and frankly, I don't give a damn. He's my man for the rest of the trip. After that, he can do him."

Toni high fived her friend and clapped her hands in celebration. They all got comfortable in their positions to talk about the men they met. Jordyn really liked Sanji and had learned quite a bit about him. Not only was he fine, but he had a lucrative career and also own a few gyms where he did personal training.

Sanji was an only child that adored his mother. He was born and raised in New York and had the body of a God. Jordyn loved his long locs and his smooth demeanor. When he touched her face, his hands were softer than a baby's ass and one wouldn't have thought he was a firefighter.

"Jordyn, I saw how you were deep in thought with—what's his name?" Toni asked tucking her foot under her butt.

"Sanji." Jordyn blushed.

"Sanji. What type of name is that? Where is he from?"

"He's from New York, and I actually asked how his mother came up with his name. I learned a lot about him tonight. His mother is black and he gets a lot of his features from her. The name Sanji is actually Japanese. Seeing Sanji and listening to him speak, one wouldn't know he was half-Japanese. Born and raised in Harlem, his father was right there with them until he passed away a couple years ago."

"No way!" both Toni and Baylei screeched.

"You're right, I would've never guessed. He's hood as hell." Baylei laughed.

"Man, Malik is hood too. When he's around his friends. But he has a freaky side that I'm going to get acquainted with before I head back to the Chi. Would you believe me if I told y'all he is a doctor?"

"Toni, that man isn't a damn doctor," Jordyn rolled her eyes. "With all those damn muscles and the way he carries himself, he's a dope boy. Plus, he has a whole woman at home. Didn't you hear Selena ask him about *Ailani*?"

"I heard that shit loud and clear. Fuck Ailani! I'm riding that dick, bitch." Toni laughed as she got on her knees, moving as if she was actually riding something. "After I'm finished with his sexy ass, he's gonna be hiring a private investigator to get in touch with me because that bitch ain't gon' be able to please him another day."

"Bihhhhh you got no shame." Jordyn laughed. "I ain't mad atcha. If he doesn't care about her, why should you? There's already trouble in paradise because she's not here with him. No man is going to leave their significant other back in the states to go out of the country to his friend's wedding. Have fun with him every day."

Baylei laughed hard while holding her stomach. Toni was a damn fool when it came to her getting sexed by a good-looking man. She didn't care about his relationship status as long as he wasn't walking around with a boyfriend. Waiting for them to finish talking about their future sexcapades, Baylei went back to the subject of Malik being a dope boy.

"Going back to the occupation of these men, Jordyn, I can honestly say, every last one of them have careers. Malik is truly a doctor, Sanji I know is a firefighter, Chade is an accountant, we didn't get into what Samir did for a living, Ahmad is a software developer, and Vincent is an engineer. Never judge a book by its cover. As my mama always says, you can take a person out the hood, but you can't take the hood out of the person. There's a time and place for everything and they're all on vacation to have a good time. They can go back to being professional when they get back home."

As soon as Baylei finished her speech, her phone chimed with a notification alert. Fumbling around in her purse, she pulled out the phone she hadn't paid attention to all night and smiled. There was a message from ChanceLover. He hadn't reached out to her since earlier that morning and she knew he had something good to tell her about his trip.

"Y'all think about what I said. I have to go talk to my friend while I get ready for bed. Are we going out to ride the jet skis?" Baylei asked as she got up from the chair she was sitting in.

"I thought we were going scuba diving,"

"No, I thought we were going on the St. John tour and snorkeling tomorrow."

"Toni, I know for sure that's set up for Wednesday. But y'all figure out what we doing because I'm sleepy. It really doesn't matter what we do, to be honest. I'll see y'all in the morning."

Baylei left them to figure out their plans as she entered her room and closed the door. She went into the bathroom and turned the water on in the Jacuzzi tub to soak while messaging ChanceLover. After disrobing, she eased down into the huge tub and one of the jets so happened to be under her. The water gushed out and rubbed against Baylei's yoni, paralyzing her momentarily. She placed her phone on the side as she held on to the bar attached to the wall.

"Mmmmm," Baylei moaned as the force of water gave her kitty attention it wasn't designed to give. Rocking back and forth, her stomach clenched causing her lady parts to erupt just as strong as the water from the jets. "Fuck! Whew."

Cutting off the water, Baylei had to empty the water and start again. The orgasm had her body relaxed, but she was sleepy as hell. A woman would find a way to please herself no matter where she was. And that's exactly what happened with Baylei. The tub filled back up and Baylei eased in; avoiding the jets the second time around and laid her head back. She picked up her phone and opened the message in her inbox.

ChanceLover: Just wanted to stop in and see how your trip was going. I hope you had fun on your first day.

LeiLeiBay: Hey you. I had a very good time. Me and the girls really enjoyed ourselves. How was your day?

ChanceLover: My day was fabulous. I met this fine-ass female and we hung out tonight.

LeiLeiBay: You don't waste no time finding a woman to occupy your time, I see. I'm not mad at'cha. At least you don't have to worry about drama coming your way once you leave your location LOL

ChanceLover: you got that shit right. I do believe if I was back home, me and this one would definitely hit it off. I'm going to enjoy her company as much as I can without invading on her time with her people. We'll see though. I just got in and a nigga tired. I'll hit you up tomorrow. Be careful, Beautiful. Don't be getting to know any niggas too soon. I'm not there to protect you.

LeiLeiBay: Hell, I'm a big girl. I can handle myself so I'm good. You not the only one that's about to get to know someone for the week. You must've forgotten that I'm single now.

ChanceLover: That may be the case. I still want you to be careful out there. When the nigga approach you, I want to know all about his ass. If he can't tell you shit, move around because nine

times out of ten, he ain't the right one to spend time with. I'll talk to
you soon, Beautiful

LeiLeiBay: Later, Chance

Baylei closed the message and went to her Apple music play list. "Get you" by Daniel Caesar bounced off the walls of the bathroom. Chade's lips upon hers were vividly in her mind. She could feel the action as if it was happening in real time. The thought of him making love to her had Baylei blushing even though she was alone.

Who, who would've thought I'd get you?
And I'll take some time
Just to be thankful that I had days full of you, you
Before it winds down into memories
It's all just memories, no

Singing the lyrics to the song made her want to spend time with Chade more than ever. They were definitely going to make memories together and she was going to make sure she would forever be on his mind. Emerging deeper into the tub, Baylei closed her eyes and fantasize about her vacation boo that she couldn't shake from her mind.

Chapter 12

Chade's night came to an end once Baylei left the beach. Everything started winding down and he wanted to head back to the hotel. It was well after three in the morning and he'd been up damn near twenty-four hours. The thought of being tired never entered his mind until the beautiful woman was no longer by his side.

Chade could still feel the texture of her lips upon his own and the tingling feeling wouldn't go away no matter how many times he licked them. As he slid inside the limo, waiting for the driver to close the door, his eyes instantly closed when his back hit the cushioned seat. When the vehicle rocked slightly, he peeked through his lids and saw Sanji and Malik sitting across from him.

"We had to make sure you were good. I've never known you to leave a party before they said last call for alcohol."

"I'm good, Sanji. It's been a long day and I just want to get some sleep before we do this shit all over again later today."

"Are you sure that's all it is? I mean, your whole attitude changed once ole girl left the beach. The way y'all was making out, I thought you would have her in your room and not leaving without you." Sanji laughed, but Chade didn't.

"She's different from the other bitches I just smash and get ghost on. For some odd reason, I want to really get to know this one. We may not see each other after this week, and that's cool with me. In the end, I have a feeling she will be a friend of mine for life. The way we clicked, hasn't happened since—" Chade cleared his voice and shook his head. "This is different."

"Take your time. I mean, it's about time you give a woman a fair chance. Even if it's for a week."

Chade looked out the window as they passed the resort Baylei was staying. His mind wanted to tell the driver to go back, but his heart didn't want to treat her like a throw away. Instead, he sat back and listened as Malik and Sanji talked about random shit.

"Hey, do either of you know what's up with Vincent? He seemed kind of standoffish tonight. Every time I spotted him, he had his phone up to his ear or his head was down while he texted a mile a minute."

Chade tried to envision what Vincent was doing all night and came up with nothing the more he thought about it. He couldn't recall shit other than Baylei. Hunching his shoulders, Chade didn't know how to answer Sanji's question.

"Vince is probably trying to make things right with his girl. She asked to accompany him on this trip and he turned her down. I guess she didn't like that shit and thought he was on bullshit."

"Malik, what girl are you talking about? We have never seen that nigga with any damn woman. The only thing he does is talk about having a bitch. His ass is worse than Tommy on *Martin* about having a job. He ain't got no girl, man." They laughed at the way Chade made fun of Vincent because he had a valid point.

"Nah, he has a girl or somebody he's getting serious about. Vincent is just keeping her away from us for whatever reason. Whomever it is got his ass trained from afar because if you didn't notice, he didn't give Jordyn the time of day when you introduced them earlier."

"How the hell you know he wasn't checking out Toni, Malik?"

"Because I told his ass when she stepped out the door, that one was mine. Vincent wasn't trying to talk to nobody from the jump, Chade. So, he definitely has somebody that he is respecting, even when she's not present."

Chade thought about what he'd heard and wondered why his long-time friend was being so secretive. He wanted all of his boys to find someone to love, everyone except himself. Baylei would be his woman for one week, then he was back to manipulating any pussy that came his way when he returned to Cali.

Pulling up to the hotel, Chade waited his turn to exit. The lobby was quiet and it took no time for the elevator to open. As the car ascended, the friends made plans to meet for lunch because they already knew, nobody was making it down for breakfast. Chade was the last person to get off and he couldn't wait to lay down in the big king-sized bed.

The first thing he did was went to his inbox on social media and hit up LeiLeiBay. They chatted for a little bit before he told her to be careful and logged out. Chade decided to take a shower and was in and out in no time. Walking into the bedroom with a towel wrapped around his waist, there was a knock on his door. It couldn't have been anybody except one of the fellas and his guess was Malik's ass.

Without asking who it was, Chade just flung the door open. He wanted to slam the door closed once he saw who was on the other side. Anger surfaced inside of him the minute he laid eyes on Sakeenya.

"What are you doing in my doorway, Keenya?"

"Can I come in so we can talk?" she asked while staring downward. Chade watched as she licked her lips and that prompted him to look down as well. Unbeknownst to him, the head of his dick was playing peek-a-boo behind the towel.

Readjusting the towel, Chade crossed his arms over his chest. "No, you may not come in. There isn't anything to discuss."

"Tell me when a good time would be because obviously, I'm interrupting whatever you have going on in your room." Sakeenya chuckled when Chade didn't blink or respond. "Let me taste him real quick," she said, reaching her hand out to stroke his manhood.

"Don't touch me, man," he said, slapping her hand away. "Go back to your room and stay the fuck away from me. You drunk, and I'm not about to entertain your bullshit. I said all I had to say earlier and I'm standing on that shit. Respect me and I won't have to embarrass yo' ass more than you doing by yourself."

"Chade, you know I love you," Sakeenya whined.

"You don't love me. I told you in the beginning nothing was going to come from fuckin' with me. I'm a toxic nigga, Keenya. I don't have a love bone in my body. The only thing I'm capable of giving his pain. Loving a woman other than my mama is not something I'm trying to do. It's not what I'm trying to learn how to do. Long as I love myself, that's all the love I need."

Sakeenya dropped to her knees and tried her best to get to Chade's python. He laughed as he pushed her away. The elevator dinged and Chade grabbed Sakeenya by the arm, trying to pull her to her feet. Ahmad and Chasity headed toward his room and stopped abruptly.

"Keenya, what are you doing?" Chasity asked.

"What do it look like I'm doing? I'm trying to suck my man's dick!" She laughed, still trying to grab the towel from Chade's waist.

"Chasity, take her to the room and put her in the bed. She's drunk as hell."

"I don't need nobody to take me anywhere! I'm right where I want to be," Sakeenya hissed at her best friend.

"You are embarrassing yourself. Can't you tell he don't want you in his face? Don't ever beg for a man's attention. It's either he wants you or he don't. In this instance, it's obvious that he doesn't want anything to do with you," Ahmad said heatedly.

"I'm going to bed. Take her away from here so she can sleep that alcohol off."

Chade stepped back into the room as Ahmad helped Sakeenya to her feet. She was talking shit while being led to the elevator by Chasity. Ahmad stayed behind and he started laughing soon as the doors to the elevator closed.

"How the hell did she end up here?"

"Man, I don't know," Chade said, walking away from the door. "I opened the door thinking one of y'all were coming to chop it up, but it was her ass. Sakeenya was like a dog in heat trying to get at my dick. I would never fuck with her again because she's too dramatic for me. She wants to be a factor in my life when in reality, she will forever be jawbone in my eyes."

Ahmad laughed as he walked into the suite and closed the door. Chade went into the bedroom and changed into a pair of shorts and a tank. He returned to the living room and Ahmad had a drink in his hand while sitting on the sofa. Chade sat across from him with a huff.

"Why you call that girl jawbone? That wasn't right." Ahmad laughed heartily.

"She lucky I didn't call her messy-ass Hoover. Bitch can suck a dick through a straw; perfectly. She can give a thick milkshake a run for its money." Chade paused as he stared at his friend. "I know you don't want to hear this, but you better be sure about Chasity. Her girl is showing her true colors, and I'm quite sure your wife to be isn't too far behind."

"Sakeenya don't have anything to do with Chasity. I can honestly say, she's nothing like her friend."

Chade could tell his friend didn't like the comparison, but he saw what Ahmad couldn't see. Them bitches were out to get a bag and Chasity was going to keep the front going until the wedding was over. She was smart about how she played her cards. Chade wasn't buying her charade though.

"I don't know what Sakeenya said to you, fam. The two of them are like oil and water. Chasity is going to school for her Master's and I'm cool with taking care of her until she reaches her career goal. After she finishes, we will both be bread winners."

Chade sat back on the sofa and crossed his leg over his knee. Staring at his friend, he searched his memory bank back to something Ahmad had told him a few months back. When he finally gathered his thoughts, he calmly threw them back at his friend.

"Didn't you tell me Chasity worked as a hotel manager? When did she stop working?" Chade asked curiously.

"That's something only I need to be concerned about, Chade. Like I said before, Chasity isn't shit like Sakeenya." Ahmad sneered. "I would really appreciate if you wouldn't judge my girl by her friend's actions. Give me that much respect."

"You got it, bro. I won't apologize and I will be right by your side when you need me. I won't bring up Chasity in any more of our conversations. My door is open whenever. You have my word though, Ahmad. Finish your drink and leave when you're ready. I can't keep my eyes open a minute longer," Chade said, standing to his feet. "Do me a favor and keep Sakeenya away from me. I don't have anything to say to her."

Throwing the alcohol down his throat, Ahmad took the glass to the kitchenette and rinse it out. Chade stood in the doorway of his bedroom as Ahmad walked toward the door. Ahmad stopped suddenly then turned toward his best friend.

"I know you mean well, fam, and I appreciate your concern. You have always had my back, right or wrong. That means the world to me. Chasity means the world to me as well and I want you to accept her as being a part of my life just as I would when you meet that special someone."

Ahmad walked back to Chade and embraced him in a brotherly hug before making his exit. Chade stood looking at the door for a spell before walking across the room to secure the lock. He thought about what Ahmad said and decided to leave well enough alone. Chade had a feeling his friend was walking down the path to heartbreak and there was nothing he could do to intervene.

Chapter 13

"Baylei, wake up."

The sound of Toni's voice jarred Baylei out of the deep sleep she was in and she was pissed. It felt as if she'd just closed her eyes minutes prior. Struggling to open her eyes, Baylei threw the cover over her head and turned over.

"Baylei! Come on, get up. Noah's on my phone for you."

With the mention of Noah's name, Baylei sat up and glared at Toni. "Why the hell would Noah be calling you? Fuck him!" she said, lying back down.

"Obviously because he can't get you on your shit. I almost cussed his ass out. He knows I don't fuck with him like that."

"Tell his ass I'm asleep," Baylei snapped.

"You think I didn't? The muthafucka ain't trying to hear that. Take this damn phone! This will be the last time he'll be able to get through because I've already blocked that shit."

Baylei held out her hand for the phone. Once Toni chucked the device at her, she left and slammed the door on her way out. Baylei groaned as she sat up and snatched the phone from the bed. Taking a deep breath, she looked at the phone and laughed. Toni had the phone on mute, but what she had Noah's name programmed under was funny as hell. "Nasty Ass White Boy" was displayed across the top of the screen.

"What is it, Noah?" Baylei asked as soon as she unmuted the phone.

"Who is the nigger you getting all cozy with in St. Thomas? You thought I wasn't going to find out? I have eyes all over that resort. Why do you think I chose the destination?"

Baylei chuckled as she listened to Noah putting a little bass in his voice. If he thought she was scared because he knew about what she was doing the night before, he had another think coming because she didn't give two fucks. She was actually glad Mark ran his mouth.

"First of all, I want you to watch how you address my people. Nigger is a word I never want to hear fall from your lips ever again.

Secondly, I don't know why you are mad about me entertaining the next man when you're lying up with your very own Alicia Silverstone in Chicago. By the way, I hope that shit was fun." Baylei cackled.

"Ashley doesn't mean anything to me, babe."

"According to your mother, that's a lie. Look, I don't give a damn what's going on between y'all. All I know is what we had is over. Thanks for the trip, Noah. When I come back home, there won't be an *us*. We are done. Finito. Finished. We don't belong together because you have shown your true colors. You can't be a racist and call yourself in love with a black woman. There's just no way the two can mesh. I'm willing to help you make the decision you are dreading. I'm out."

"Bitch, it's not over until I say it's over. Your black ass needs me. Without me, you're not shit. I will make sure you don't make another dime in this city, nigger!"

"Well, well, well. The true Klansman emerges once again. Tell me how you really feel, Noah. Make that the last time you call me a nigger. I'll respect you more if you referred to me as nigga. Far as needing you, I've worked hard for everything I've accomplished. If you think the money you were dishing out monthly kept me afloat, think again. You just started a beautiful nest egg that's going to have me sitting nice for a very long time. Thanks, boo. I appreciate that shit."

"I'm going to allow you to enjoy your vacation. But if I hear about you being with that ni—that man again, when you get back, there will be hell to pay."

"Is that a threat? See, I haven't told any of my family members about you putting your hands on me. All it would take is one phone call and yo' ass will come up missing. Please don't threaten me with a good time, Noah. You don't want these types of problems. As far as the man I've been entertaining, tell Mark to pay attention so he can get graphic pics of me riding his dick. Fuck you, Noah."

Baylei hung up on him and threw the phone on the other side of the king bed. Closing her eyes, sleep was the furthest thing from her mind at that point. She stared out the window and got out of bed.

Walking onto the balcony outside of her room, she stared out into the ocean and Chade invaded her thoughts. The feel of his lips made hers tingle with the slightest touch of her tongue. The conversation with Noah was erased from her memory bank as if it never happened.

As Baylei looked out into the blue water, a vision of herself and Chade lying on the white sand played before her eyes. The way they stared at one another was a picture-perfect scene that was destined to be. Soon as she blinked, the image disappeared and the sound of the hotel phone ringing had Baylei turning around to head back inside. Just as she stepped back into the room, Toni entered without knocking.

"Respect my shit. I could've been in here playing in my love box."

"Ewww, that's nasty as hell, you freak. Chade is on the phone. Maybe he can play in your cooch for you and save you the trouble of trying to do it yourself." Toni grinned devilishly.

Baylei grabbed Toni's cell phone off the bed and pushed it into her chest as she all but ran to the table to pick up the receiver. She had no intentions of sleeping with Chade, but the way they were kissing and groping one another at the beach had her ready to change her mind. The way Noah called himself checking her made her decision that much easier too.

"Hello," Baylei said trying to hide the excitement in her voice.

"Good afternoon, Beautiful. I was wondering if you and your girls had anything planned for the day."

"Actually, we do. We are going out to ride the jet skis and do a little snorkeling."

"Oh, okay. That sounds like fun. When you're done with your excursions, I want you to go back to your suite and get some rest. You'll be going with me later on tonight. Ahmad and Chasity will be celebrating their upcoming nuptials upon a yacht, and I want you to be my plus one. It's a black-tie event by the way."

"Awww that's sweet of you. Thanks for the invite. I didn't pack anything to wear to such an event. I'm going to have to pass. Maybe we can get together tomorrow or something. Plus, I don't want to leave Toni and Jordyn behind. We came here together and I would feel bad having fun without them." There was a knock on the door as Baylei finished explaining why she couldn't accompany Chade for the night.

"Hold on a second. Someone's at the door."

"Take your time," Chade replied patiently.

Baylei placed the receiver on the table and made her way to the door. Looking through the peephole, she saw a woman on the other side waiting patiently for her to open the door. She was hesitant to open it, but curiosity got the best of her.

"May I help you?" she asked, peeking out of the small gap of the door.

"Yes, I have a delivery for Baylei, Toni, and Jordyn."

In a state of utter confusion, Baylei opened the door wider and her eyes widened at the sight of the cart the woman had sitting against the wall of the hall. There were boxes that appeared to be shoes along with three garment bags and three smaller gift bags. Baylei knew she hadn't ordered anything and wondered where the items came from.

"Um, this must be a mistake. No one here placed an order for anything."

"Is this Baylei, Toni, or Jordyn's suite? Maybe I have the wrong room." The woman turned to walk away but Baylei's voice stopped her from going too far.

"No, I'm Baylei. I just need to know where these items came from."

"Ma'am, the only thing I'm in charge of is making the delivery. I've done my job. Have a nice day and enjoy your gifts." The woman smiled and left the cart in the hall and walked away.

Baylei stood staring at the items as if she had committed a crime. Hurriedly, she pulled the cart into the suite and closed the door quietly. Her hands started sweating and she wiped them on the hem of her nightshirt. Turning to her left, she noticed the phone lying on the table and she gasped. She'd left Chade on hold the entire time she was going back and forth with the lady at the door.

"Hello? Hello?" she said into the receiver.

"I'm still here. Is everything okay?" Chade asked smoothly.

"Yes, everything is fine; I think. The weirdest thing just happened. There were some things delivered here that I know neither my friends nor I made. I'm so scared to open them because maybe it's a set-up or something."

Chade laughed, causing Baylei to frown. This was not a laughing matter. She was really afraid of going to jail for fraud. Her first mind was to hang up on him.

"It's not a set-up. I had a feeling you would have an excuse to not go with me tonight so Sanji, Malik, and myself made some shit shake. You don't have to worry about not having anything to wear or leaving your friends behind. We will all turn up together under the moonlight as we sail the ocean. What do you say about that?"

The smile on Baylei's face stretched from ear to ear. Knowing the effort Chade put in to spend time made her feel giddy inside. She was overly excited to see what he had purchased for her to wear.

"I think it was a great gesture. Hopefully whatever you had delivered fits. You don't even know my size."

"See, that's where you wrong, Beautiful. I sized you up from the moment I laid eyes on you at the beach. From your head down to your pretty feet. Tell me if I'm wrong. You are a size ten, about a thirty-six C in bra size, and your feet are about an eight and a half. Am I right?"

Baylei was amazed at how accurate he was without knowing her more than a day. Noah's ass couldn't surprise her with a pair of panties if he wanted to and she had been with him for years. Chade had rendered her speechless.

"Does that mean I got everything correct?" he asked.

"You just about summed it up. I wear an eight, depending on the shoe. Everything else is very accurate. How did you do that?"

"I'll just say, I know women. Be ready about eight. Don't have me waiting, Beautiful. I can't wait to see you. Oh, and, um, pack a bag. The party is an overnight affair. Talk to you later."

Before Baylei could protest about the overnight sneak he threw in there at the end, Chade hung up. Since she didn't know the number to his hotel room, she couldn't call him back. After all she had gone through, both of her friends took the liberty of coming out of their rooms at that precise time.

"What is all of this?" Jordyn asked, walking deeper into the living area of the suite.

"We have been invited to a black-tie event—on a yacht! Chade and his boys took the liberty of shopping for us so we wouldn't turn down their invitation." Baylei was excited and her friends had the same look on their faces that she'd had when the delivery arrived.

"You have to be shitting me!" Toni exclaimed. "Let me see what we got here." She walked to the cart and grabbed one of the garment bags. "This one is yours, Lei."

Toni handed Baylei the bags and a box with her name on it. She did the same for Jordyn before retrieving her own items and scurried to the sofa. The ladies were quiet as they all hesitated to open their gifts.

"Shid, y'all may not want to see what's in these packages, but I do," Toni said as she unzipped the garment bag. Her eyes widen once she saw the contents. "This is a bomb-ass dress! Oh my God, I love it!" Baylei and Jordyn strained their necks to see for themselves, but Toni had yet to reveal the fabric.

"Take it out so we can see, damn." Jordyn stood from the sofa and stood over Toni.

Reaching inside, Toni stood, removing the dress from the hanger and let the garment bag fall to the floor. She held a rose-colored dress with shiny sequins swirling from the top left shoulder, across the midsection, and traveled to the bottom of the dress. The material on both sides were none existent and it was backless.

"Okay, Malik! I see you. I'm about to rock this muthafucka." Toni held the dress up to her body with a huge grin on her face. She immediately went for the shoe box and the rose-colored open-toed sandals were cute too. "Wait, there's a note, bitches!" Tearing the envelope open, Toni read what it said out loud.

I hope this is enough to get you to come out and enjoy this night with me. Spending time with you was a night to remember. I've never had a woman that could have fun and hold a conversation the way you did. Getting to know you on another level is something I truly look forward to in the future. Toni, I know we just met, but I don't want St. Thomas to be our last stop. There's so much I have to tell you, but I also have to clear my plate before I approach you in the way I would like. But I want to enjoy the here and now with you. See you tonight with your sexy ass. -Malik

"Awwww, that's what I'm talking about. I'm excited to see what Sanji's taste looking like." Jordyn rushed back to her packages fast as hell.

When Jordyn pulled her dress out, the sparkle in her eyes told everybody she liked Sanji's dress choice for her. He went with a simple black bodycon dress that would fit Jordyn's curves like a glove. The dress was floor length. One arm was long sleeved and the material would wrap around the left side of her neck. The split was damn near to the waistline of the dress. Jordyn wasn't an underwear type of woman, so the dress was right up her alley.

"I'm gon' have to be careful with this one. My yoni is going to be able to breathe in this here dress. My boob is gonna be playing peek-a-boo too. I wouldn't change nothing about this get-up."

Jordyn picked up her shoebox because she was eager to see the shoes. Sanji had selected a pair of clear stilettos with black six-inch heels. Jordyn searched for her note, but there wasn't one in the box. She frowned, but grabbed the smaller bag that she had set on the table. Inside was a diamond tennis bracelet, and that's where her note was found. She read the note aloud just as Toni had done.

Jordyn! First, I want to say, your short ass is the epitome of beauty to me. This dress is a symbol of how sexy you are in my eyes. I can't wait to see you walk up the steps to the yacht. All eyes will be on you, baby. I'm confident that I made a great choice in the dress and the woman that would be wearing it. I'll be waiting for you. P.S. don't thank me for none of that shit. It's all about you. -Sanji

"Ohhhhh I hear you loud and clear, Mr. Sanji. He gon' wet these cookies up tonight!"

Baylei laughed and got up while grabbing her packages. Her friends looked at her as if she was stealing. When she had everything in her hands, she headed toward her room.

121

"Where the hell you going? We want to see what the hell you gon' be wearing and I know damn well Mr. Lover Man had plenty to say in his note," Toni snapped.

"See, the difference between you and me, I want to be surprised. I'm not looking at any of these things until we are getting ready. Is that okay with you?"

"Man, that's dirty, Lei. But I'm gon' let you have that shit. I hope there's a church dress in that bag." Toni cackled.

Baylei threw up her middle finger and walked off holding it in the air. When she got to her bedroom door, she turned around, glancing over her shoulder. "Be ready in an hour. We have an excursion to enjoy. All this other shit can wait." Walking off, she closed the door and smiled to herself. She was low-key excited about their impromptu invitation and couldn't wait to slide into the gown Chade bought for her.

***

Baylei was tired as ever after the fun that she and her friends had throughout the day. The best part was racing on the jet skis. They were out there like professional drivers and even ran into a couple cuties that tried to sweep them off their feet. Turning the men down nicely, they weren't trying to have too many men in one spot because the ones that were on their radar would be waiting for them at the dock later that night.

They went shopping at a few shops that they ran into as they dried off. There was a day party which they attended and had fun with other vacationers on the beach. Baylei's mind went back to the conversation she'd had with Noah earlier, but she shook it off. Baylei and her friends took many pictures as they laughed and had fun in the sun until they tired themselves out, working up an appetite.

Once they made it back to the hotel, they ordered food and showered while they waited for it to arrive. Wasting no time after eating, they all fell face first into their beds. Energy was going to be needed to party hard later.

Baylei jumped up hours later as her alarm alerted her that it was time to get up. Looking at the time on her phone, she stretched and climbed out of the bed. Baylei sat at the vanity and thought about how she was about to beat her face. "Damn, I have to peek at the damn dress." She sighed as she got up.

Unzipping the garment bag, she saw that the dress was red and turned away from it. Baylei knew exactly how she was about to apply her makeup. She moisturized her face first, then she applied a light primer before going to work. When she finished, she smiled and winked at herself. There was a light knock on her door before it opened.

"Damn, Lei. I've never seen your makeup like that before. Chade done brought out a different side of you! I love that look. It's the smoky eyes with the red shadow for me, sis! Toni, come look at Lei!" Jordyn yelled.

"Fuck, Lei!" Toni bellowed back. Within a few minutes she was standing in the doorway being nosy. "Who the fuck is that? What you do with my friend? You look good, bih! Chade done called the devil out to play around this muthafucka!"

"That's what I said! She acting up in St. Thomas! I'm here for it though. That lil pussy about to get bust opened tonight!"

"Jordyn, you two sluts will be fuckin'; not me."

"Let me see the dress, Lei. That will determine what type of night you will have tonight." Toni laughed.

"I have to curl my hair first. I haven't looked at the whole dress. I took a quick peek to see what color it was. That's about all." Baylei explained as she plugged her curling irons up. "You will see it when I put it on. Now, go get dressed. Chade will be here at eight."

Baylei styled her hair in big curls that flowed down her back. She felt beautiful in that moment and was eager to really see the dress that awaited her. After oiling her body with shea butter, Baylei walked toward the garment bag and took the dress off the hanger. She slipped the dress over her head and it hugged her body tightly without giving away too much. The asymmetrical off the shoulder neckline, a slightly scrunch of the material on the sides, and the high slit showed off her toned thigh.

Baylei ran her hand down the dress and she was pleased with what she saw as she looked at herself in the mirror. She opened the shoebox, seeing the red stiletto red bottom sandals that laid in the box looking cute as hell. Glancing down at her French manicure, Baylei wiggled her toes before sitting down on the side of the bed. She slipped her feet into the shoes and fell in love.

Standing to her feet, Baylei walked back to the box and searched for Chade's note. Like with Jordyn, there wasn't one in the box. There was another gift box in a Jared's bag. Baylei was shocked because she didn't notice where the gift was from until that moment. She slowly opened the box and inside was a diamond choker with a diamond and ruby charm attached.

"I'm going to wear this tonight, but Chade is going to take this back because it's too much. I can't accept this."

"You can't accept what?" Jordyn asked, causing Baylei to turn abruptly as she entered the room.

"This diamond choker. It's too much."

"Damn, that's beautiful, Lei. I know you're going to go through the whole 'I'm not a materialistic woman' speech. Go easy on him, sis. Everyone is not Noah. Accept the gift and don't think too much into it."

"I'm not thinking about Noah's ass. He has nothing to do with any of this." Baylei's mood soured from just the mention of her problem back home.

"Anyway, you look good, girl. I love this new Baylei, and Chade will too. Mark my words; that dress coming off."

"You ain't short stopping. That dress is everything, but you wear that type of shit all the time for those corporate parties you're always rubbing elbows with. Where the hell is Toni? We have about fifteen minutes before we have to go downstairs."

"I'm right here, divas," Toni said, sashaying through the door holding a rose-colored clutch with a Louis Vuitton tote bag draped over her shoulder. "Y'all look good!"

"Oh shit! I forgot to pack a bag! Please unplug all that on the vanity while I pack real quick," Baylei said, scrambling through her luggage. "That clutch is pretty, Toni."

"I know. It was an added gift from my vacation boo." She smirked.

"Hell, Lei. What's in this orange box?" Jordyn asked, walking back into the room. Baylei hadn't noticed she'd even left until she returned.

"What box?" Baylei asked quizzingly.

Jordyn placed the box on the bed and gasped. "This is a Birkin box!"

"I know like hell he didn't! I definitely can't accept *that* gift. Chade is out of his mind!"

"Lawd, Chade is about to *get it wettttt,*" Toni sang the words from Twista's "Get It Wet" song.

Lifting the lid of the box, Baylei's hand flew to her mouth when she saw the bag inside. The Bleu Indigo travel bag was one that was on Baylei's wish list, but she wanted it in black. She knew why it was still a wish in the making. She wasn't too thrilled about paying four thousand dollars for a damn bag. It didn't sit well with her that a man that she barely knew went out of his way to buy the expensive piece for her.

"Nope! The choker is one thing, but this is too much! Chade will be getting these gifts back soon as I see him. I'm not accepting this!"

"Give it to me then," Toni said with a smile.

"No, it will be returned to the man that spent his hard-earned money."

Baylei walked away from the bed and went back to picking out an outfit for the next day. After gathering all of her toiletries and a swimsuit just in case there was a pool or a Jacuzzi, she packed everything in her Michael Kors tote just as the phone rang in the other room. She closed the lid on the box and walked right out the door to answer the phone.

"You're thinking too much into this, sis." Toni said behind her. Baylei didn't respond as she sat the box down and pick up the receiver.

"Hello."

"Hey, Beautiful. Your ride is downstairs." Chade's voice did something to her lady parts soon as she heard it.

"You not down there?" she asked nervously.

"No. I had the driver drop us off first. I'll be waiting for you at the yacht."

"Um, okay. About the gifts you bought—"

"We can talk about that when you see me. Get to that damn car, woman. See you in a minute." Chade ended the call before Baylei could protest.

"Come on. The car is waiting for us."

Baylei led the way out of their suite and wanted to turn back around to go back inside. She didn't even attempt to renege because both Toni and Jordyn would've drug her out by her long tresses. Instead, she willed herself silently to walk one foot in front of the other. As the trio excited the resort, Baylei came to the conclusion that she was going to enjoy herself without thinking too much about what Chade had in store for her.

Chapter 14

Chade ended the call with Baylei quickly because he knew she was about to complain about the expensive gifts he sent her. He wasn't trying to hear anything she had to say. Money wasn't an issue for him and he liked to spoil any woman he deemed worthy, and Baylei was for sure worth every dollar spent.

As he stood at the opening of the yacht, the party was in full swing. Everyone in the wedding party and the guest that traveled to be there for the bride and groom were already aboard.

"What are you doing out here? Come dance with me."

The sound of Sakeenya's voice irked the hell out of Chade. He'd told her to stay away from him, but she was back pushing her luck. Chade ignored her and continued looking down at the dock, hoping the limo would be pulling in sooner than later.

"So, you just gon' act like I'm not talking to you?"

"Keenya, go find somebody to do. I've already told you what it is with us."

"I didn't get the memo. Tell me again."

Chade turned to face her. "It ain't shit. I told yo' ass to stay away from me. I'm trying to be nice. Don't make me embarrass you in here. Now, get away from me."

Sakeenya laughed, but it didn't last long when she saw the limo pull up. The sound of her smacking her lips didn't go unnoticed when Baylei emerged, followed by her friends. Chade's eyes were glued to the beautiful woman he couldn't wait to wrap his arms around. The interaction between him and Sakeenya was long gone from his mind until she opened her mouth.

"You invited that bitch to celebrate with my best friend! Chasity don't even know them hoes," Sakeenya seethed.

"Nah, I invited *Baylei* to celebrate with the best man. Jealousy don't look good on you, shawty. Go wash that shit off," Chade said, glaring in her direction. When Sakeenya didn't move, his voice raised an octave higher than before, "Go the fuck inside and stop being stupid!"

Sakeenya stalked inside with a huff and Chade shook his head at how ignorant she was acting. If seeing Baylei had her feeling some type of way, just wait until she was standing on the sideline watching him love on the woman that was heading his way.

Baylei was wearing the shit out of the dress Chade chose for her. Every muscle down to her calf flexed with every step she took. His dick matched the rhythm as he thought nothing but nastiness in his head.

Chade had a temporary case of tunnel vision because he was focused hard on Baylei. As she climbed the steps, it dawned on him that instead of walking her pretty ass up the stairs with the Birkin bag hanging from her arm, she carried the box in her hands. Maybe it was damaged or something, he thought to himself. Opening his arms wide, he waited for Baylei to walk into them as she stepped up onto the landing of the yacht.

"You are beautiful." Chade beamed.

"Thank you," she said holding the box out to him. "Thanks for the bag, but I can't accept such a gift. I loved the thought you put into it though."

Taking the box from her, Chade wrapped his free arm around her shoulders and pulled her into his chest. "Yes, you can and you will. We have all night for you to talk about this material shit that means nothing to me. Tonight is about fun and enjoying the moment." Chade glanced behind Baylei and smiled. "Hello, ladies," he said, addressing Toni and Jordyn.

They spoke and then Chade led the way inside the vessel. As they stepped inside, the decorations took Baylei's breath away. The mahogany and black theme with specks of white gave the environment a sexy feel. Looking around, all eyes seemed to be on them as they made their way through the room. Chade held on to Baylei the entire time. The whispering and gestures from many kind of made Baylei nervous on the inside. She didn't let that shit show openly, but the jitters were definitely in her stomach.

After climbing another flight of stairs, the group walked out onto the upper deck. Sanji stopped talking when Vincent nudged him and nodded his head in the direction of the entrance. He and

Jordyn made eye contact at the same time and the sexual connection could be felt from afar. Licking his lips, Sanji tweaked his beard before making his way to the woman he'd been waiting for. Jordyn looked good enough to eat and his stomach growled; not because he was hungry for food. Sanji had a taste for her sweet nectar.

"Damn, baby. You looking good. Are you here alone or do I have to toss ya man overboard to make you mine?" Sanji nuzzled his chin into the top of her head as he hugged her closely.

"Nah, you don't have to do all that. I'm here looking for this sexy man from Harlem, New York. I met him last night, but I had one too many drinks and don't remember what he looks like. The only think I can recall is his cologne. He smelled so good," Jordyn said, inhaling Sanji's scent. "As a matter of fact, he smelled kind of like— you. Is that Tom Ford, Black Orchid?"

"As a matter of fact, it is. I love a woman that knows fragrances. Since that nigga ain't here to stake claim on your fine ass, how about you just chill with a real one for the night?"

Sanji caressed the side of her face and a shiver rippled down her spine. His hands were soft and Jordyn wanted to see how they felt on other parts of her body. There was no denying the sexual connection both of them felt. By the end of the night, they would be ducked off somewhere working up a euphoric sweat.

"I can't just walk around with you without knowing your name. I'm Jordyn, by the way." She kept the charade going to see how far he was going to take it. Jordyn could play with him anyway he wanted. She had nothing but time.

"Nice to meet you, Jordyn. I'm Sanji."

Jordyn was stuck on the way he licked his lips then smiled. The dimple in his left cheek was calling for her to stick her tongue in it. All the nasty shit she wanted to do with him clouded her senses. She went deaf for a few seconds because she didn't hear anything Sanji was saying to her. The only thing she could do was watch his mouth move without sound.

"What do you say?" he asked, squeezing her hand.

"I'm sorry, what did you say?"

"Do you want to take your bag to the cabin you will be staying in for the night?"

"I wasn't given that information with my invite." Jordyn smirked. "Who would I have to talk to in order to find out the sleeping arrangements?"

"How would you feel about staying with me in my cabin? I mean, you are my plus one."

Jordyn's inner body was doing a happy dance. She didn't have a problem with the arrangements at all. If anything, she welcomed it because she did come to St. Thomas to get laid by a handsome man.

"Lead the way. We are both grown and whatever happens, happens. Let's get this out of the way so we can eat, drink, dance, and whatever else is in store for us."

Jordyn's words were music to Sanji's ears and he loved the sweet melody. Doing as she requested, he led her in the direction of what he thought of as the love cove. Sanji was thinking of all the ways he was going to caress Jordyn's mind, body, and soul.

Passing Chade and Baylei, Jordyn stopped to let her friend know where she was going. After the exchange, the two of them continued on to their destination. The frown on Baylei's face concerned Chade and prompted him to question her facial change.

"What's on your mind, Beautiful?" Chade asked standing close to her.

"Are we sharing a room as well?"

"Yeah. Is that a problem for you?" Baylei turned and looked out into the darkened ocean. Her silence let Chade know she wasn't comfortable with the idea of spending the night with him. He should've told her beforehand, but didn't think it would be a problem. "If it makes you feel any better, the cabin has a small sitting area with a sofa. I'll sleep there while you take the bedroom. Baylei, I didn't invite you here tonight to have sex with you. I just wanted to spend more time with you and have fun while doing it."

"It would've been nice to know about this earlier. I won't let this ruin the night. You want to have a good time and so do I. It's been a while since I've let my hair down and just enjoyed life. But when it's time to call it a night, I hope that sofa is long enough for your tall ass."

Baylei's laugh warmed Chade's heart and he was a little terrified. He'd known this woman two days and she had him cheesing like a Cheshire cat. Baylei's presence was one he had never encountered and he was intrigued beyond belief.

"That's cool by me. I didn't always have money. I know what it's like to sleep on a pallet on the floor. A little sofa ain't shit to me. With a beautiful chick like you in the same vicinity, I should sleep like a baby."

"We'll see. For now, I need to put this bag down so I can dance circles around your smooth ass. This DJ is showing out."

Chade glanced around until he spotted someone trustworthy that would keep an eye on Baylei's belongings. He took Baylei by the hand and lead her over where the tables were set up. Miss Betty was bobbing her head to the music while eating as they approached her. Sakeenya took that moment to approach the table and the look on the woman's face told anyone that was paying attention how she really felt about Sakeenya's presence.

"Now, she knows damn well Miss Betty don't care for her or Chasity's ass," Chade scoffed.

Baylei didn't know who Chade was referring to and she was curious to find out. "Who is Miss Betty?"

"Ahmad's mom. Sakeenya still on her bullshit," he said with an attitude.

"That's *your* girl." Baylei's lips quirked in amusement.

"My girl for the week is right next to me. I don't have any intensions of dealing with anyone other than yo' fine ass."

Baylei was smiling inside but she didn't show him how much his words affected her. "Mm-hmm. That's fine by me. You better make the next five days the best they can be. When we depart, we will be distant thoughts for one another."

Chade stopped and Baylei was forced to do the same. He looked down at her and Baylei felt as Chade's eyes penetrated her soul with the intensity of his stare. His eyes roamed over every part of her face and her skin felt extremely hot. Taking a deep breath, Chade opened his mouth to speak but instead, he shook his head and began walking again.

Sakeenya kept looking in their direction the closer they got to the table. When they got within earshot, Miss Betty had gotten fed up with Sakeenya's lurking.

"Chile, take your ass on away from here nah. You been standing over me five minutes and ain't said a damn word yet. You ain't slick. Running your stupid ass over here soon as you saw Chade's fine ass coming to pay me a visit. You are yesterday's trash because my baby got a beauty on his arm tonight." Miss Betty laughed in Sakeenya's face with no shame. "Go 'head nah. Don't make me cuss you out, little girl."

Sakeenya glared at Baylei until she and Chade paused on the other side of the table. Miss Betty's voice snapped her out of her jealous trance. "There's plenty of men 'round here. Find you one, because my baby is off limits for the night. This was a much-needed trip for him. Maybe he will finally settle down and leave all these good for nothing girls alone for once."

Sakeenya sucked her teeth as she stood to her full height. Always needing to have the last say, she opened her mouth and put her foot right in it. "*Your* baby can play the role of being the doting boyfriend for a week, but I've known him longer. Miss Prissy don't know what she's getting herself into. Chade will be hitting my line soon as his balls start tingling."

"Get your trifling ass away from here before I smack the piss out of you. Didn't nobody teach your disrespectful ass to respect your elders?"

"Man, Sakeenya. Gon' with that mess. You need to grow the fuck up, for real."

"Chade, let me handle my own affairs," Miss Betty said, standing up with her fork clenched in her hand. "See, I tried to be nice. Get yo' hoe ass away from here, and that's the last time I'm going to say it. What you about to do is make me stab yo' ass then help them look for your retarded ass after I push you in that black-ass water out there."

Sakeenya backed away from the table, but her focus was on Chade. When she finally left without another word, Chade looked down at his hand, which had gone numb from the grip Baylei had on it. Wiggling free, the scowl deepened on Baylei's face as she watched Sakeenya and Chasity stealing glances in their direction.

"Baby, you're too pretty to be frowning. That shit causes wrinkles. Straighten your face. That chile ain't worth a pot to piss in, so don't give her the satisfaction of seeing you upset." Miss Betty turned to Chade with fire in her eyes.

"And you! Stay the fuck away from that girl. I told you when you met her at my damn house, she was gonna be a problem. You and Ahmad gon' get enough about not doing your homework on these bitches. Now his stupid ass about to marry the ringleader and shit. A hard head makes a soft ass, and he's going to come crying to me and I'm gon' punch him in his shit! I hope his stupid ass got a prenup in place."

Chade was glad he wasn't the only one feeling Ahmad was making a mistake. It was one thing for Ahmad not to take his concerns into consideration, but his mama's? Everybody at least soaked in what was being said when their parents tell them something isn't right. Chade wanted to be a fly on the wall when shit hit the fan.

"Enough about that madness. What's your name, baby? I'm Mama Betty." Miss Betty's voice softened as she introduced herself.

"Nice to meet you. I'm Baylei." Miss Betty looked at her outstretched hand and pulled Baylei into her bosom.

"I hug, especially when the energy is positive. You just might be what the doctor ordered to get this hoe out the streets. He needs a good woman by his side."

"I don't know about all that. He's just my boyfriend for the duration of this trip."

"Yeah, I like you. Gon' 'head and get your swerve on and leave him with his dick swinging between his legs. He's gonna remember you for sure, Suga."

"Miss Betty, you trippin'." Chade laughed. "Would you mind keeping an eye on Baylei's things while we dance?"

"What cabin are you in? Give me the damn key and I'll secure it for you. That lil hussy made me lose my appetite and my food is cold." Chade reached in his pocket and gave Miss Betty his keycard. "Thank you. Now go make that pissy-tailed gal jealous. By the way, Baylei, you wearing the hell out of that dress. The lady in red has arrived."

"Thank you! Chade did good for himself." Baylei smiled.

"Yes, Chade has an eye for beautiful things when he's thinking clearly. Leave your mark, baby. Go 'head and have a good time. I'll put this away for you." Miss Betty winked as she headed for the sleeping quarters.

The DJ mixed his music and the beat for "Money" by Cardi B blared from the speakers and Baylei's ratchet side emerged without thought. In her mind, she was about to be petty as fuck while she had an audience. She swiveled her hips as she placed her hands on Chade's shoulders, dancing in front of him. She rapped the lyrics as if she wrote the song herself; putting a little icing on the cake for her admirers.

"*Look. My bitches all bad, my niggas are real. I ride his dick in some big tall heels.*" Baylei turned her back and grinded into Chade's midsection, causing him to grab her hips while watching her ass. "*Big fat checks, big large bills. Front I'll flip like ten cartwheels. Cold-ass bitch, I give Ross chills. Ten different looks and my looks all kill.*" She faced Chade, smiling. He knew she was on that good bullshit and was lovin' every bit of it. When Cardi said, "*I kiss him in the mouth—*", that's exactly what Baylei did. Chade parted her lips with his tongue and the two of them got lost in one another right in the middle of the area.

Baylei pulled away first because she couldn't believe she went from not having sex on the trip to initiating the shit. "Don't start nothing you can't finish, Beautiful. There's room in that big-ass king-sized bed for two."

Ignoring his slick comment, Baylei walked away to find a drink. She was hot and bothered. A cool drink would do the trick of cooling her off. Chade watched every sway of her hips and that ass was sitting right in that dress. Miss Betty's words filled his head and he agreed. He sure knew how to pick 'em when he was thinking clearly.

Meesha

Chapter 15

"So, Toni, tell me a little about yourself."

Malik and Toni decided to eat before going to the open bar to get their night started. The steak, broccoli, and baked potato Toni ordered was hitting the spot for her. Ahmad hired a full kitchen crew to cook for the event into the next day. The kitchen was open for whatever you wanted for the duration of the night and well into the morning as long as it was an hour before they docked back at the starting point. Malik had a juicy cheeseburger along with thick steak fries in front of him and he was smashing as he waited for Toni's response.

"Hmmm. I'm thirty-two, single with no children. I was born and raised in Chicago and I work for a well-known law firm as a paralegal. I'm the middle child of three. My two sisters are married with children. I like to have fun and as you can see, I love to eat."

Malik nodded his head as he chewed the food in his mouth. "That's what I'm talking about. Beauty and brains; my type of woman." Taking a sip of water then clearing his voice, Malik folded his hands together and stared intensely at Toni. "So, the women that you came on this trip with are your friends and not your sisters?" he asked.

"We are a little more than friends. They are my sisters; just not by blood. Our sisterhood started over a decade ago while in college. We met at orientation at the University of Chicago and the bond has been solid ever since."

Toni hoped like hell Malik kept his line of questioning on her because she didn't know what Baylei and Jordyn were telling his homeboys. Watching as Malik chewed his food, Toni took in his caramel complexion and how his skin tone complemented his eyebrows. The deep waves in his head were deeper than the ones the yacht slowly cruised on. His muscular body was lean and Toni could tell he worked out regularly.

"With all girls, I know your father kept his pistol locked and loaded," Malik said, bringing Toni back to their conversation. The mention of her father took Toni from being happy to a somber place.

"My father was very protective of us girls; until he and my mother went away four years ago." Toni swallowed the lump in her throat.

"Awww, your parents raised you to be the strong woman you are today. No need to be sad. All you have to do is take time out to go visit them. I can tell you miss them so much. Where did they move to, another country?"

"No, they are still in the States. In Chicago, to be exact," Toni said with a slight smile. "Malik, my parents were killed by a drunk driver as they were heading home from celebrating their thirty-second anniversary." Toni pushed her plate away as she picked up her glass of water and took a sip. "The twenty-one-year-old woman was the daughter of a sheriff. She was given three years' probation, doing no jail time for the death of my parents."

"I'm so sorry, Toni."

"You didn't know; it's alright. I need to talk to someone about that night. I haven't grieved at all. Not one tear, screaming episode, nothing. I've been holding this shit in for four years and I try to stay away from any altercations that would set me off. Somebody would feel my wrath. Since we are on the subject, I want you to tell your people to keep that hoe away from my friend. She don't want no smoke."

Malik loved the way Toni went from a little vulnerable to straight hood. That shit made his dick hard. She was not to be fucked with. Toni was the type of woman that wanted better for herself and went out and got it, but at the same time she was straight street outside of the workforce. Sakeenya better stay away from Baylei if she knew what was good for her.

"I understand what you're saying, and my heart goes out to you. We have more than enough time to talk whenever you're ready. Tonight, is about putting a smile on your face and keeping it there. As far as Sakeenya, that situation will play out as it may. I don't have anything to say about it. Are you finished eating? If so, it's time to get this party started."

Toni liked the idea and pushed her chair back from the table. They went to Malik's cabin to put her bag away after ordering their food. Toni didn't mind spending the night in the same room. If anything, she welcomed it. She came on the trip for that purpose alone and to have a good time. Malik put his hand on the small of her back and led her over to where everyone was congregating and dancing. The music faded out and Ahmad was standing on the stage next to the DJ with Chasity by his side.

"Thanks everyone for coming all the way to St. Thomas to celebrate with my soon to be wife and I. We really appreciate the love we've received and wouldn't have wanted to share this moment any other way. Saturday can't get here fast enough for me. Having this woman by my side for the rest of my life," Ahmad said, pausing to hug Chasity and planting a kiss on her temple, "is a dream come true. Thank you, Mr. Driver, for trusting me to do right by your daughter. Mrs. Driver, I won't disappoint you and your husband at all. The love I have for Chasity is over the moon and I will cherish every day that she's my wife like it's my last."

The crowd's applause was very loud and the support of the couple could be felt around the entire yacht. Toni clapped slowly out of respect as she glanced at the people around her and her eyes landed on Sakeenya, who had a smirk on her face. She mouthed, "You got him, bitch" and Toni followed her gaze as Chasity nodded her head. Something wasn't right about that interaction between them and Toni peeped that shit off top.

"Baby, we are going to be together forever and I love you," Chasity said. They shared a long kiss and the cheering got louder. Chasity's short response was an embarrassment to Toni. Ahmad poured his heart out and she said little to nothing.

"Let's get this party started the right way," Ahmad said with a smile, gazing in Chasity's eyes. "If you haven't eaten, the kitchen is open all night and the drinks are endless. Drink up and have a good time; on ya boy!"

The couple walked off the stage and the DJ started the music up. DMX's deep raspy voice belted out with "What These Bitches Want." Toni started bouncing to the beat, then started rapping along with the rap legend. Malik admired her demeanor and joined in on her fun.

"Ayo, dawg, I meet niggas, discreet niggas. Street niggas slash Cocoa Puff-sweet niggas. Make you want to eat niggas, but not me y'all niggas eat off the plate all you want, but not T. I fuck with these niggas from a distance. The instant they start to catch feelings, I start stealing they shit. Then out just like a thief in the night, I sink my teeth in to bite. You thinking life, I'm thinking more like, what's up tonight?"

Toni changed the words to fit her criteria and it only made Malik grin. She was letting him know he was entitled to get what he wanted while they were together on the trip, but she had a thing or two to learn about him. He had plans to dick her down so good that she was going to feen for his touch well after she was back home tucked between the sheets of her bed.

Malik and Toni were having the time of their lives. He held her close and whispered sweet nothings in her ear, making her laugh. His mission was to get her mind off the death of her parents and back on enjoying herself to the fullest. Baylei found them on the dance floor and bounced to the music until she was in their space.

"Move over, bacon, it's my turn to tear up the floor with my bestie."

Baylei smirked as she nodded her head at Toni. One thing the women loved was to dance; especially line dancing. Before going to find Toni, Baylei went to the DJ table to see if he had any line dance music. The only one he had was the "Wobble" and "Cupid Shuffle". That was a no-go for Baylei. She found what she was looking for on her phone and the DJ was gracious enough to play what she wanted to dance to.

Walk it to the right, now move it on up, move it on up.

Walk it to the left, now, bring it on back, bring it on back

Big Mucci's voice turned Toni up and Jordyn wasn't too far behind. The three ladies were tearing the floor up as everyone else gathered around the dance floor to watch. Even though the song had been out since 2016, it was new to the other attendees.

"Oh, shit! I wanna learn that!" a woman yelled, running to the floor.

Baylei had no problem teaching anyone that wanted to dance. Kicking off her heels, she put a little sass in her movements. She could feel all eyes on them and knew Chade was amongst the onlookers. When she turned, their eyes connected as Chade watched her while licking his lips.

"Damn, bro. Here's a napkin to catch the drool that's about to fall from your lip." Vincent laughed. "You're really feeling her, huh?"

Chade ignored the wisecrack his boy threw at him and continued watching Baylei on the dance floor. The DJ slowed it down just a little by playing "Before I Let Go". The crowd thinned, but the ladies had to do the line dance for that one as well.

Chade hadn't been away from the Chi too long. He knew that dance. He walked slowly onto the dance floor, leaving Vincent where he stood, and found his spot behind Baylei. The two of them turned the dance into one with a lot of sex appeal. They were in sync with one another and were giving a hell of a show, especially for Sakeenya, who was seething on the inside as she sat tossing back Remy shots like water.

"That muthafucka throwing it on thick for that ugly bitch."

"Sakeenya, your hate is shining through," Chasity said, rolling her eyes. "You're not going to win him over being nasty. Stop that shit. She's not going back to California with Chade. We both know he's putting up a front on this trip. You will be getting a call once they part ways."

"Fuck him! He bet' not call me after playing me for her broke ass." The liquor Sakeenya consumed was flowing through her system rapidly. "I didn't want his ass anyway," she said, reaching out to hug Chasity.

Pulling away from her best friend, Chasity stepped away slightly. "Okay, if you're going to start that drunk bullshit, stop drinking now," Chasity gritted. "You will not fuck up my party, Keenya."

Sakeenya frowned and stood from her seat. Before she could open her mouth, Chasity grabbed her arm and rushed toward the nearest restroom. Sakeenya tried her best to shrug out of her grasp, but she couldn't because of the intoxicated state she was in. As they passed patrons, there were whispers and pointing as Sakeenya tugged at her dress as it rose above her naked ass.

Toni danced for a couple minutes then excused herself through the crowd. She had to piss like a race horse and needed to find a bathroom quickly. Malik cut her off and pulled Toni into his chest.

"Where you off to in such a hurry?" he asked.

"I have to go badly." Toni danced around like a toddler and Malik laughed. "Move before I pee on myself."

"Hurry back. Baylei and Chade is out there stealing the show. I can't have that. There's a bathroom downstairs to the right of the narrow hall."

"Okay, handsome. Thank you."

Toni followed Malik's directions and found the bathroom with no problem. As she neared the door, loud voices echoed in the hall. Others couldn't hear because of the music. But when Toni placed her hand on the door to push it open, she paused because she heard the words clear as day.

"I want you to kill the noise, Keenya. You have to come down off the alcohol before you blow my shit up. Acting stupid over Chade is not a good look for you right now. It's embarrassing. Chade isn't naïve like Ahmad. I lucked up and put the right dose of pussy on his ass. Long as I'm getting money, you straight."

Chasity's proper tone was gone and her ghetto side emerged instantaneously. Toni was stuck with her mouth wide opened, forgetting all about the reason she came to the bathroom to begin with. Turning to leave, Sakeenya started slurring her words as she spoke, causing Toni to stop in her tracks.

"Chasity, I only went after Chade because you asked me to. Sucking his dick was foreign to me, but I learned how to master that shit for you! Why you think I haven't fucked him yet? Because I love pussy! Preferably yours!"

Toni was stumped because the tea she'd heard was piping hot.

"You were supposed to date the nigga, not marry him! That wasn't part of the plan, Chasity." Sakeenya was hurt and it could be heard in every word that fell from her mouth. The shit went on deaf ears because Chasity wasn't trying to hear none of what her friend said.

"See, now you talking too fuckin' much! Get all that shit out now because it bet' not go beyond the walls of this bathroom. If it's mentioned on this trip, that's your muthafuckin' ass!" Chasity pushed Sakeenya into the wall with her finger deep in her forehead. Sakeenya winced in pain as her back connected to whatever was protruding from the wall. "I'm marrying Ahmad and still gon' eat yo' pussy every chance I get. Now what? We hit a lick together and you better continue to play the role of best friend, bitch!"

Toni couldn't handle any more of the shit she'd heard. Bad as she wanted to stick around to listen, her bladder was screaming for her to relieve it. Damn near running to the cabin she and Malik was sharing for the night, Toni tapped the keycard that she stored in her bra and raced to the bathroom. As she sat on the toilet, the conversation she overheard played in her mind.

"These bitches ain't shit. I can't keep this to myself. Ahmad needs to know about the woman he's about to marry. He can't go through with this wedding."

Toni didn't know Ahmad, but she wouldn't want any man to commit to a woman with ill intentions. The way Ahmad admired the bitch was something any woman would want from a man. He catered to her without being asked; the shit was automatic. Chasity didn't deserve the love she was getting, and Toni was going to make sure to put a halt to her deception.

Chapter 16

Baylei finally made her way to the kitchen to put an order in for food. She was hungry as hell and the last thing she wanted to do was keep drinking on an empty stomach. That would've been grounds for destruction, and she wasn't about to embarrass herself by having Chade take care of her while she was drunk and praying to the porcelain gods.

Baylei's mouth watered just thinking about the ribeye steak, mashed potatoes, and asparagus she ordered. It was damn near midnight and she was about to tear that food up. She ordered Chade the same but with fries because he hadn't eaten anything as far as she knew. A shudder went up her spine as she thought about all the nasty things he whispered in her ear on the dance floor.

Baylei played it cool because she wasn't trying to sleep with Chade. Her lady parts had a different plan for them though. The thong Baylei wore was soaked and if she didn't know better, Chade smelled all her sweet essence in the air as he cradled her in his arms. The smell of Black Phantom cologne alerted Baylei that the very man she was thinking about was within reach.

"Hey, Beautiful. What you order to eat?" Chade asked walking around to sit across from her at the table she snagged to eat.

"Steak, potatoes and asparagus."

"That sounds good as hell right about now. I'm about to place my order." Chade moved to get up but Baylei caught him by the hand.

"I already ordered for you. They will bring it out with mine."

Chade sat back down slowly and peered into Baylei's eyes. He'd never had a woman be so attentive to him before. It was always him trying to make them smile and thinking of them first. The other day at the beach, Baylei had a drink waiting for him after his altercation with Sakeenya, then she asked if he was okay once he was settled back with his boys. She was pulling out a lot of firsts and it had Chade feeling some type of way. A way he told himself he would never allow happen again.

After ending things with his ex, Chade became the biggest man whore in California. The Birkin bag wouldn't have been returned if he had given it to anyone else. That alone told me a lot about Baylei. She wasn't a materialistic type of woman and she could hold down her own.

The cook coming out onto the deck caught Chade's attention and he waved him over when he saw the two steak dinners on the plates. The smell of the food filled Baylei's nostrils as the cook placed the plate on the table and her stomach growled loudly.

"Damn, Beautiful, if you were hungry, we could've eaten before now. Are you sure that's going to be enough for you?"

"This will be plenty." Baylei cut into her steak and closed her eyes as she placed the tender meat in her mouth.

Chade got up and headed to the bar. Ordering two glasses of water, a double shot of Remy, and a pineapple Amsterdam with a splash of piña colada juice for Baylei. That had been her drink for the entire night so he stuck to it so she wouldn't be mixing dark and light. When he returned to the table, he noticed Baylei had kicked her heels off.

"Your feet hurt or something?"

"A little bit. I've been on them all night. This is the first time we have sat down. We were tearing that dance floor up," Baylei laughed. "That DJ been spinning nothing but hit after hit."

"You damn sure know how to dance. If you, Toni, and Jordyn hadn't kicked shit off, these muthafuckas would've still been sitting down doing nothing. This steak is good."

"It sure is. Can I have one of your fries?"

"You can have them all. I would've preferred mashed potatoes myself."

"Pick up your steak."

Chade looked over at Baylei but did as she asked. She switched the plates and placed her steak down and started eating the fries. Baylei was a selfless person and it showed in her actions without her trying. There was nothing about her that screamed fake. Genuine is more of the word that described the beauty that sat across from him. Breaking his stare, he scooped up a spoonful of potatoes.

"Let's talk about the gifts I purchased for you. Why didn't you rock the bag instead of bringing it in the box?" Chade asked.

"I preferred to bring the bag back because it was too much. The bag cost four thousand dollars for Christ sakes, Chade. You don't even know me like that to buy such a gift."

"I don't know you, but I want to get know you in every way possible. Stop focusing on the monetary value of the gifts. You have shown what type of woman you are and I wanted to do something nice for a beautiful woman. I want you to accept the bag, Beautiful."

"Chade—"

"Chade nothing. Finish eating so we can end the night on a good note. I'm going to say this, then that's the end of it. If you wake up in the morning and still want to give the gifts back, I won't argue with your decision. Just know that they are yours to keep. Fair?"

Baylei nodded her head and they finished eating in silence. Chade thought about what she said to Miss Betty and it didn't sit right with him. Baylei wasn't trying to keep in touch with him after the trip and he didn't know how to feel about it. That's probably how females felt when he never called them again once he had fun with them. Chade was definitely getting a dose of his own medicine without the sexual contact.

As Baylei downed her drink and chased it with water, the DJ put on an old school jam by Johnny Gill. The music for "My My My" started playing and Chade smiled. Reaching over the table he grabbed her hand and stood to his feet. Baylei was the epitome of the woman Johnny sang about in that song.

"Can I have this dance?"

"You're so silly. Yeah, let's do this." Chade helped her slip on her shoes and wrapped her in his arms and started crooning in her ear.

Put on your red dress
And slip on your high heels
And some of that sweet perfume
It sure smells good on you
Slide on your lipstick
And let all your hair down

'Cause baby, when you get through
I'm gonna show you off

Baylei and Chade rocked to the music and her yoni was thumping a mile a minute. His voice was soothing and sensual. The image of her standing in front of him naked was vivid in her mind. Chade placed his hand on the top of her butt and she wanted him to go lower for some odd reason. She was playing with the devil on one shoulder and the angel on the other. She wanted to let everything go and have fun, but on the other hand, she didn't want to give in to temptations of letting Chade have her in every way imaginable.

Opening her eyes, Baylei searched the dock and neither one of her friends were anywhere to be found. She knew they were in their cabins with their asses in the air. Chade's voice brought her back to their dance and she melted into his body.

My, my, my, my, my, my, my,
Sure look good tonight
I wanna love you
I wanna love you in every way, every way
Let me, let me show you how sweet it's gonna be

Baylei was shivering because she was aroused and didn't want to be. The devil won because she was all in and ready to bust it open. Chade serenaded her through the entire song. Baylei stepped out of his grip and held his hands as they stared at one another. Without a word, she guided him to the exit of the deck and Chade knew exactly where she wanted to go.

***

Chade tapped the keycard to unlock the door of their cabin and gestured for Baylei to enter first. As soon as she stepped inside, she could hear the notifications going off on her phone. Searching for a light switch, the room brightened after Chade did the honors. Baylei looked around for her bag and spotted it on a chair by the door. She hadn't checked in with her mom and thought that was who would be blowing her phone up, but that wasn't the case. All of the notifications came from her social media messenger inbox. Baylei opened the messages and Noah was on a warpath.

Noah Connery: Where the fuck are you, Baylei? Mark came to your room and you're not there!

Noah Connery: Unblock me now! I need to talk to you.

Noah Connery: You better have fun because when you get back to the States, you're going to wish you never crossed me!

Noah Connery: Bitch, I'm booking a flight and I better not find you with that nigger! You are playing with a world of fire and you have never seen this side of me! There's no leaving me alone, Baylei!

"Everything okay, Beautiful?" Chade asked. walking up behind her.

Baylei closed the messages and turned to face Chade. Nodding her head, she picked up her bag and walked toward the bedroom. Her mood had changed in the blink of an eye and Chade could sense she wasn't alright. Following her into the room, Baylei sat on the side of the bed while staring at the wall. Chade sat next to her, lifted her leg, and removed her shoes from her feet.

"Do you have anything to drink? Preferably tequila," Baylei asked softly. Chade rose from the bed to go into the other room to make her a cocktail. "Bring the bottle."

Chade walked to the bar and grabbed a bottle of Remy along with the tequila Baylei requested. As he headed for the bedroom, he doubled back and snatched up two glasses. Putting everything on a cart, Chade went to the kitchen and added pineapple juice, a can of Coke, and a small container of ice to the cart.

Entering the room, Baylei was laid back on the bed with her eyes closed and her arm over her head. She looked sexy and relaxed with her pretty toes on display. Chade poured tequila into the glass and reached for the juice.

"Straight, no chaser," she said, sitting up as she positioned herself against the headboard.

Chade placed the juice back on the cart and handed the glass to her the way she requested, even though he didn't want her to get drunk. Baylei accepted the drink and threw it back then held the glass out for another. "Slow down, babe. I don't want you to get sick behind this alcohol."

Ignoring his concern, Baylei took it upon herself to pour herself another shot; a double, and then downed that one too. She followed it up with another before Chade took the bottle and put it on the dresser out of her reach. He and Baylei stared at one another. Chade with concern and Baylei with sadness.

"Tell me, what's bothering you, Beautiful? Drinking is only going to take your problem away temporarily. We're not going that route. I'm here to talk to you about whatever it is without judgement." Baylei's chin fell to her chest and Chade rushed to her side. "Always hold your head high; no matter the situation. Adjust your crown and wear that muthafucka with pride and grace, Beautiful."

A tear fell from Baylei's eye and Chade used his thumb to wipe it away when she looked up at him. Her lip quivered but she fought hard to keep from crying like a baby. The alcohol was working overtime because her emotions were front and center. Chade gathered her in his arms and allowed her to cry it out. When Baylei cried most of her pain away, she shrugged out of Chade's hold. Never glancing up, she focused on the makeup stain she left on the left side of his dress shirt.

"I'm sorry for messing up your shirt. I'll have it cleaned for you when we get back to shore. I've messed up your night, and I didn't mean for things to end this way. Not to sound standoffish, but I don't want to talk about what I read in my phone. If it's alright with you, I'd rather we just enjoy the rest of the night without the complications that I'm going to face when I get home. Another drink would make me feel a lot better though."

Baylei smirked because she tried to sneak the last part in quickly. Chade wasn't giving her anything else to drink. Instead, he walked to his luggage, removed his shirt, and threw it on a chair that sat in the corner. The muscles in his back flexed as he bent down and pulled a pack of cigarettes from the bag. Baylei's nose turned up instantly because she couldn't stand a man that smoked those stinky ass things. She watched as Chade removed a pack of woods and everything started coming together.

Chade took out one of the wrappers and emptied a few of the cigarettes onto it. Baylei was amazed because she wouldn't have known the difference had she not seen it for herself. Instead of tobacco, Chade had a full blunt in his hands that he rolled perfectly. Raising the wood to his lips, he ran his tongue along the edge, making her yoni do a happy dance in her thong. Grabbing a lighter from a pocket of his bag, Chade held his hand out to help Baylei from the bed.

Making sure to grab the bottle of Remy, Chade led the way out of the cabin. As they walked past the dresser, Baylei swiped the tequila in her free hand, never missing a beat. They walked up a flight of stairs to the upper deck. There were lounge chairs that overlooked the black water line along the wall. Chade walked until the pair was in a semi dark area before he chose the spot they were going to chill. He sat down without releasing Baylei's hand and guided her between his legs.

Baylei stalled momentarily because his chiseled chest was giving her all types of vibes and she didn't trust herself to chill so close to him. Baylei's instincts took over and she found herself admiring the imprint of his dick that sat like a lump of coal in the front of his slacks. Turning her head, she contemplated going to the lounge chair next to the one Chade was already comfortable in, but he wasn't down for the separation.

"We just chillin', Beautiful. I promise, I won't try anything inappropriate with you."

Baylei unscrewed the top to the bottle she was holding and turned it up without much thought. "It's not you I'm worried about," she said, shaking her head. "You have been a gentleman from the day I met you." Taking another swig of the liquor, Baylei was getting a new buzz on top of the old and her body was heating up fast.

"When did you grab that bottle?" Chade chuckled. "Give it to me. You've had enough, Beautiful. Seriously. I want you to remember every second we spend with each other."

Before handing over her poison, Baylei took three long sips from the bottle and called it quits. She gave Chade the bottle and plopped down on the lounge chair between his legs. Adjusting himself so they would both be comfortable, Chade lit the blunt and inhaled deeply. He blew the smoke away from Baylei, but she instantly got a contact. Baylei hadn't smoked since the day she put her father in the ground, but she got the urge that day. Turning around, she placed her chest on his lower region and smiled.

"Let me hit that." She smirked.

"You don't look like the type that smokes."

"Neither do you, but here you are smuggling weed into another country. That was clever as hell, by the way. Now pass that shit."

Chade hesitated because Baylei was already borderline drunk. He didn't know what she was on but he wasn't about to fight with her; she was a grown-ass woman. Baylei took the blunt when he passed it and hit it like a pro. The smoke came out through her nose and she hit it long and hard once more before giving it back to him.

Baylei laid her head on Chade's stomach and his dick thumped her left breast. She rubbed his member as if it was a puppy's head. Chade fought to compress the groan that was stuck in his throat. He took a deep pull of his blunt to keep his mind off the dirty thoughts running through his mind. Snubbing out the wood, Chade placed his hands on each side of Baylei's head. He forced her to look up at him and she held his gaze seductively.

"Come put that pussy in my face, Beautiful."

The smile on Baylei's face dropped like the ball in Times Square on New Year's Day. She tried her best to stick to her word of not having sex with Chade, but her love box wasn't trying to hear her inner thoughts. In fact, she was having a huge debate in her head.

"Bitch, you better see what that fine man got to offer. You felt the firehose in his pants. Ride it girl, ride!"

"I'm not about to be out here acting like a hoe! I've only known him a couple days."

"So. The. Fuck. What! Noah's lil puny-ass dick wasn't hittin' on nothing. I don't know why you tortured yourself long as you did. Black is the way to go, Lei. I'll put my insanity up if you prove me wrong. It's time for you to get on that pogo stick and show the fuck out! Stop being a punk, bitch!"

There was no way her inner self was going to call her out like that. Baylei was mad because she couldn't slap her for talking out the side of her neck. The mixture of alcohol and marijuana was the thinker for Baylei. She fell right into the trap her inner self set up. Chade motioned for her to come to him and just like music, she moved to his tune.

Baylei stood between Chade's legs and eased toward his head. Holding his left hand out to assist her, Baylei crept slowly so she wouldn't step on any parts of his body. Standing in front of him, Chade let go of her hand and rubbed her calves softly. With every touch, his hand went higher up her leg, lifting her dress inch by inch.

"Mmmm, you smell so good." Chade reached over and hit the lever to let the chair fall back a little bit as he motioned for Baylei to move forward. "Bring it to me, Beautiful," he said, licking his lips.

Baylei's thong was soaked with excitement of what was about to happen. They were alone on the deck, but knowing anyone could come out to get air at any moment made the act more intriguing. The freaky side of Baylei was winning the race because now she wanted to feel Chade's mouth on her. Standing over his head, Baylei's squatted down onto Chade's awaiting tongue and a shiver traveled down her spine.

Using his fingers, Chade moved her thong to the side and licked her slick center slowly. Baylei's knees buckled and he cupped her ass cheeks to keep her steady. Chade wrapped his lips around her bud and sucked lightly. Baylei lost all mobility of her legs causing her to collapse. It was a good thing Chade was holding her, other-wise he could've been hurt.

"I'm just getting started, Beautiful. It's too early for you to tap out," Chade mumbled against her clit.

The vibration of his lips jump started the movements of her hips. Chade's tongue invaded her lower lips and the feeling was just what the doctor ordered. Baylei's eyes closed as she fell forward grabbing the chair to hold herself steady. Using her upper body, she used the arms of the lounge to go into a full split giving Chade all access to her goodies.

"That's what you doing now? I love that shit. Your pussy is so damn pretty."

He dove in head first as he sucked her soul through her yoni. Baylei's legs shook with every stroke of his tongue and she was losing control. Not knowing how long she would be able to hold the compromising position she put herself in, Baylei brought her legs down and grounded her goodies into his mouth while moaning seductively.

"I'm cummin', Chade. Shit. damn. Ssssss."

Baylei held the side of his head as her juices marinated his beard. Chade didn't let up. He kept going causing her to cum again within seconds. Backing away from his mouth, Baylei placed her foot on the floor of the deck and attempted to get up. She had to get away from his lethal mouth while she had the opportunity. Chade laid back and rubbed her sweet nectar into the hairs on his chin with a smirk on his face.

"Where you going, Beautiful? Don't run from me now. You opened the door for me to make you forget about all your problems."

"Run? I don't run away from anything. You've ignited a fire that only you would be able to distinguish. I have on too many clothes," Baylei said as she slipped the beautiful dress over her head.

Her body was sculpted like a goddess. She wasn't too small nor was she too big. She was just right in Chade's eyes. He stood from his position and made his way over to where she stood. Turning her around, Chade placed his hand around her neck and gently pushed her into the wall of the deck. Running his hand up and down the crack of her ass, he pushed his thumb inside and Baylei tensed up because her sacred hole had never been tampered with in such a manner.

"Relax. I got you," Chade whispered as he continued exploring her secondary hole and she pushed back on his thumb.

That was his cue to go forward because at that point, Baylei was all in. Using his free hand, Chade unbuckled his pants but grabbed the gold wrapper from the pocket before allowing them to fall to his feet. He kicked them away, removing his thumb. Baylei looked back with her bottom lip locked between her teeth. Covering his manhood with the condom, Chade ran the tip along her wet lips. Lining it up with her opening, he pushed forward and damn near lost his shit.

"Damn, it's tight and warm. Just the way I like it." Cradling Baylei's right leg in the crook of his arm, Chade pushed deeper and cursed through gritted teeth. "Fuck!"

He needed better access, so he lifted her other leg while she placed her palms on the wall. Baylei was convinced he could hold her weight and went with the flow Chade set in place. He hit crevices she forgot she possessed and she was definitely getting the pleasure she desired. Noah would never do anything spontaneous; he was a missionary kind of man. Baylei was never going back to having a boring sex life. Chade had let the sexy lioness out and she was overly ready to play.

"Stop playing down there, Chade. Give me what you gave that bitch that's stalking your ass. I want the G14 classified dick."

"Nah, she didn't get none of that shit, Beautiful. That's the reason she's acting stupid. I got you though. You won't have to stalk me. After this, you can have any and everything your heart desires," Chade said, churning her yoni like butter as he kissed the back of her neck.

The sexual act went on for what seemed like forever. Baylei and Chade was so engulfed in each other that they didn't know they had an audience. Sakeenya was standing in the cut with her phone in hand as she recorded the couple. Inside she was seething because she wanted so badly to be the woman Chade was sexing, but every time Chade tried to initiate the act, she had an excuse for why she couldn't go through with it. His bank account was what she really wanted and letting him fuck would've been the key to achieving it. Since that wasn't how she rolled, Sakeenya had everything she needed in the palm of her hand to put Chade's business out for all to see.

Chapter 17

Baylei and Chade went back to the cabin moments after their session ended. They didn't bother getting dressed because everyone was tucked away in their own living quarters. After showering and making love again, they slept the rest of the morning away. By the time they had awakened, it was lunch time and the captain of the yacht had docked the boat on the island of St. John. Chade woke up first and left Baylei sleeping while he went to get some food for them to eat.

He was met by Sanji at the kitchen. By the smile on his face, Chade knew his boy had one hell of a night with Jordyn. Sanji sat with his head held high and his chest poked out. Chade sat on the stool next to him and waited for one of the staff members to take his order.

"What it do, fam?" Sanji asked, sipping his glass of water.

"Shit. Just enjoying life. What got you smiling like you hit the jackpot?"

"Jordyn." Sanji had a faraway look in his eye when he said her name. "That woman is it, man. There's no way I'm going to be able to let her walk away from me after this trip. Don't even say it. I know it's too early, but I felt this way before we called it a night and left the party. The sex was an added bonus. Jordyn is a keeper and I'm claiming that."

Malik walked up with a replica of Sanji's smile on his face. Chade shook his head because his brothers couldn't hide what type of night they had if they were paid to disclose that shit. It had been a long while since Malik seemed utterly happy.

"What you shaking your head for?" Malik asked, slapping hands with Chade then Sanji.

"You got the 'I shot out a few nuts' look in your eyes." Sanji laughed.

"Nah, he got that 'Toni fucked the shit out of him' look going on," Chade retorted.

"Fuck both of y'all. Don't come for me like that. All I can say is, we had fun. Now I have to feed her so she can get up and tour this island with me."

"How long are we going to be here? I need to know how much time I have to play with."

Sanji looked down at his watch and back at Chade. "It's almost noon and we're here until about four. By the time we get back to the starting point, it will be well after dark."

The cook came out and stood in front of the counter. "Good afternoon, what can I get for you?" he asked.

"I would like two cheeseburgers with lettuce, tomato, and onion on the side. I would also like ketchup, mustard, and mayonnaise packets, fries, and two pink lemonades please. Oh, and I would like those burgers well done."

The cook wrote down everything on a notepad and did the same for Malik's order. Sanji rose to his feet when his food was brought out on a tray. He waited until Malik finished putting in his order before he bid his farewell.

"Aye, I'm about to go feed Jordyn. We can meet up in about an hour to enjoy the sights as a group. We should invite the ladies to the wedding. What y'all think?"

"I'm good with that," Chade said, giving Sanji a brotherly hug. Don't get caught up in the bedroom. We have to show them a good time."

"Yeah, I'll try." Sanji smirked. "Well, I'm out. Catch up with y'all in a minute."

Sanji left, heading back to his cabin, and it was just Chade and Malik. They sat in silence for a few, giving Chade the time to reminisce about Baylei. He didn't get the answer to his question of what was bothering her last night. Chade wasn't going to push her to tell him, but he would try his best to keep her mind off of it for the duration of their trip.

"Man, Toni is a real-ass chick. She is the ideal woman to have by my side. She's easy to talk to and I like that about her. Ailani could never hold an intellectual conversation with me. She hasn't been able to talk about anything other than ways of spending my money without bringing any back into the home. Ailani hasn't worked for damn near a year and I don't see that changing anytime soon. What one woman won't do, another will."

"What are you going to do?" Chade asked.

"I'm leaving Ailani alone, man. She's been calling me every other hour since we left Vegas. I went home and she wasn't there. I packed for this trip and went to Samir's crib and went to the airport from there." Malik had a faraway look in his eyes that Chade had never seen before. "Selena told Samir that she saw Ailani in the store with another nigga. The bitch been cheating for the longest. That's the reason she's never home. I don't have shit to say to her when I get back. Hopefully, she understands what I haven't told her because Ailani has to go."

"Damn, Malik. That's fucked up. I agree, it's time to put a stop to that shit. You should've installed those cameras when you had suspicions last time. I'm glad you know what's going on and you can address the situation with her," Chade said quietly.

"I'm not addressing nothing! I'm just going in there and packing my shit. She can have that crib; I'll get another one. I'm not about to argue with her; I'm just gon' leave. Ailani will cause me to do something my mother wouldn't be proud of. Plus, I have a career to think about."

"If you need me, I'm there, bro."

Their food came at that precise moment and they dapped each other up and went their separate ways after agreeing to meet up for the tour. The things Malik said about Ailani didn't surprise Chade at all. He always said she wasn't shit, but kept his thoughts to himself after Malik didn't listen. Everything done in the dark, always came to light. Chade knew about that first hand and it was the reason he was skeptical about getting in another serious relationship. Baylei was changing his perspective slowly.

When he got back to the room, Baylei wasn't there. He panicked, but calmed down when he realized she couldn't be too far away. She had to be somewhere on the boat. As he went to look for her, the door opened and in walked Beautiful. She was adorned in an olive-green two-piece swimsuit that showcased her toned body.

The olive-green cover-up didn't hide much, but made the swimsuit appropriate enough to walk around in. She had a pretty tattoo of little flowers surrounded by tribal symbols that went from her navel around her side and disappeared around her back. Chade didn't notice it until that moment and loved it.

"Hey, I got you some lunch. I thought you ran off on me," Chade smirked.

"Now, why would I do such a thing? I went to see my girls. We're going to take advantage of this tour. Sanji told us that you guys will be accompanying us."

"Yeah, that's the plan. Come on so you can eat. I need you to have all of your energy. It's kind of warm out there." Chade's eyes roamed her body seductively. "You are so beautiful."

"Aht aht. I know that look. We have plans and you still have to shower and get dressed. By the way, I'm energized to the max, thanks to you. I wanted to tell you that you got all the kinks out of a sister's body. I needed that."

Baylei walked across the room and wrapped her arms around Chade's waist. Standing on her toes, she kissed him on the chin until he lowered his head allowing their lips to connect. They locked lips until Baylei stepped away and slapped him on the ass.

"Nah, that's something you can never do again. The shit is gay as fuck, Beautiful."

Baylei laughed because men thought everything was gay nowadays. To her, it was just a playful gesture, but whatever. She picked up the containers and took them to the breakfast nook. Opening the first container, she was glad Chade didn't get any condiments on her burger because she wouldn't have eaten it. Baylei took a fry and popped it in her mouth and chewed slowly.

"Are you going to stand there looking at me, or are you going to join me?" She asked with a smile.

"I can't help looking at you, Beautiful." Chade sat next to her on a stool and opened his own container. Assembling his burger, he put ketchup, mustard, and mayo on it and Baylei turned up her nose. Chade glanced in her direction and laughed. "Why are you looking at me like that?"

160

You better brush, gargle, and brush again because you won't be able to kiss these lips with all that shit on your breath. That's disgusting."

"Here's your pink lemonade. You're gonna need it eating that dry-ass burger. Get with the program. This shit is about to hit, baby."

"There's moisture from the lettuce, tomatoes, and cheese. All that other stuff is nasty as hell, but that's your food; enjoy."

Chade ate his food while shaking his head. Baylei's phone started ringing and she got up to get it from the room. When she returned, she sat down, putting her Airpod in her ear.

"Hey, ma."

"You must've found you a fine island boy to entertain because I haven't heard from you. What happened to you calling me once a day, Lei?"

Baylei looked at Chade and her cheeks reddened as she smiled from ear to ear. "Something like that. It's nothing though. I was going to call you later today, I swear."

"Yeah, tell me anything. Long as I know you're alright, that's all that matters. I'm going to leave you alone for now, but I better get a call tomorrow, Baylei Marie."

"No, you didn't just call me by my government." Baylei laughed as she ate her food. "You will hear from me, Slim. I love you. I have to finish eating so I can hit the beach. I'll be going shopping to get you a lot of souvenirs."

"You don't have to worry about buying me anything. I want you to have a good time and it seems as if you're doing just that. Please stay safe and don't roam around alone. I love you too, Lei. I'll be waiting on your call."

Baylei's mom ended the call and she went to her social media inbox to see if ChanceLover had reached out to her. When she saw that he hadn't, she smiled. He must've been having just as much fun as she was on his vacation. Baylei couldn't wait to hear about the many bitches he'd entertained on his trip. She had to see how things went with Chade before sharing the details with her online friend. The last thing she wanted to do was come off as a hoe.

"You and your mom seem like you're pretty close." Chade said getting her attention.

"I love that lady with everything in me. She's always looking out for me."

"That's the way my mother and I are. I'm surprised she hasn't called reading me my rights because I haven't called her. I'll send her a few pictures while we're on the tour. Speaking of the tour, we better get a move on before we're late."

"Chade, I'm already dressed. You still have to shower and get yourself together." Baylei laughed.

"You're right. I'll go handle that real quick."

Chade got up and took his container to the garbage. As he exited the kitchen, he stopped and planted a kiss on Baylei's forehead before disappearing into the bedroom. The night they had was amazing, but Baylei felt bad for Chade because she had no plans of taking things any further than St. Thomas. She'd already went against what she believed in by having sex with him; and she was going to do it again.

Passing up the opportunity to feel that way again was something Baylei wasn't going to do. She hadn't been that aroused in a very long time and she was going to milk it for all it was worth.

As she sat picking at what was left of her food, there was a light knock on the cabin door. Baylei got up to answer and didn't ask who it was before swinging it open. Sakeenya was standing before her with a smirk on her face. Baylei tilted her head to the side without uttering a word.

"Are you going to just stand there, or are you going to invite me in?" Sakeenya sassed.

"Invite you in? You not coming in here. What can I help you with?"

Baylei didn't move an inch. Dating Noah changed her into the mild-mannered woman she was from back in the day. The saying was true, "you could take the girl out of the hood, but you can't take the hood out of the girl". Sakeenya was forcing the girl that was born and raised on the southside of Chicago out to play.

"Whatever you and Chade had going on back in California is something that won't be addressed here. Take that shit up with him at a later date, because he belongs to me for a few more days. After that, he's all yours. Now, get the fuck away from this room!"

Sakeenya snickered as she scrolled through her phone. She raised the device and turned it for Baylei to see. Sakeenya had posted a video on her social media of Baylei against the wall in a split while Chade stirred her coffee. Seeing the video didn't bother Baylei at all because her face wasn't visible. Anyone that knew her could probably tell it was her, but she wasn't worried.

"You did that for what? I'm a grown-ass woman that takes care of herself. I can't get in trouble by anyone, if that's what you thought." Baylei's eyes traveled to the post under the video and laughed. "What Chade is doing with me should be your least concern. For a bitch that wears Jordans but spells 'Nike' Niki, is a damn shame. Go find you somebody else to play with, Sakeenya." Baylei slammed the door and when she turned around, Chade was standing in the doorway of the room.

She went to the breakfast nook and cleared the table. Chade had a towel wrapped around his waist and small specks of water were visible along the tattoo on his chest. Baylei kept herself busy in the small kitchen so he couldn't see the lust in her eyes.

"Was that Sakeenya at the door?" he asked.

"Yep. Chade, she better find herself some business because I won't be able to compose myself the next time she steps to me. She uploaded a video on social media with us having sex on the deck. She's a fucking stalker." Baylei chuckled.

"I'm gon' tell her to take that shit down! What the fuck was she thinking?"

"She doesn't have to take it down. Let her be great. Your psychotic boo doesn't have me on her social media and our faces aren't visible so, it's nothing to me. The video could go viral for all I care. Just keep her away from me before I get locked up. I have no problem slapping somebody's child; that's exactly what she's acting like."

"I'm sorry she was spying on us—"

"No, she was following *you*. I have nothing to do with y'all situation, but what she's not going to do is keep involving me in the bullshit. I'll see you on the island. I need some air."

Baylei grabbed her beach bag from the couch and left the cabin. Chade was left fuming because once again, Sakeenya was being messy. The thought of her posting their intimate moment was a low blow. Chade turned to get dressed so he could get of the yacht to find Baylei and confront Sakeenya.

Chapter 18

Jordyn and Sanji were hugged up, waiting on Chade and Baylei to come off the yacht. Sanji hadn't fallen for a woman so quickly in all of his years of dating. Watching Jordyn sleep after he caressed her body and soul, Sanji was in love. He couldn't see himself allowing her to get on a plane going back to Chicago. Sanji wanted Jordyn with him at all times but, he knew there were so many things he had to put in place beforehand.

"I really enjoyed myself last night," Sanji said, kissing Jordyn's lips.

"Same here. We can have fun for the rest of the trip, if that's what you want to do. I'm not talking about just sex either."

"Jordyn, you initiated the intimacy. I could've gone without, to be honest. I'm interested in *you*, not what's between your legs. Truthfully, you are the type of woman I need in my life. The type I can take home to meet my mama. That shit hasn't happened in a very long time."

Sanji looked down at Jordyn with the look of love in his eyes and Jordyn felt every bit of it through her pores. She wanted to express herself to him as well, but it was too early for all of that mushy shit. Instead, Jordyn smiled and puckered her lips for a kiss. Sanji obliged and gave her what she wanted. They were so engulfed in one another that when Baylei approached them, she had to clear her throat to get their attention.

"Ahem." Jordyn stepped back with flustered cheeks and leaned into Sanji's chest to hide her face. "Y'all better go back inside with all of that public display of affection." Baylei laughed.

"Where's my boy?" Sanji asked as he looked around for Chade.

"He should be coming out shortly, I guess." Baylei hunched her shoulders. "Where's Toni, Jordyn?"

"Divas!" Toni shrieked walking toward them in a swimsuit in the same color as Baylei's, but a different design. Malik was behind her with his eyes glued to her voluptuous ass. "Y'all ready to get in this beautiful water and take some pictures?"

Toni's smile dropped from her face as she looked to her right. Baylei and Jordyn followed her gaze and Sakeenya and her crew were eyeballing them with scowls on their faces. "These weak ass bitches. Man, let's take a walk," Toni said, turning to Malik." I'll be right back. Y'all better tell Ahmad to call off his wedding because Chasity ain't where it's at."

Toni walked away but Malik grabbed her by the arm with a concerned look on his face. "What do you mean?"

She wanted to fill her girls in on what she'd overheard at the bathroom door, but her anger got the best of her when she told Ahmad's friends to warn him. It didn't occur to her that they would want to know more about what she was talking about. Toni wanted to tell Baylei and Jordyn first, but there was no way Malik nor would Sanji allow them to walk away without spilling the beans.

"Last night I overheard some information that I sat on longer than I should have. Ahmad is making a mistake marrying Chasity." Toni turned her back to Chasity and her herd because they were all in her mouth trying to read her lips. "The chick that has been hassling Chade—"

"Sakeenya," Malik cut in.

"Yeah, her," Toni said, rolling her eyes. "She and Chasity were having a heated discussion in the bathroom and I was stuck in place listening to what they were saying. To make a long story short, Chasity used Sakeenya to go after Chade so both of them would have a man to take care of them. Sakeenya obviously couldn't get into Chade the way they planned because she's too tied up with her feelings for Chasity."

"I know you lying!" Jordyn exclaimed. "Toni, I know you're not saying what I think you're saying."

"Y'all heard me right. Chasity and Sakeenya are carpet munchers, bumpin' cats, you know, fuckin' each other. I didn't have to put two and two together because Chasity confirmed my suspicions by saying, long as she marries Ahmad, they were both going to come up from that alone. Sakeenya confessed that she hasn't slept with Chade because she likes eating the twat, preferably Chasity's."

"That's dirty as hell," Baylei said, trying her best not to scowl in the group's direction. "If she is in love with Chasity, why is she doing so much to get Chade's attention? The shit isn't making sense to me. She almost got her head knocked off when she thought posting a video of me and Chade was going to worry me."

Chade finally found his way off the yacht and headed right in the direction of Sakeenya. "Go grab him, Sanji. He's going to hurt that girl." Baylei didn't want Chade to get in any trouble behind Sakeenya.

"Aye, bro. Come here for a minute." Chade ignored Sanji, which caused him to jog over to his friend before he made it to his target. "It's not worth it, man. Let her ass be great and think she has the upper hand in the situation." Sanji positioned himself in front of Chade and ushered him in the opposite direction.

"Sakeenya is going to stop playing with me!" Chade fumed.

"All that shit she's doing is a front for Chasity. Toni shared some news with us and it's not good for Ahmad. We have to tell him what's up so he won't go through with this wedding."

Stopping where he stood, Chade turned to Sanji, confused. "What do Sakeenya have to do with Ahmad and Chasity?"

"Man, everything. Those two are snakes and you can hear their hisses a mile away. Sakeenya and Chasity are lovers. They are playing Ahmad and you were part of their plan, but Sakeenya didn't follow through."

"What you mean she didn't follow through? I've never gotten past her giving me head. Any time I went in for the pussy, she always had an excuse. Hell, I thought she was a virgin and wasn't ready for the shit I'm packin' down below. The thought of her being a lesbian never crossed my mind."

Chade glanced in Sakeenya's direction and she was grilling Ahmad as he loved on Chasity's shiesty ass. "I've been telling Ahmad something wasn't right with that girl, but he didn't listen and I have a feeling he won't take well to the information I'm going to lay on him about his wifey. I forgot to ask Baylei if she would accompany me to the wedding."

"Don't worry about it. Jordyn already said they were going to sit that one out. She feels Sakeenya's actions warranted they wasn't wanted at the wedding. I told her it wasn't a problem, but with the news we just learned, Ahmad isn't going to be walking down the aisle anyway."

"Chasity can do no wrong in Ahmad's eyes. He's not going to believe anything thing that's told to him about her. I don't know what she has done to him, but she has him wrapped around her finger."

"Maybe if we all talk to him, he'd hear us out. We have to deal with this shit before we get back on the yacht. The wedding is in two days and the truth must come out. In the meantime, let's enjoy the time we have with the beauties that's waiting on us."

Sanji led the way back to their group. Baylei was talking lowly to Jordyn and Malik was kissing Toni all over her face, making her squirm and giggle like a schoolgirl. Baylei pointed toward the water and turned in Chade's direction as he approached. She wanted to take pictures underwater with the fish. It was always a dream of hers to swim in clear blue water alongside the water creatures.

Chade grabbed Baylei's hand and walked toward the equipment booth to start their adventure for the day. Trying to push the problems at hand to the back of his mind, he wanted to have fun before the storm. The way Baylei was looking at the water let Chade know she really wanted to get in and experience what awaited them. When they arrived at the booth, Chade requested a couple of waterproof cameras and the oxygen equipment they would need to breathe underwater.

"Are you ready to do this?" Chade asked.

"How did you know? I never mentioned it." Snorkeling was something Baylei always wanted to do and she was about to knock it off her bucket list.

"The way you kept looking at the water, I knew you wanted to go in head first. You no longer have to wait. I've made it happen. Do you need a life jacket? In other words, can you swim?"

"In the water, I'm a human mermaid." Baylei laughed. "We won't be going in too deep anyway, but I'll be alright. It's you I may have to worry about. You know they say black people can't swim."

"That doesn't pertain to me, Beautiful. I was on the swim team all through high school and college."

"We'll see. I may have to make this competitive somehow. You sound like you're bragging and shit."

Malik stopped their playful interaction when he came over with Ahmad in tow. Chade huffed as he tried to control his anger. He'd specifically said he would deal with telling Ahmad anything until after they enjoyed the tour of the island. Chade knew if they discussed Chasity's indiscretions and her infidelity, no one would have fun.

"What's up, y'all? Malik said there's something you want to talk to me about," Ahmad said calmly.

Baylei, Toni, and Jordyn took that moment to go into the water without the men. Chade smiled because he didn't have to ask to give them a minute. As he watched the sway of Baylei's hips, Ahmad's voice brought him back to the situation at hand. Clearing his throat, Chade rubbed the back of his head trying to figure out how he was going to tell his friend what he knew. Sanji laughed and took over because he felt they were wasting time trying to lay it out gently.

"Say, Ahmad. I'm not about to sugarcoat shit for you. I've always been straight up and I'm going to give it to you straight with no chaser. I learned something about your woman that doesn't sit well with me."

"What could you have possibly heard about Chasity?" Ahmad crossed his arms over his chest as his eyebrows furrowed together.

"There's no need to get defensive, bro. Deflate ya chest, because we're better than that. All I want you to do is hear us out," Chade said, trying to defuse the attitude that Ahmad obviously had. "Chasity isn't marrying you because she loves you, man. She's using you."

"We've been through this shit before, Chade. I thought we'd agreed that we wouldn't bring up your assumptions about Chasity anymore."

Malik shook his head because Ahmad always shied away from any conversation about his soon to be wife. He wasn't about to let him dodge that shit again. Usually he stayed out of it, but he couldn't bring himself to do it that time around.

"There's no assumption, Ahmad. Chasity and Sakeenya aren't just best friends; they are lovers. They approached you and Chade for financial gain. You have to call off the wedding, bro. There's no way I can participate in a wedding which in the end, you will be hurt."

"Where are you getting your information from? Chasity don't like women! This is what I'm talking about. Y'all always talking about being there for me but something negative comes up every time. Stop looking into the social media bullshit and believe in what I tell you!"

Ahmad was pissed, but his friends weren't buying into his tirade. Since Ahmad wanted to try making them out to be liars, the time for them to tell him everything they knew was at that moment. Chade stepped to his long-time friend and placed his hand on Ahmad's shoulder. He slapped Chade's hand off him and took a step back.

"Don't touch me, dawg. I'm sick of this shit! Why can't y'all just be happy for me?" Ahmad snapped.

"I'm not the snake in your camp. The bitch you going to war for is the one you should be huffin' at! I'll beat yo' ass out here!"

Sanji stepped between the two of them so things wouldn't get worse than what it already was. "We are not about to fall out over this! Both of y'all needs to pipe the fuck down. It has always been bros before hoes, and you muthafuckas seems to have forgotten that shit. We gon' talk like brothers and leave this shit right here," he said, grilling both of them simultaneously. "Ahmad, we wouldn't be coming to you if we didn't give a fuck about the mistake you are about to make. I don't know Chasity from a can of paint, but I know what I heard ain't cool."

"When have we ever believed hearsay? When y'all get proof, holla at me, because I *will* be getting married in two days." Ahmad stormed off without saying much more.

"Fuck! What's up with bro and shawty?" Sanji screamed.

"I don't know, but Ahmad got his head so far up that bitch's ass that he can't see. I didn't like her from the moment he showed me the woman he met online. Chasity had raunchy videos and pictures on her page. She and Sakeenya was always together and the caption always mentioned niggas and money."

"Why would that automatically cause you to dislike the woman?" Sanji laughed.

"Ahmad told us he had been conversating with Chasity for months and really liked her personality. He said she had so much going on for herself in Michigan, but I know that was game. She said everything to get her foot in the door and been milking his ass ever since. He told me he was supporting her while she's in school, but the last I heard, she was working."

"Maybe they came to an agreement for her to get her education to better herself and he would be the sole provider. Don't get me wrong, the whole situation is fucked up on all levels, but we can't make Ahmad call off the wedding. He's going to have to see the shit on his own and I hope nobody gets hurt in the process. That's our brother, and he's getting married in two days. Are we there or not?" Sanji asked seriously.

"I'm done talking about that bullshit. I'm about to enjoy this tour. I don't know about y'all," Chade said, walking away.

"Chade is right, Sanji. Let's get back to the ladies. This isn't the last time we will be addressing this issue. Shit is going to hit the fan and it's going to be a whirlwind." Malik and Sanji walked across the sand behind Chade, leaving the conversation back at the booth.

Chapter 19

Ahmad was fuming as he made his way back to the yacht. He wasn't in the mood to do the tour after his boys tried telling him about what they heard. Ahmad didn't appreciate how Chade brought everyone into the mix of basically ganging up on him about Chasity. Ahmad understood the reason as to why Chade didn't get close to women, but he didn't need him trying to shove his logic down Ahmad's throat.

As he stepped on the first stair of the yacht, he looked over to where Chasity and her friends were chilling with drinks in hand. The things that were said flooded his mind and he couldn't shake the shit for nothing. Stalking across the sand, Ahmad approached Chasity in a haste.

"Fuck this tour. I need to holla at you back in the cabin," Ahmad said angrily.

"Babe, what's wrong? Is everything okay?"

"Now, Chas! Save the questions," he said, walking off. Ahmad didn't hear any movement behind him and turn abruptly to see what the holdup was. "Did you hear what I just said to you? Get up and let's go, Chas!" The bass in Ahmad's voice shook Chasity and she scrambled to her feet.

Sakeenya sprang up and grabbed Chasity by her arm. "Since when do we jump when a nigga tell us to? That's not how we get down."

"Say what?" Ahmad asked with a raised eyebrow.

"Let me handle this. I'll be right back," Chasity said, twisting out of her friend's grasp. Sakeenya finally released the hold she had on Chasity, but she grilled Ahmad with pure hate.

Ahmad pushed Chasity in the direction of the boat; not to hurt her, but to get her ass moving. The sun that beamed in the sky had nothing on the heat that resonated from his body. As they were walking up the stairs, Chasity turned to say something to Ahmad and then thought twice about it when she saw the scowl on his face. Keeping quiet was the best option for her at that time. It didn't take long for them to get back to the cabin. The minute the door closed

behind Ahmad, he didn't waste any time with his line of questioning.

"Is there anything you want to tell me, Chas?" Ahmad stood
with his back against the wall and his arms folded over his chest.

"Anything like what? We just had a wonderful morning together and now you are upset, handling me as if I did something to
you. I don't know where any of this anger is coming from, Ahmad."
Chasity's words seemed sincere and it softened Ahmad up a little
bit. "Tell me what's on your mind and come right out with it."

Ahmad played things over in his head because he didn't want
to come off as being aggressive. Even though he didn't believe any
of the things he'd heard about Chasity, Sakeenya's actions moments
before had him second guessing himself. The way she got mad had
Ahmad thinking of other times he'd caught Sakeenya peering at him
in a disgusted way. He always brushed it off because when he
thought he'd seen the expression, it would disappear just as fast,
making him believe he'd imagined it.

"Chasity, yes, we've had a wonderful week thus far and I'm
pissed at myself for even bringing this bullshit up. I need to know
that you are being truthful with me all around. Now, I'm going to
ask you one more time. Is there anything you need to tell me? I'm
giving you the chance to come clean about any discretions you may
have hidden away."

Chasity's eyes turned to slits and Ahmad knew he had pissed
her off. Shaking her head, Chasity paced the floor as she bit her
bottom lip. "When I met you online, you won my heart fairly
quickly, Ahmad. You were there for me when I was struggling to
find my place in this dreadful world. You believed in me when I
didn't believe in myself. It was your encouraging words that made
me move my ass and get back in school. I would be a fool to deceive
you in kind of way." A lone tear cascaded down her face. Ahmad
walked toward her slowly and reached out to embrace her.

"No, Ahmad! I don't know what happened when you went to
talk to your friends, but I know they don't care for me. I've known
this from the moment you introduced me to Chade and I knew from
day one how he felt without him even opening his mouth."

"I'm sorry you felt uncomfortable for the past six months, Chas. There were things mentioned when I talked to the guys and I need you to answer truthfully to what I'm about to ask." Ahmad took a deep breath as he stared deeply in her eyes. "Have you ever slept with Sakeenya?" Ahmad was searching for any signs of deceit as he waited for Chasity's response.

"Sakeenya? She's my friend, Ahmad! And if you hadn't no-ticed, she's a female! I have never been with a woman in my life. Sakeenya has and always will be overprotective of me. That will never change, but accusing me of having a sexual relationship with her is ridiculous. She was having relations with Chade! Why the hell would you even assume something was going on between the two of us?"

The tears dried up and all Chasity saw was red. Ahmad tried to console her, but his bride-to-be wasn't having it. "Let me guess. One of them hoes brought this crap to the attention of your friends, huh? They don't know shit about me, Ahmad! As a matter of fact, they don't know them niggas either! I'll say this shit one more time; Sakeenya and I are friends. You don't have to worry yourself trying to figure out what we have going on because ain't shit to worry about." Chasity softened her tone and walked into Ahmad's arms.

"If I had something else going on in my life, I wouldn't be ex-cited about you asking me to marry you. Ahmad, we are set to walk down the aisle on Saturday. We can't allow negativity to steer us away from our happily ever after. I love you and only you, baby."

Ahmad held on to Chasity tightly and rested his chin on the top of her head. He had made up his mind that he would believe in his fiancé and let any doubts blow in the wind. The love he felt for Chasity was the same type of love he felt generating from her vibes. She hasn't given him any reason to question her and Ahmad was going with his gut on this one.

"Come on so we can enjoy the tour," Chasity said, looking up at him.

"Nah, you go ahead and enjoy yourself. I'm not in the mood to be around anybody right now." Ahmad kissed Chasity on the lips and stepped back. "Go ahead. I'll be here when you come back. I love you, Chas."

"I love you too, Mr. Sanford." Chasity smiled, stealing another kiss. She walked toward the door and looked back at Ahmad as he walked slowly to the bedroom before she left to find Sakeenya.

***

Chasity kept looking back to make sure Ahmad wasn't behind her as she rushed through the yacht. She took deep breaths in an attempt to stop the rapid beating of her heart. It was a good thing she'd learned young to make herself cry. When Ahmad asked about her relationship with Sakeenya, Chasity almost messed her pants. She didn't have any other choice other than to get mad, then hit his ass with the tears. The main thing she needed to know was, how the hell did anybody know about her and Sakeenya's discretions?

"The only person that knew about that shit was her ass!" Chasity said lowly.

Charging off the yacht with a vengeance, Chasity scanned the beach in search of Sakeenya. The section she left when Ahmad came over was empty and it frustrated her terribly. She looked out into the water, not recognizing anyone except Chade and the other guys. The hoes they were with were irrelevant, so she moved along before the temptation to approach them became stronger.

"Chasity!"

Hearing her name being called, Chasity turned around in circles like a lost child trying to figure out who was calling her and where they were. She finally spotting her cousin Krystal sitting on a stool at the beach bar. Making her way over, Chasity sat down with a thud.

"What's with the long face?" Krystal asked, taking a sip of her frozen drink.

"Too damn much. I don't have time for messy-ass people, Cuz. Where the hell is Keenya?"

"She went back onto the boat not long after you and Ahmad. She was pissed about the way he handled you in front of us. I had let her know that she needed to stay out of your business and allow you to take care of that on your own. Whatever's going on is y'all business. Keep Sakeenya out of it, Chasity."

"Girl, you know how Sakeenya is. We've been there for each other through the mud. She's gonna ride down on whoever comes off as a threat. She was just looking out for my well-being and I would've done the same for her."

Chasity did her best to explain Sakeenya's actions, but the expression on Krystal's face told her she wasn't buying into it. Her cousin had her own suspicions of Chasity and Sakeenya's relationship and had asked many times if there was something going on between them. She always denied any involvement. What she and Sakeenya did behind closed doors wasn't any of her concern. Chasity had to talk with Sakeenya and fast because the jealousy she hid so well in the past wasn't quite hidden anymore. The last thing she needed was people looking down their noses at her built on mere speculation.

"Alright, Chasity. You're my cousin. I've known you my entire life and I know your history." Krystal rolled her eyes. "Do you truly love Ahmad? If not, please don't continue to lead that man on. Walk away before you commit to a marriage you have no plans of following the rules God set in place. It is He you will have to answer to; not just Ahmad."

Chasity chuckled nervously. "Fuck you. Since you know and no one has ever confronted me about my sexuality, keep it that way. In other words, continue to act like you don't know, Krystal." Chasity glared at her cousin with pure hate in her eyes. "You're my cousin and you know firsthand I'll crush your ass if you fuck this up for me."

"Save your idle threats, Chasity. You don't need any help fucking up what you have with Ahmad. You're doing a fine job of that yourself with your conniving ways. God don't like ugly and he's not too fond of pretty either. The two of you snake ass bitches got this shit in the bag. When your bullshit comes into the light and smacks you in the face; and it will. I'll be front and center to wipe the egg off."

Krystal snatched her drink and left Chasity sitting alone at the bar. To hear her cousin say she knew what was going on made Chasity nervous. There was no telling who else had speculations about the subject, but hadn't spoken on it. Ahmad coming to her about the information that was brought to him wasn't by chance. Somebody was running their mouth.

"I gotta find this bitch. She's fucking up big time." Chasity finished her drink and set off to find her homie, lover, friend.

As she walked back to the entrance of the yacht, Sakeenya emerged wearing an orange maxi dress. The sun radiated off her brown skin and she was beautiful. The situation at hand snapped Chasity out of the lustful state she almost got lost in. Waiting for her friend to descend the steps slowly, Chasity strummed her fingers on the railing as her patience thinned.

"Hurry the fuck up off them damn stairs. You ain't in no beauty pageant."

"Oh, so Mr. Man chewed yo' ass out and now you want to come at me sideways? Take that shit up with the nigga you're about to say I do to. You don't want to go that route with me, Chasity."

Glancing around to see if anyone was within earshot to hear Sakeenya's rant, Chasity grabbed her by the arm and damn near dragged her to a secluded area on the beach. Sakeenya snatched away and slapped Chasity across the face. Her nostrils flared wide and her hands balled up into fist.

"Keep your fuckin' hands off me, Chasity. I'm not going to continue to let you talk to me as if I need you. Did you grab on Ahmad's ass when he embarrassed your ass on the beach? I bet a million dollars you didn't! Stop coming for me, because I'll kill yo' ass on this damn island and leave you here to rot."

"Pipe that shit down, bitch. You do need me; stop fronting. Let's not forget, you need me when we get back to California. How else are you going to pay for the apartment you live in that's in my motherfucking name? Or the car that you drive that I pay the note and insurance on? I'm the reason your ass came to California in the first place. If it wasn't for me sending for you, you'd still be living in your mama's basement eating noodles!" Chasity snapped. "Make that your last time putting your hands on *me* and shooting out threats. I'm going to let that shit slide, but don't let it happen again."

The anger dissipated from Sakeenya's face with every word Chasity spoke. There weren't any lies detected and she didn't have a combat to defend herself. Many on the outside looking in would think Chasity was using Ahmad for his money, but honestly, she wasn't. Chasity took care of Sakeenya back in Michigan with the money she finessed from niggas. Sakeenya, on the other hand, sat back and watched her come up without having to work hard at all. That was part of the reasons she agreed to go after Chade, so she wouldn't have to depend on Chasity and have shit thrown in her face.

"Now tell me how the fuck Ahmad heard about us being lovers? Didn't I tell you I bet not here about that shit on this trip?" Sakeenya had a look of shock on her face at Chasity's choice of words. She racked her brain far too long for Chasity's liking because before she knew it, her neck was being squeezed tightly. "Bitch, answer me!"

"I don't know," Sakeenya finally forced out while struggling to get Chasity's hands from around her neck. "I promise, I didn't say anything to anyone." Chasity pushed Sakeenya back into the trees, releasing the hold she had on her.

"He knows, and I had to lie my ass off to get out of the jam obviously you put me in. Why I say it was you is because I know damn well *I* didn't say shit to anyone!" Sakeenya started crying as she walked toward Chasity. "Stay away from me, Keenya! I told you not to fuck this up for me and your drunk ass ran your mouth to some damn body. Now, Ahmad is probably in the cabin wondering if he still wants to marry me. I swear if this wedding doesn't happen, we are done!"

Chasity turned and walked away as Sakeenya yelled her name. She wasn't trying to hear shit Sakeenya had to say. The only thing she worried about was finding a way to ease Ahmad's mind about the love she had for him. she needed him as the breadwinner and there wasn't anything that would get in the way of them getting married.

Chapter 20

Baylei and Chade were on their second lap of swimming back to the shore. There was loud cheering as the onlookers waited to see who was going to win as if they were competing in an Olympic swimming meet. Both of them were going hard because the wager was one neither one wanted to lose. To everyone else, the prize was five hundred dollars, but only the two of them knew what the real reward would be. Privately, they agreed whoever won would have to give the winner head for two hours without a break.

"Bitch, swim!" Baylei said in her head. "You can't afford to have jaw spasms for the duration of this trip from sucking Chade's big ass dick."

Swinging her arms vigorously, Baylei swept the water behind her and pushed forward with all her might. She was determined to win. Losing was not an option. Soon as her feet hit sand, Baylei took off running and slapped Malik's hand for the win.

"Who run the world?" Toni sang as she jumped up and down on the sand wildly.

"Girls!" Jordyn chimed in. All of the guys stood shaking their heads as Chade emerged from the beautiful waters. Wiping the water from his face, Chade shook his finger at Baylei ignoring his friend's reactions.

"She cheated! When I was swimming, she kicked me and I thought a shark or something was about to eat my black ass up." Everybody started laughing because they knew Chade was lying through his teeth.

"Nah, bro, she was nowhere near you the entire time y'all was in the water. She smoked yo' ass, so come up off that chedda," Santi laughed. "I've never seen anyone smoke you like that in the water. To make matters worse, it was a woman that fucked up your streak."

"Whatever," Chade laughed. "I want a rematch," Chade smirked in Baylei's direction.

Baylei took off her swim cap and started drying off with a beach towel. "No can do, patna. I won fair and square. I'll be in the cabin waiting for you to come in to pay me."

She winked at him as she picked up her belongings. Chade was stuck watching her ass sway back and forth as she walked away. As soon as Baylei disappeared through the entryway of the yacht, Chade turned around with his hand cupping his dick.

"Yeah, boy, you got it bad for that one right there," Sanji cracked. "You better take it easy, because Baylei didn't come on this trip to play with ya."

"Shut the hell up, Sanji. I won't even front, baby girl got me in a headspace I've never been in. Truthfully speaking, I can see myself settling down with her."

Sanji put the back of his hand against Chade's forehead. "Are you sick? You gotta be sick. Come on so I can find a hospital to have you checked out." Sanji grabbed him by the arm and started walking toward the yacht.

"I'm not sick." Chade laughed. "Baylei is the epitome of the woman I need in my life. I won't rush into anything, but I know what I want, and it's her. In fact, I'm going to get her right now."

"Nah, I know where you're going, and it's not to pay her the five hundred dollars. Yo' ass bet that woman something sexual for that win."

"See, that's where you're wrong. She bet me something sexual, nigga." Chade walked away smoothly and Sanji couldn't do anything but laugh.

"You've met your match, Chade. She even thinks like you. Be careful with that one. She definitely has the potential to have you walking around with ya dick between your legs. I want to be the best man at the wedding."

"Fuck you, Sanji," Chade said with his middle finger in the air. He kept walking without looking back.

The sun beamed down on Chade's back and he was relieved when he stepped onto the air-conditioned vessel. Strolling through the lobby, Von stepped out of the stairwell with a drink in his hand. He stopped to wait for Chade to get closer as he took a sip from the tumbler.

"What up, Chade? That set was off the chain last night."

"You did yo' thang. Thanks for showing up for us. I knew I had to have you on the turntable for this one," Chade said, giving him a brotherly hug.

"Say, I need to holla at you about some shit."

"Don't tell me that nigga Ahmad didn't pay you. Shit, we need you for the damn reception on Saturday. How much did he promise you?"

"Hold on, fam. I was paid in full once I was set up here. That's not what I want to talk about." Von threw the drink back and leaned against the wall. "After I finished editing video, I noticed there was an audio file that I didn't realized I recorded. When I hit play, everything was cool until I got about twenty minutes in. There were some things I heard that I shouldn't have had access to. Going into detail is something I won't do, but I will say, I don't think your boy will be getting married in a couple days."

Chade was curious to know what Von was actually getting at. Before he could ask him to elaborate, Von cut into his thoughts. Rubbing the back of his neck, Von pushed off the wall and patted Chade on the shoulder.

"Don't ask. I sent both files to your email and only the video to Ahmad. One thing I will say is the content is going to blow your mind. My name Bennett, and I ain't in it," Von said, laughing. "I'm about to go out here and workout under this hot ass sun. Hopefully, I'll find a female that's willing to let me crawl between her thighs before we set out to return back to shore."

Von left Chade wondering, but the thought of Baylei waiting on him pushed the shit he brought to his attention aside. Making his way to the cabin, Chade swiped his keycard and the sounds of Tank filled his ears. It only meant one thing. It was freaky time, and his joint was already leading the way. He grew harder with every step he took because he could taste the sweet nectar of her kitty on his tongue already.

Nearing the bedroom, the music got louder and the steam thicker. Baylei was in the shower singing her ass off. Chade removed his clothes fast as he could and inched toward the sliding door. He opened it and Baylei turned around quickly.

"It's just me," he said, stepping further inside.

"You scared the hell out of me! Announce yourself next time," Baylei said, striking him on the chest.

She stepped back under the water with her back turned and continued washing her body. Chade took the loofah from her hand, taking the liberty of finishing the deed for her. When he slid the loofah between her ass cheeks, Baylei moaned lowly. Her head fell forward and the water soaked her hair. Chade caressed her outer lips and she lifted her leg onto the ledge. Rinsing her off, Chade hung the loofah onto the showerhead and picked Baylei up in a swift motion.

"Now that you're clean, it's time for me to pay my fare, Beautiful." With her back against the cold tile, Chade placed her legs in the crook of his arms and lifted her higher until he had her yoni directly in his face. "Damn, you're pretty," he said, planting light kisses on her lower lips.

Baylei held the back of his head for leverage even though Chade's muscular arms held her body weight effortlessly. Burying his head into her tunnel, Chade maneuvered his tongue around with smooth strokes across her clit. He must've been famished from their competitive swim because he was eating like it was the Last Supper.

Baylei moaned lowly as her eyes fluttered closed. "Nah, open your eyes and watch me devour this pussy," Chade said, taking his mouth off her. "And I want you to let me know I'm doing this shit to your liking."

Doing as she was told, Baylei pulled his head back into her sweet pot and Chade latched on like a baby. Rolling her hips, she fought hard to keep eye contact with the sexy man that was pleasing her better than she'd ever been pleased. The water ran down on both of them. A shiver ran down Baylei's spine and she arched her back as her sweet nectar slid down Chade's throat.

"Oh, Fuck! Yes!" Baylei screamed as she attempted to push Chade's head away.

"Move your muthafuckin' hands, Beautiful. This pussy is mine for the taking. I'm just beginning. I still have an hour and forty-five minutes to drown in this shit."

184

Using his hand to open the sliding door, Chade stepped out onto the rug with Baylei's legs wrapped around his head. He bent down so her head wouldn't hit the door frame and led the way to the bedroom, all while slurping up Baylei's juices. His skills were at an all-time high and Baylei didn't want him to stop. Chade laid her on the bed and ran his hand up and down her slit. Putting his fingers in his mouth, he sucked all of the secretions from them with a smile.

"I'm about to suck your ass into submission. Get ready, because you will be all mine after this is over."

The devil had made a permanent appearance because Baylei spread her legs wide with a grin. She rubbed her perky nipples between her thumb and forefinger before bring one of them to her mouth. Flickering her tongue over her bud, she bit down slightly and moaned.

"I'm ready for all you got, daddy. Bring that shit here."

Chapter 21

"Congratulations on your win, Connery," one of Noah's colleagues called out before he could get into his office.

"Thank you! That one was easy." He laughed.

Noah had just won a high-profile medical case and won millions for his clients. He was on an all-time high and had added a lot of money to his bank account.

Things had been pretty rocky between him and his parents. Noah ignored all calls, texts, and invites to spend any time with them. His mother cried in every voicemail she left on his phone, but the minute he felt any sympathy for her, his father would come along with threatening messages of his own. Noah automatically said fuck him and went about his business.

Sitting behind his desk, Noah kicked his feet up and thought about his big win. With a smile on his face, he retrieved his phone and called the one person that would sure to be happy for him. When he received Baylei's voicemail, his joy turned to anger instantly. Noah specifically told her to take him off the block list and she gave him her ass to kiss. Noah would feel the heat coming from the collar of his shirt hitting his face. As he opened his social media account, he received a text from Mark.

Mark: Hey, I know you may be in court but I couldn't see this without passing it along. Is this your woman?

Noah opened the video Mark attached to the message and pressed play. The image in front of him only infuriated him even more. without a doubt, Noah knew the woman that was spread eagle on the wall was indeed Baylei. The angle of the camera captured the tattoo she had wrapped around her waist perfectly. There was no way she'd be able to deny it wasn't her.

"This bitch is going to make me kill her!" Pressing on Mark's name, Noah listened to the phone ring as he waited for him to answer.

"Yeah, is that her?" Mark asked.

"Oh, it's her alright. I thought I told you to keep an eye on her! How is she out giving my pussy away to that black motherfucker?"

"Noah, I don't know at what point she left her room Thursday. I went to take care of business after dropping them off from their excursions. When I returned later in the evening, they weren't in the suite. I can only do so much when I know where she will be. I had no idea she had plans because she didn't use my services to get to her destination," Mark explained.

"If you didn't drop her off, who did?"

"Maybe the guy that's having the time of his life with her. Hell, I don't know."

"Where did you get the video, Mark?"

"I was scrolling on my social media and it popped up. The video has gone viral with over fifty thousand shares. It was posted by a woman whose location is here in St. Thomas. My guess is, she has some type of connection with the guy and is pissed off because he's not drilling her instead of your girl."

Noah was madder than King Kong when Godzilla tried to drown his ass. "Find that slut and tell her to call me! If she doesn't, I'm going to make her wish she had."

Noah hung up and went to Baylei's inbox and started typing out his message. Stopping abruptly, he erased everything he wrote and exited the app. Instead, he called Ashley to meet him at his house. Answering on the first ring, Ashley agreed without hesitation.

Ashley had been staying out of Noah's way since the incident at his home and was ecstatic when she saw his name appear on the screen of her phone. She was sitting in his mother's living room talking about him then boom, he called. Half listening to the conversation that resumed after she ended the call, Ashley cleared her throat.

"Elizabeth, I have to go. That was Noah and he wants me to meet him at the house. I'll talk to him about calling you because it's not right that he's been ignoring you the way he has." Ashley got up from the sofa and gathered her purse.

"You don't have to say anything to my son for me. When I see him, he's going to wish he never chose a Negro over me. Let him be, Ashley. What I do want you to do is seal your position in his life. That's the only way he will get a dime from me and his father," Elizabeth seethed.

"Elizabeth, you do know Noah makes good money as a lawyer, right? He's not interested in the family's money. You're going to have to come better than holding a trust fund over his head. He's not me."

"I didn't ask for your input, dammit! Go to my son and do whatever you must to get him to leave that bitch alone!" Elizabeth said, pointing her finger in Ashley's face. "Get on those bony-ass knees and suck his dick like a nasty porn star. Better yet, let him fuck you in the ass. I don't care, just get the job done. Now, get the hell out of my house!"

Ashley stood red-faced with tears in her eyes. She couldn't believe Elizabeth said the things she had. She didn't have a choice but to do what his mother insisted. That was the only way Ashley would continue to get the monthly payout she'd been getting for the past six months. Noah was certainly the bigger payout, but the money his mother was dishing out held her over until she received her allowance from her father.

Leaving Elizabeth's home, Ashley sat behind the wheel of her car and cried her eyes out. She had to put a few drops of Visine in her eyes to get rid of the evidence of her breakdown. Ashley started the car and backed out of the Connery's driveway. Glancing back at the house, Elizabeth was standing in the window with an evil grin on her face. Ashley had signed a deal with the devil and was going to walk through hell to get out of the contract.

It took a bit longer for her to arrive at Noah's home because she actually thought about turning around to go home. When Ashley pulled into Noah's driveway, his car was nowhere in sight. Picking up her phone to call him, the light of headlights beamed through her back window. She shut off the car and got out, waiting for Noah to make his exit.

"You look great," Noah said as he walked up and hugged Ashley. "Come on inside.

Ashley smiled. "Thank you. You don't look so bad yourself. How have you been?"

"I can't complain. I won my case today, so that's a plus for me."

Noah's voiced sounded happy about his win, but Ashley noticed the excitement didn't reach his eyes. Whenever Noah put another victory under his belt, he beamed with happiness. Not that evening. Something wasn't right.

When they entered Noah's home, Ashley sat at the island and watched Noah grab a tumbler from the cabinet and poured a hefty portion of scotch in a glass. It was unusual for Ashley because Noah wasn't much of a drinker. After downing the contents, he poured another before joining Ashley.

"You want something to drink?" he asked lowly.

"No. What's going on, Noah? Did something go wrong at the firm?"

Shaking his head, Noah sipped from the glass and placed it on the counter in front of him. "Everything at work is great," he said, clearing his throat. "How much do you love me, Ashley?"

"You know I love you with everything in me." Ashley stared at Noah and he had a faraway look in his eyes that she'd never seen before. "What's wrong? You're scaring me, Noah."

Noah drank the alcohol from the glass then grabbed Ashley's hand. Running his thumb over the back of her hand, his chin fell to his chest. Lifting his head, the hurt was evident in his eyes and Ashley waited patiently for him to tell her what was going on.

"She hurt me and must pay, Ash. If you love, help me make the bitch pay for deceiving me."

A wicked smile crossed Ashley lips. She was finally about to have Noah to herself and Baylei was going to be out the picture for good. Standing to her feet, Ashley walked over to Noah and wrapped her arms around his neck. Pressing her lips to his, she rubbed her hand down his face.

"Gladly."

Chapter 22

Chade woke up the minute his alarm sounded. Looking over to the beautiful woman that rested next to him, he smiled as he admired her beauty. The time he has spent with Baylei has been the best he'd ever experienced with a woman. In spite of all the drama Sakeenya tried to instill in his life, the trip was one he would never forget. All the great times with a woman that he had the opportunity to connect with from the moment he met her were worth locking in his memory.

"Why are you staring at me like a creep?" Baylei asked as her eyes fluttered open.

He was caught red-handed lusting over the woman he dreamt about loving the night before. Chade knew Baylei said what they experienced in St. Thomas wouldn't go any further. After all the years of hoping from one woman's bed to the next, Chade was finally experiencing the want of commitment.

"I can't help myself. You're so beautiful to me." Chade ran his hand across her cheek. "You hungry? I'll go get breakfast."

"You don't have to do that, I'm not hungry for food," Baylei said devilishly as she massaged his joint.

"Don't start nothing you can't finish."

"Ain't nothing like a long piece of wood first thing in the morning."

Baylei and Chade made love until almost one in the afternoon. If it wasn't for Baylei's friends calling, they would've gone a couple more rounds. Chade watched as Baylei moved effortlessly around his hotel room and wanted to mount her ass like a stallion.

"No, for real though. Jordyn and Toni want to take time today to go shopping. Did you get your suit back from the hotel cleaners yet?" Baylei was talking as she bent over into her overnight Birkin bag to get what she would need before going to the shower. Chade had convinced her to accept the gift and she ran out of reasons as to why she shouldn't. He won with flying colors and was quite proud of himself.

"Enjoy your outing. I'm not rushing to get to that damn wedding because I truly believe everything that was said about Chasity's snake ass. I will be there for Ahmad, but I truly think he's making a mistake. But what can I do about it? Not a damn thing. He has to deal with the decision he makes; not me. I'll be there to pick up the pieces when she breaks his heart." Chade thought back to the conversation he'd had with Von and remembered the email he still hadn't checked out.

"You are correct. There's nothing you can do to make him cancel the wedding. Continue to be his friend and support him on his day. You don't have to like it, but you will respect it, right?" When Chade didn't respond, Baylei turned to face him with an eyebrow raised. "Right?"

"I will never respect that bi—"

"Aht, aht. Don't do that, Chade. This don't have anything to do with Chasity. Your loyalty doesn't lie with her. Leave Chasity out of the equation. Ahmad is your brother and that should be your primary focus. Today is his day. You are the best man and you will stand up with him with your head held high. I wish I could be there with you, but I don't want any problems. I'm going to trust you to be on your best behavior. I want to hear all about the fuckery when I see you later."

"It's gonna be a shit show for sure. I'm quite sure there's going to be a lot to tell," he said getting up from the bed. "Go ahead and take your shower. I have a few things to do before I head out."

"Your clothes are—"

"I know, downstairs at the hotel cleaners. Thanks for taking them down to get pressed. I can't go to the venue without them, Beautiful."

Once Baylei disappeared into the bathroom and closed the door, Chade grabbed his phone and plopped on the bed and searched for the emails Von sent. Bypassing the video, Chade went straight to the audio and put in his earbuds. Bopping to the music that began to play, he was jammin' to the beat until the music stopped. Chade was stunned by what he was hearing and his anger returned full force.

Standing to his feet, he paced back and forth as he kept going back a few seconds to make sure he wasn't hearing things. Chade crawled back in the bed and laid on his back. He tossed his phone to the side and pinched the bridge of his nose.

"This shit is about to crush Ahmad badly. I don't know how I'm about to present it, but he has to know. He wanted proof, and Von came through with it," Chade mumbled to himself as he closed his eyes. the wedding was set to start at four and it was already a quarter to two. "I'll get to that bitch when I feel like it. Fuck that wedding."

Thirty minutes later, Baylei emerged from the bathroom and found Chade snoring as if he didn't have any place to be. She dressed and pulled her hair into a ponytail because all the sex she had engaged in had her mane puffy as hell. Thinking about waking Chade, she decided to just leave and let him deal with timing on his own. Toni was sure to call any minute if she didn't leave and head back to their suite.

***

Sanji assisted Ahmad with his cufflinks as the rest of the groomsmen finished getting dressed. Ahmad was sweating like he was about to take his last walk on the green mile. His uncle Stewart was constantly wiping his forehead and neck so he wouldn't ruin his clothes.

"Come on, Nephew. You chose to do this and it's a little too late to turn back now. This suit wasn't cheap and I'm not walking down the aisle representing yo' ass if you have ring around the collar." Everybody laughed, including Ahmad.

"I'm gon' be cool, Unc. Maybe I just need a shot or two. Then I'll be all good. You feel me?"

"Hell nawl, I don't feel you. I wasn't sweating like I was walking through hell on my day. I knew my woman was for me, so being nervous wasn't something I experienced. What the fuck you scared of? You test drove the pussy, right?"

"Man, that ain't none of your business." Ahmad laughed nervously as his eyes shifted around the room. "Where the hell is Chade?

The wedding starts in thirty minutes! His ass is always late for some shit."

"He's on his way. I just talked to him," Vincent said as he poured shots of Hennessy. "Come on so we can toast it up to the man of the hour!"

Ahmad's cousin Nick held his arm in the air. "I got this shit since the best man isn't here to do the honors. Y'all ready?" he asked looking around to make sure everyone had a glass.

"Ahmad, I never thought you would find a woman as beautiful as Chasity to tie the knot with. Being here with you today made me realize, you are no longer the same little cousin that I used to beat the fuck up." Ahmad shot him a dirty look but laughed along with everyone else. "Nah, for real. I'm proud of the man you have become, Cuz. I want you to love, cherish, and honor that woman that's on the other side of this building. Remember, a happy wife, makes a happy life. Cheers and congratulations!"

As soon as the guys threw their drinks back, Chade walked in fully dressed with a frown on his face. The room fell silent and Chade stared Ahmad down like he was ready to put hands and feet on him. Turning away, Ahmad took his jacket off the hanger and flung it onto his back.

"Can everyone except my brothers leave the room please? We will meet y'all in the hall. We are about to line up in a few anyway."

The other groomsmen left, leaving the six friends alone in the room. Chade rubbed the back of his neck as he slowly moved to the window. The set-up outside on the beach was beautiful, but the day was about to get ugly. Without turning around, Chade cleared his throat, "Ahem, ahem. So, Ahmad, you really want us to support this fuck shit today?" Chade asked, facing his long-time friend.

"Man, not today. I'm about to get married in a matter of minutes!"

"Yeah, Chade. This ain't the time, bro." Samir walked up to Chade, grabbing his arm. In return, Chade snatched away laughing.

"I'm cool. You don't have to grab on me." Turning back to Ahmad, Chade reached into his breast pocket with his phone in hand. "You right, you are *supposed* to get married today, but I want you to do me a solid and listen to this file first. And if you still want to take this broad's hand in marriage, I'll be right there backing your decision. We out so you can be alone to figure out what you want to do. Come on, y'all."

"What the fuck is going on, Chade?" Samir asked with an attitude.

"Obviously, Chade is the only one that knows what's going on and I respect how he came to Ahmad with whatever it may be. Respect the shit and move the fuck around! It's time to line up."

Sanji led the way out and the others followed. When Chade was about to cross the threshold, he looked back at Ahmad and nodded his head. Ahmad looked at the front of the phone and pressed play once the door was closed.

At first all he heard was music, but when he skipped several minutes, his heart started beating fast. Hearing Chasity admit to what his boys had already told him hurt his heart. With every word, it felt as if a knife was being twisted in his chest. Shaking the feeling away, Ahmad knew Chasity was the woman for him regardless. He had gotten this far and he wasn't going to bail out.

"Fuck this shit. The show must go on," Ahmad said to himself, leaving out the door and walked right past the rest of the grooms-men. He walked outside and down the aisle to the front of the make-shift altar that was setup on the beach.

"Best of Me" by Tyrese blared through the speakers and Chade made his way down the aisle to stand beside one of his best friends even though he didn't agree with what he was doing. When he made it to Ahmad, Chade gave him a brotherly hug and they dapped it up as they watched Sakeenya taking her time walking slowly down the aisle with an animated smile on her face. Ahmad didn't even look at her when she ventured off to the left and took her spot.

The music switched and "Spend My Life with You" by Eric Bonet and Tamia guided the rest of the party out. The song played out and everyone in attendance were smiling big as day except Mama Beverly. Ahmad knew his mother didn't like Chasity, but he did, and that was all that mattered. His mother knew he didn't care what her thoughts were. Like she said, he was grown and had to learn on his own.

"When You're in Love" by Karina Pasian started to play and everyone rose to their feet. Chasity appeared holding her father's arm for dear life. Ahmad had tears running down his face as he admired his soon to be wife in the beautiful white and mahogany gown. Her hair was in a neat bun on top of her head and her makeup was flawless. Ahmad couldn't lie; she was beautiful.

Chasity and her father made their way to the alter and the minister was smiling from ear to ear and stepped forward to take his place. Chasity's hand was placed in Ahmad's and he smiled. His wife to be reached upward and wiped the tears from his face before taking his hand again. The minister said a few words about marriage, but everything sounded like gibberish to Ahmad.

"Chasity, I was told the two of you will recite your own vows and you would go first. Is that correct?" The minister asked after he finished. Chasity nodded her head yes and stared Ahmad in his eyes.

"Ahmad, you have been nothing short of great since the day I met you. I didn't think I would fall in love with a man I'd met off the internet, but you proved me wrong. You have loved me, cared for me, and been everything a girl could ever want in a man. You are my everything and I look forward to spending my life with you for many, many, many, years to come."

Smiling with a few tears escaping her eyes, Chasity waited for Ahmad to give her the same treatment she had given him by wiping her face, but it never came. It was now his turn to recite his vows and there was complete silence. Waiting patiently, Ahmad finally cleared his throat as he swiped a hand down his face.

"To the first woman I've loved and who has had my heart from the start. I'd never leave your side and go against the grain when it comes to you. You told me to leave the garbage outside, and I didn't listen." Chasity's smile slightly dropped as she listened to Ahmad's choice of words. Ahmad showed his first sign of happiness when he looked at his mother.

"You warned me that something wasn't right about this conniving, no job having, gold digging, manipulative-ass woman standing

196

before me. You always said she would never be your daughter-in-law and you were correct."

Chade stood tall with his head held high. He was proud of his boy and didn't think he had it in him to expose his trifling-ass fiancée.

Chasity tried to pull back, but Ahmad held her hand tightly. There were gasps and whispers from some of their disreputable audience members. No one could tell Ahmad that her family and friends didn't know what was going on with Chasity and her so called best friend.

"Nah, where you going? I'm not finished. Mama told me there would be days like this, but I didn't think you would play me the way you did. Was it worth it, Chasity?" Ahmad laughed.

"We already discussed this, baby. I told you it wasn't true. Please don't embarrass me like this," Chasity whispered.

"Embarrass? What about how I felt when I learned the truth firsthand?" Ahmad sneered. "Did you consider my feelings in all of this bullshit?"

"Son, there is a time and place for—"

He cut the minister off with a stern glare. "I'd advise you to mind the business that pays you. This is definitely the time, homeboy." Ahmad was on a roll and beyond pissed. The tears that rolled out of Chasity's eyes didn't move him one bit. "If Sakeenya was the person you wanted to be with, why take things with me as far as you did?"

"Sakeenya? That's my best friend, Ahmad!"

"So, you still want to stand in my face and lie, right?" Removing Chade's phone from his breast pocket, Ahmad passed the device to his best friend and Chade hurriedly unlocked it. "See, I gave you two opportunities to come clean with me, and you didn't. Your time is up, Chasity." Ahmad grabbed the microphone and pressed play on the recording.

"I'm marrying Ahmad and still gon' eat yo' pussy every chance I get. Now what? We hit a lick together and you better continue to play the role of best friend, bitch!"

"Chasity, you know I love you and I will do whatever it takes to make you happy."

The sound of loud kissing could be heard. Low moans followed and the look of horror was on the faces of Chasity's parents.

"Suck that pussy, Keenya. Yeah, just like that."

Sakeenya dropped her bouquet and bolted across the lawn to get out of the spotlight. Chasity was stuck in place, eyes wide like a deer caught in headlights. Stopping the recording, Ahmad addressed the guests.

"There won't be a wedding today. Checkmate," he said, dropping the microphone and walking off.

Chapter 23

"This is cute. Anita will definitely love this chain and bracelet set, Lei."

Jordyn admired the gift Baylei had picked for her mother with approval. They had gone to a small shopping center to buy souvenirs to pass time while the guys were at Ahmad's wedding. Along with the jewelry, Baylei purchased some shirts and shot glasses for her mother and Justice, a pack of cigars for Wes, a couple T-shirts for their son Sage, and a little outfit for their daughter Faith.

"Get whatever y'all want. It's on me," Baylei said as she glanced around to see if there was anything else she liked. "I may as well put another dent in Noah's card. This time, I don't care the cost."

"Well, let's go to the store with the high-end shit in it," Toni said wickedly.

"Lead the way, friend." Baylei paid for the items and they left, heading to their next destination.

The weather was mild that day. All three ladies had on pretty sundresses with open-toed sandals. Toni walked into the store first and ran straight for the wall that held sunglasses and purses. Jordyn went across the room where the Gucci items were. Baylei, on the other hand, wanted to buy something special for Chade. With him being an accountant, she wanted to get him something he could use for work. She spotted a black Louis Vuitton messenger bag and knew right away that was the perfect gift. Baylei also selected a black wallet that matched the bag perfectly and decided to get that too.

Baylei cringed at the total when the clerk finally finished ringing up their items. As she handed Noah's credit card over, her phone rang, but she ignored it. Once finished, the trio left to get something to eat.

"What do y'all have a taste for?" Baylei asked as her cell phone rang again inside her purse. "Who's blowing my line up like this?" she mumbled, looking at the unidentified number. A strange feeling ran through her and that alone pushed her to answer. "Hello."

"Is this Baylei Jefferson?" the caller asked.

"Yes, this is she. May I ask who's calling?"

"This is Sara from University of Chicago Medical. We have you listed as next of kin for Anita Jefferson. We need you to get to the hospital soon as possible."

Time stood still and so did Baylei as the words registered in her mind. "What's wrong with my mama?" Baylei's voice caused Toni and Jordyn to halt their conversation and double back to their friend.

"Ma'am, I can't discuss that information over the phone. We are located 5700 S. Cottage Grove Avenue. How long will it take you to get here?" Sara asked.

"I'm not even in the States, but I'm going to book a flight soon as I can to get there. Is there a number I can call you back on to get updates until my arrival?"

"Actually, your mother is in surgery right now. There won't be an update for several hours. I will gladly give you a call when I learn any new information."

"That would be fine. Thank you so much, I'm on my way." Baylei ended the call and the tears she was holding back rolled down her face.

"All I needed to hear was mama and hospital. We have to get back to the hotel," Jordyn said, frantically dialing on her phone. "Mark, come pick us up from the shopping center. Make it quick," she barked into the phone.

"I'm not too far away. I'll be there in about three minutes."

Toni was looking for flights as Baylei paced back and forth. Jordyn dropped her bags and embraced her friend in a tight hug. Sobbing uncontrollably, Baylei's knees buckled. Toni stopped what she was doing to help Jordyn sit her down on the sidewalk.

"Lei, you have to be strong. We're going to make it to her; I promise."

"I can't lose my mama! She's all I have left!" Baylei cried.

"Anita is one stubborn mule. She's not going anywhere fast; believe me when I tell you. There's Mark," Toni said, pointing down the street.

Gathering the bags, Jordyn and Baylei wasted no time jumping in the back of the limo when Mark opened the door for them. Toni on the other hand discreetly watched him place their bags in the trunk as she continued searching for flights. The costs to change their flights were pretty costly but she knew Baylei wouldn't care.

"I found flights, but they are costly. The next one isn't leaving until about ten o'clock tonight." Toni explained.

"That's not going to work!" Baylei wailed. "I need to get back to Chicago in the next couple hours. It's three o'clock here, so it's two back home. I want to get there some time tonight."

"It's impossible, Lei, if there aren't any flights. We're gonna have to book these tickets and fly out when we can. Other than that, it's out of our control."

Mark closed the trunk and walked over just as Toni finished trying to explain things to Baylei. "I thought you ladies were here until Tuesday. Why the need to rush off? Did someone hurt one of you?" Mark was very concerned and looked like he was ready to attack whoever caused Baylei pain.

"No, everyone has been nice to us. Baylei has an emergency back home that's cutting our vacation short. We can't get a flight out until tonight and that's too late for my friend."

"I may be able to help you," Mark said, taking his phone out. "Hey, fuel up the jet. I have an emergency and need to get to Chicago ASAP. How long will it take?" Mark listened as the person on the other end spoke and Baylei was holding her breath while praying for a miracle in the back of the limo.

"See you in an hour." Mark ended the call and ushered Toni into the limo. "I'm going to get you all back to your suite so you can pack. I'll be back to take you to my jet and get you all back home safely."

"Thank you so much, Mark. I don't know how I'll repay you, but I promise I will!" Baylei cried.

"There's no need to repay me. Your gratitude is enough for me."

Mark closed the door and rounded the car. When he was seated in the driver's seat, he looked in the rearview mirror to make sure the partition was closed. Pushing a button on his phone, he started the car while he waited for the call to connect.

"She will be there in about five hours. You owe me big time." Mark hung up and peeled away from the curb to get the ladies back to their suite.

***

Five and a half hours later, Mark's jet landed at the air strip. He stood and turned to the ladies, "I have a car waiting for you. It's a black Mercedes Benz, license plate number HZ9813. The keys are under the driver's mat and the code for the door is 1125. It's parked right outside so you won't have to look for it. Here's a card with all the information you will need on the back and the number to the company when you're done with the vehicle. It was nice meeting you all, and I hope you enjoyed your stay at my resort."

Baylei took the card and thanked Mark for his help. Rushing off the plane, the only thing on her mind was getting to her mother. As they descended the stairs, Toni hugged Baylei from behind.

"Everything is going to be alright, Lei. Mama Anita got this, okay?"

Baylei nodded and spotted the vehicle soon as her feet hit the pavement. The workers had their luggage sitting on the ground behind the Mercedes waiting for Baylei to pop the trunk. Just as Mark said, the code worked with no problem. Once the luggage and all of their packages were loaded, Toni hopped in the driver's seat and Baylei and Jordyn followed.

"What hospital is she in?" Toni asked putting the car in drive.

"The University of Chicago on 57th."

"Why would they bring Mama Anita all the way to the city? This doesn't make sense, Lei. They could've taken her to South Suburban," Jordyn exclaimed.

"I was thinking the same damn thing. Maybe she has some type of trauma that only the doctors at the University could handle. Just get me there fast as you can, Sis. I need to see my mama."

Toni pulled up into the door of the hospital about twenty minutes later. "I'm going to find a park and we'll be right behind you." Baylei acknowledged Toni and jumped out. When she reached the service desk, the employee behind the desk smiled.

"Welcome. How may I help you?"

"I received a call this afternoon stating I needed to get here because my mother, Anita Jefferson was brought in. I'm her daughter."

As the woman tapped away on the keyboard, Baylei felt a presence behind her. Not bothering to turn around, she waited patiently for the woman to tell her what room her mother was in. The lobby was quiet and Baylei's nerves were in overdrive.

"I don't see anyone by that name in the system. Are you sure she was brought here?"

Before Baylei could respond, an object was pushed into her back and she froze in place. Someone was breathing heavily onto her neck making her skin crawl. She moved to turn and an arm encircled her neck, followed by a kiss to her temple.

"You thought I was joking, didn't you, Baylei?" The sound of Noah's voice sounded demonic and Baylei feared for her life.

"Please help me," she pleaded with the woman behind the desk.

"It's above me now." She laughed wickedly. "Noah, take your problem outside. You have about three minutes before the surveillance system comes back up. Oh, I want my money within the hour."

"You bitch!" Baylei struggled to get out of Noah's grasp.

"Shut your ass up and move!" Noah pushed Baylei towards a side exit. She turned slightly and was met with a gun pointed in her face. Don't make me shoot you, Lei. All I want you to do is walk and we won't have a problem."

Baylei moved toward the door on shaky legs. The last thing she thought she was going to do that night was come face to face with Noah. She'd ignored every attempt he made to contact her and now she didn't know what his plans were. The emergency door was pushed and Noah's car was parked right outside. In the driver's seat sat Ashley's bum ass.

Noah opened the back passenger door and shoved her inside. In the process, Baylei purposely dropped her phone, praying it didn't fall out of the car. As soon as he got in behind her, Noah punched her in the face.

"Drive this motherfucker, Ash!"

Doing as she was told, Ashley peeled out into the parking lot. Jordyn and Toni were seen walking into the hospital and Baylei couldn't even call out to them. Blood trickled down her chin from the blow Noah landed to her jaw. "I sent your black ass to St. Thomas and you gave my pussy away! How dare you, bitch! I hope that nigger was worth me kicking your ass!"

Noah punched Baylei repeatedly in the face as she cried out in pain. The hits were coming so fast, she didn't know which way to begin blocking them. He banged her head against the window, causing Baylei to black out. Ashley glanced in the rearview mirror in horror. Baylei was unresponsive when Ashley pulled onto the street. Noah checked her pulse and it was barely there.

"Pull back around to the side entrance. Go to the dark area right there." Ashley slowly followed his directions and Noah opened the door and pushed Baylei onto the pavement. "Get the fuck out of here!" He yelled as he slammed the door closed. "I told her ass not to play with me. Now look what she made me do."

Inside the hospital, Toni and Jordyn were trying to figure out where Baylei had gone. The man at the desk explained that he never saw anyone who looked like the person they described and he had just gotten back from a quick bathroom break. Things became more confusing when he told them there wasn't a patient by the name of Anita Jefferson that had been admitted.

"I just dropped her off and watched her walk in with my own eyes! She came into this hospital, sir!" Toni was now screaming, because something wasn't right.

"I'm sorry. I don't have anything more for you. Maybe your friend found out her mother wasn't here and stepped outside or went to the restroom. You can check for yourself. It's down the hall to your left."

Toni ran in the direction of the restroom while Jordyn stayed behind. Taking her phone from her purse, she went to the find my phone app to track Baylei's phone. Her location said she was outside of the hospital, so maybe the employee wasn't lying about what he'd told them. Jordyn quickly called Toni.

"Did you find her?" she asked.

"I tracked her phone and her location is right outside. Come back so we can see what's going on." Jordyn said quickly.

The two of them followed the dot on Jordyn's phone but couldn't go out of the emergency door without the alarm going off. They went back to the desk and asked if they could go out of that door. The employee told them no so, they headed out the front to go around. When they got to the spot, Baylei's phone was lying on the ground, but she was nowhere in sight.

Panic came over the two friends because women were coming up missing on a daily all over the country. The thought of their friend being kidnapped scared the shit out of them. Toni looked back and forth around the area and took off running.

"Toni!" Jordyn screamed. Watching Toni fall to her knees next to what looked like a body, Jordyn ran in her direction.

"Go get help! Baylei, wake up, sis. Oh my God, who did this to you!" Toni sobbed.

Chapter 24

Chade was sitting at the bar nursing the Remy he had sitting in front of him. After the drama settled down from the wedding that didn't happen, the friends enjoyed everything from the reception that was in place for afterward. It took all of them to hold Mama Betty off Chasity's ass. She wanted to beat the hell out of that girl. Mama Betty did get a good hit in with Chasity's mother because she got in Mama's Betty's face talking mad shit about Ahmad.

Chade and Sanji snuck away for a few to go get Baylei and her friends to party with them. But when they went to their suite, the men were told that the trio had checked out. Chade was puzzled because Baylei never said anything about leaving. He knew for a fact she was supposed to stay until Tuesday.

"You aight over here, brah?" Sanji asked sitting next to him.

"Yeah, I'm good. I'm just trying to figure out why she would just up and leave without a word."

"Something had to happen. Jordyn would have found me if she knew they were leaving. We had a conversation about trying our hand at a relationship. Did you get a number for Baylei? I have Jordyn's somewhere in my room."

"Nah, I thought we had time for all that shit. I guess I was wrong," Chade said, looking at his phone.

LeiLeiBay came to mind and he went to her inbox to see how she was doing. The time spent with Baylei kept him away from his online friend and he regretted it now that she'd ran off on him. LeiLeiBay was going to talk shit but I had something to talk to her about. His trip to St. Thomas had been nothing short of amazing, humorous, and adventurous that he could admit.

ChanceLover: Hey, Beautiful. I hope your trip is all you thought It would be. I have so much to tell you about mine and can't wait to hear from you.

Malik sat on the other side of Sanji with a drink in his hand. Everyone was trying not to talk about how things went down at the alter but that came to a halt with an alcohol filled Malik. Vincent wasn't too far behind him and Ahmad followed suit.

"Man, Ahmad, you good, brah?" Malik laughed.

"Go ahead and say I told you so," Ahmad said to Chade. "That bitch almost caught my ass like a big catch. I can't believe I was loving on her while she slurped on Sakeenya behind closed doors. Chasity pulled the wool over my eyes and I couldn't see any wrong in her. I feel like a damn fool."

"I won't say anything of the sort. There was no way I was going to sit back while you sold your soul to the devil's little sister. You live and you learn in this dreadful world we live in. You should've let your mama whoop that trick though."

"I agree," Malik laughed. "Mama Betty was ready to rip her head straight off her neck. I wanted to accidently let her go."

"We didn't need her out there like that," Vincent chimed in. "Y'all should've called one of them girls y'all met here to put them hands on her trifling ass. Ahmad, you're good, because it couldn't have been me. I would've choked the slob out of her."

"Nah, he did right. Chasity and Sakeenya is going to hide their faces for a long time after this trip. Maybe they will think about what happened here before they try it on the next man. To be honest, they got lucky because the average man would've killed them and hid the body." Sanji was speaking nothing but truth with what he'd said.

"Let me go find Toni's freaky ass. Maybe she would give me a threesome with one of these island girls."

"Good luck with that, Malik. Toni and her crew bailed on us. They checked out of their hotel sometime today."

"Damn," he said shaking his head. "What the hell you do to ole girl, Chade? I know you the reason they followed their girl out of here."

"Nah, I didn't do shit. If anything, I did everything right." Chade looked down at his phone and frowned. LeiLeiBay didn't respond to his message and that was unlike her. To think about it, he hadn't heard from her in a couple days, but he didn't think anything of it because she was enjoying herself on vacation. Opening the app, he sent another message.

ChanceLover: You cool over there? I want to tell you about the woman I met in St. Thomas. I think she stole my heart, Beautiful. She's one I could take home to meet my mama and that hasn't happened in a long time. To be honest, I want more than just sex from her. She's the one. The only thing is, she and her girls bailed on a nigga without saying a word. I know she said there would be nothing after this trip, but she was supposed to have been here until Tuesday. What do you think? Get back with me, Beautiful, I need advice.

They had been sitting around chilling for hours and it was a little past eight. Chade was about to call it a night because he was beyond tired. He sat listening to his guys talk more about Chasity and Sakeenya when his phone chimed with a notification.

LeiLeiBay: What is your real name?

Chade was confused because LeiLeiBay had never asked his name before. It was out of the norm for her to ask that question. Not that it was a problem; but for some reason it didn't sound like something she would say to him. The two of them were friends and getting to know each other on a personal level hadn't come up. Chade paused for a moment because LeiLeiBay didn't even acknowledge anything he said in his last message.

ChanceLover: Let me find out you're trying to learn more about the Lover Man, Beautiful lol

LeiLeiBay: What's your real name?

ChanceLover: Where's the humor, Beautiful? What's wrong?

Chade was worried for real at that point because LeiLeiBay would've had a great comeback for him.

LeiLeiBay: I need to know your real name. Please.

ChanceLover: My Name is Chade. Why is that so important to you? You have me over here in another country scared shitless now.

LeiLeiBay: Chade, what a small fuckin' world! You are in St. Thomas, right? You met a girl and her two friends. You were at your friend Ahmad's wedding and he married a bitch named Chasity, right?

Chade sat reading the message over and over trying to figure out how LeiLeiBay knew all of this shit. He had never told her anything about Chasity, hell he didn't think he even mentioned Ahmad's name for that matter.

ChanceLover: Where did you get that information?

LeiLeiBay: This is Toni. Baylei got a call that her mother was in the hospital. We rushed out and caught a flight back to Chicago. Chade, it was a set-up. Baylei was attacked outside of the hospital and she was hurt badly. They are working on her now. If you truly feel that way about my friend, get here! We are at the University of Chicago Medical on 57th and Cottage. Baylei told Jordyn and I that you are from here, so you should be familiar with her location. I have to call her mother and her boss. Hit my line when you touch down in Chicago and I'll fill you in. (773)555-0319. Oh, yeah. Bring Sanji and Malik with you.

"Aye, we gotta go!" Chade said, jumping to his feet.

"What's going on?" Malik asked.

"Remember the chick I was talking to online? I just hit her up and Toni ended up responding. LeiLeiBay was Baylei the whole time. She didn't ghost me like I assumed. She received a call that her mother was rushed to the hospital. Toni believes she was set up. Baylei was beat up pretty bad and we have to head to Chicago."

"Wait, you spoke with Toni?" Malik asked.

"Yeah, she told me to bring you and Sanji along with me," Chade said, turning to Ahmad. "Bro, I hate that I'm cutting my trip short, but I have to make sure she's okay."

"I understand. I think she's the one, to be honest. She kept yo' ass in line and brought out a side of you I've never seen before. Even my mama says you met your match and hopes Baylei sticks around with you. She's a winner, Chade. Allow yourself to love again, man. Go check on your woman."

Samir joined the crowd and pat Chade on his back. "Y'all go ahead and make the preparations. I'll stay back and keep an eye on this one here," he said pointing his thumb at Ahmad. "I have to make sure he doesn't kill Chasity and her people. Plus, Vincent will be here with me."

"The hell if I will! I'm rollin' with the homies. I want to see Miss Capri. It's been a while." Vincent shot back.

"What the fuck you trying to see my mama for, nigga?" Chade asked furiously. "Let me find out you're trying to move in on Ma Dukes. I'm gon' beat yo' body!" The hood made its way out with force. Chade's proper tone was long gone and his gangsta was on full display.

"It ain't even like that," Vincent said, fidgeting his fingers. "Man, I'm rolling out. What's the plan?"

"There's a flight that's heading out for Chicago at ten o'clock. I think if we head back now, we can pack and make that flight," Sanji said reading from his phone. "Am I booking these tickets or not? Y'all can pay me back later. We just got to get out of here."

"Do that shit. Ahmad. We will make this shit up to you once we get back to Cali. Stay away from Chasity, man. There's a reason you didn't get married today. The future Mrs. Sanford is out there somewhere. You just have to be patient and she will come right to you."

"Listen to the overnight Love Doctor giving out prescriptions and shit." Vincent laughed.

"Fuck you! I hope you're listening, because you got me looking at yo' ass sideways with yo' standoffish ways. All this pussy in yo' face and you haven't batted yo' eyes or licked your lips in lust. You playing on the other side of the field, Vince?" Chade asked seriously.

"Don't play with me, Chade. You know I don't do the homosexual jokes."

"Well stop acting as if you don't like pussy then," Chade said, walking off.

***

Chade fished his keys out of the side pocket of his bag and unlocked his mother's door. Entering the security code on the alarm, everyone quietly made their way into the living room. It was five o'clock in the morning and the men were beyond tired. Chade sat in his mother's favorite recliner and laid back. The rest of his friends found a spot so they could rest as well. They were being quiet as they could so they wouldn't wake Chade's mother.

"You better have a damn good reason why you chose my house to break into."

Chade opened his eyes as he tried to adjust them to the darkness. When he heard the gun cock, he sat up and reached for the lamp.

"Move another inch and you will meet your maker. "Why are you in my damn house?"

"Ma, it's me. Put the gun down, please," Chade pleaded.

"Chade? That's you?"

"Yes, woman!" he said, turning the light on. Capri looked around the room and lowered her weapon.

"All of my babies were about to get blown away." She laughed. "Now, y'all know not to come to my castle without phoning me first. I had six bullets and four was going into all of your black asses. Well, good morning."

"Good morning, mama," they all said in unison getting up to give her hugs.

"What the hell are you boys doing here? I thought you all were in St. Thomas."

"We were, but we had to fly out because a friend had an emergency and had to cut her trip short. I'm here to make sure she's okay."

"Chade, didn't I tell you to leave these pissy-tailed-ass girls alone? Wait a minute, you came all the way home to check on a woman? Are you sick, baby?" Capri placed the back of her hand on Chade's forehead, making his boys laugh.

"I met her in St. Thomas. Actually, I met her beforehand, but that's another story that I will fill you in on later," Chade said.

"Are y'all hungry? I can make breakfast if you want. Chade, don't think you are getting off easy not telling me about this woman that has you at my house at the crack of dawn."

"Who you talking to, Ma?"

All heads went to the stairwell as Chade's sister Chaya walked slowly down the stairs wiping sleep from her eyes. When she spotted her brother, she darted down the stairs full speed. Chade smiled big at the sight of his little sister. With his arms outstretched, Chade stood ready to embrace Chaya, but his happiness was halted as he watched her jump into Vincent's arms and wrap her legs around his waist.

"Baby! What are you doing here? I've missed you so much."

Chaya and Vincent stood kissing as if they were alone. Chade moved in their direction and Sanji grabbed him before he could snatch his sister out of the arms of his friend. Chaya pushed off Vincent and turned slowly to face her brother. Seeing the rage in his eyes, her head dropped to her chest.

"How long has this shit been going on?" Chade snapped more so at Vincent than his sister.

"Chade, don't start, okay? Your sister is twenty-five years old. She's grown," his mother said angrily. "You have to let her grow up. She can't be your baby sister all her life."

"This man is seven years her senior! And he knows she is off limits to any of my fuckin' friends!"

"Watch your mouth in my house, Chade Marshawn Oliver. You ain't too grown to get your ass whooped by me! Go upstairs and blow off some steam."

"Nah, get out, Vincent. You broke the code and I ain't dealing with you no more. My sister is the reason you were breaking yo' neck to get on that plane." Chade laughed.

Chaya stood holding Vincent's hand as she cried silently. "Chade, Vincent wanted to tell you, but I didn't want him to. I wanted to be the one to tell you what was going on between us for the past two years. Don't blame him for something I took part in. I love him, bro, and there is nothing that's going to stop us from being together. That includes you. Chade, you always told me long as the man I fall in love with treats me with the upmost respect, take care of me, and keeps his hands to himself, go for it."

"That didn't include my friends, Chaya! Do what you want to do. You don't have my blessing." Chade stormed up the stairs and slammed the door to his old bedroom, leaving everyone standing in the middle of the living room.

"Don't worry, baby. Your brother will come around. Vincent, thank you for loving my baby from afar. I appreciate you for that."

"No need to thank me, Ma. I got Chaya whenever she needs me. You don't have to worry about that at all. As far as Chade, he will forever be my brother and he know I'll never do Chaya wrong."

"On some real shit, Vince, you should've talked to that man regardless of what Chaya wanted. Two years? I would be pissed off too," Sanji said, giving his input on the situation.

"One thing I can say is this. Chade should know why Vincent didn't try to get with any of the women in St. Thomas. He has mad respect for Chaya, and I tilt my hat to him. That's strong loyalty even when his woman was all the way in another country. Any other man would've been trying to hit whatever. Instead, Vincent sat off to the side acting like Little Richard's gay lil brother or some shit."

"Gon' with that gay stuff. I told y'all I'm not on that." Vincent got mad every time he thought about what Chade said before they left St. Thomas.

"Chaya, come on so you can help me cook for these knuckleheads."

Capri and Chaya left the men alone and they all sat down comfortably on the furniture. Vincent kept looking at the stairs, hoping Chade would come back down, but he never did. He would talk to him later because their friendship meant more to him than anything except Chaya.

Chapter 25

Anita showed up at the hospital as soon as Toni called to tell her what happened to Baylei. The doctors allowed her to sit with her daughter for thirty minutes before she had to leave. She was told that Baylei suffered a broken nose, two black eyes, a busted lip, a concussion and bruised ribs. When she saw the condition her only child was in, she broke down crying. The city of Chicago wasn't the same from back in the day. The people that lived there didn't value life. There were too many crimes, especially gun violence happening every day. Anita never thought her daughter would be a victim of the streets. She was glad that she survived the attack and lived to see another day.

"Mommy."

Anita jumped from the seat she was sitting in and sat on the edge of the hospital bed. "I'm right here, baby. I'm right here." Baylei started crying and the tears struggled to come out of her swollen eyes. The sight pained Anita causing her to fight back her own emotions so she could be strong for her daughter. "Who did this to you, Lei?"

"I thought you were hurt. He lied to me." Baylei sobbed uncontrollably as she held her head. "I need something for this pain."

"Okay, calm down," Anita said, pushing the call button for the nurse. "Someone will respond in a moment. "Who is he, Baylei?"

The door opened and in walked Wes and his brother Donovan. When they saw Baylei's condition, the look of death was displayed on both of their faces. Turning away from her visitors, Anita stared at the two men for a few seconds before she recognized her daughter's boss. The door opened a second time and in walked her best friends. Toni ran around to the other side of the bed hugging Baylei tightly.

"Hello, Mrs. Jefferson. It's good to see you again."

"Hey, Weston. Thanks for coming to check on my baby as usual. Hello to you as well, Donovan."

"Hi, ma'am. How is she and did she tell you what happened?" Donovan whispered.

"No, I asked, but all she said was 'he hurt me'. I don't know who *he* is though," Anita said lowly. "The police came in about an hour ago. I told them to come back because Lei was sleeping." Anita got up and pulled both men to the other side of the room.

"Have a talk with her and find out what happened," Donovan spoke quietly. "If she doesn't know who did this to her, talk to the police. But if not, call me and don't say anything. I'm quite sure you know where I'm going with this."

"I have a feeling she knows. She said something about thinking I was hurt. I don't know if it's from the concussion or if she was trying to tell me something."

"Why would she think you were hurt?" Wes asked.

"I have no clue."

Anita was interrupted from a light knock on the door. The nurse walked in and looked around the room. "Oh my, there's a lot of love in this room today. How are you feeling, Miss Jefferson?"

"My face hurts. Can I have something for the pain?"

"Sure, I can get that for you. I want to check your vitals quickly then I will bring something back for you." She smiled. "Would you ladies stand for a second for me?" Jordyn and Toni moved just as Toni's phone started ringing.

"Hello?"

"Hey, Toni, it's Malik. We are in the hospital. What's the room number?"

"She's in room 319." Toni smiled.

"See you in a bit, love. Oh, don't tell anyone we're on our way up. Chade wants to surprise Baylei," Malik added.

"Okay," she said hanging up.

The nurse returned and administered the medication. She left and Chade appeared in the doorway with a huge bouquet of flowers and a teddy bear. He spotted Wes and Donovan dapping, both of them up before moving across the room where Baylei was lying with her eyes closed. He waved to Toni and Jordyn as they made their way to Sanji and Malik. Anita was staring with a slight smile on her face while Chade made his way to the bed.

"Beautiful, I'm here."

216

Chade was fighting to not show emotion as he moved the hair off Baylei's forehead. The bruises and the swelling of her eyes and nose had his blood boiling. He had been thinking about what could've transpired all morning while alone in his room. Chade remembered one of the conversations he'd had with LeiLeiBay about her sorry ass man putting his hands on her. It couldn't have been him; or could it?

"Chade, how did you get here?" Baylei asked, grabbing his hand.

"Toni got in touch with me via your social media. She told me what happened and I got on the first thing smoking. Are you alright?"

"I don't have you on my social media, Chade." Baylei tried to sit up but he put a halt to her movements and sat down beside her.

"Yeah, you did. It's ironic and we will talk about it later, but I'm the one and only ChanceLover, LeiLeiBay."

Baylei giggled a little and squeezed Chade's hand. "You knew who I was all this time! You sneaky devil you. Why didn't you just tell me?"

"I didn't know until last night. Back in St. Thomas, I went to your suite and you were gone. I thought you left to get away from me. Toni answered the message I sent telling you how the woman I met ghosted me, only to find out you were both the same person."

"Wow, that's crazy. Thank you for coming to check on me. It means a lot." Baylei yawned. "Would you guys give me, Chade, and my mom a minute, please? Actually, Wes and Donovan, you stay as well."

The door opened and closed and only the people Baylei named stayed behind. Taking deep breaths, she finally opened her eyes wide as they would allow and a lone tear trickled down. Chade wiped it away and kissed both of her eyes, nose, and her lips.

"First of all, Mom, this is Chade, the man you said took up all my time in St. Thomas. Chade, this is my mother, Anita Jefferson."

"Nice to meet you, ma'am," Chade said, shaking Anita's hand.

"Nice to meet you too. You're handsome. I see why my daughter was never available to talk to me. Hell, I wouldn't have called either if I was in the company of a man like you," She chuckled. "Anyway, Lei, what do you want to talk about?"

"I need to tell you all what happened to me, I've been silent for far too long. Whatever you do with the information I provide is fine with me." Baylei paused then continued talking. "I've been verbally abused by Noah's family from the start of our relationship. I dealt with it because I was with him and not them. Noah would slip up and say some racial things that I would catch on to, but he would swear up and down he didn't say it.

"The night of his parents' anniversary dinner, Noah put his hands on me and tried his best to apologize by buying me gifts. He booked the trip for me and the girls to go to St. Thomas as a peace offering. I knew I was done with him before I left, because I couldn't overlook the fact that he had hit me. To make a long story short, he had someone watching me in St. Thomas and knew everything I'd done on the trip. Noah would leave all types of threatening messages in my inbox because I'd blocked him from my phone. Hand me my cell, Mom."

Baylei went to the app and pulled up messages between she and Noah. She held the phone out for her mother to read, but Donovan intercepted the exchange. As he read the thread, Wes turned to Chade with a sly grin.

"How do you know my favorite architect, Mr. Lover Man?"

"That name travels the seas. You really are a man whore, huh?" Baylei asked.

"I used to be a man whore before this beauty caught my attention." Chade's words made Baylei blush and the cat caught her tongue. That gave Donovan the opportunity to jump back into the conversation leading it back to what happened to Baylei.

"So, are you telling me that this nigga Noah is the reason you're laid up in a hospital bed?"

"Yeah. Someone called while Toni, Jordyn, and I were out shopping and said my mother was rushed to the hospital and I needed to get here soon as possible. I called our limo service and the driver Mark, who is an acquaintance of Noah's, offered to bring us back to Chicago in his jet. I think Mark had a hand in Noah catching me because I wasn't in this hospital five minutes before I was escorted out at gunpoint."

"How did he get you out of the hospital without being seen?" Chade asked. "There has to be video surveillance in the lobby."

"The woman behind the desk was being paid by Noah. He set it all up. She told him he had three minutes before the cameras came back on. That's when he pushed me out of the emergency side door. His car was parked outside and his side chick Carrie Underwood was behind the wheel."

"Carrie Underwood. How ironic she has a famous name. She's going to make headline news when I catch up with her and your boy." Donovan was itching to come out of retirement. He couldn't stand when a man couldn't accept the fact a woman was done with him.

"Her name is actually Ashley, but I call her any and everything but that." Baylei yawned again, prompting Chade to wrap her in his arms. "I'm okay. I'll sleep once I'm finished telling this story because I don't want to ever have to tell it again. One of you will have to fill Toni and Jordyn in on what occurred." Baylei snuggled against Chade's chest as she tried to appear as if she was fine.

"Noah punched me in every part of my face while screaming about the nigger I was entertaining on a trip he paid for. I don't remember anything after he banged my head against the window. I don't even know where I was found."

"That's all I need to hear," Donovan said, holding his hand up to stop Baylei from going any further. "I need to know everything about Noah. His address, workplace, parents' address, and anything on the bitch that helped him. Leave the rest to me. When the police come back to talk to you, you don't know anything!"

Donovan turned to head out the room but came back. "Take care of her, Chade. Don't worry about this cat because you know how I handled things back in Cali. You have too much to lose. I got this."

"I hear you loud and clear, Dap. Good looking, and I owe you for this."

"Nah, you don't owe me anything. The only thing I want you to do is set your playa card on fire; you won't be needing it anymore after today. Baylei is a real one and you know how I feel about family. You don't want this smoke."

"Believe me, I know she's something special. There's not a woman on this earth other than my mama and sister who could get me to cut my vacation short and end up in Chicago without much thought. My Beautiful is in good hands, no doubt."

Baylei lost her fight with the medication she was given. Chade eased her onto the pillow and pulled the covers over her. Anita sat in the chair beside the bed and watched her daughter sleep. Wes tapped Chade on the shoulder and motioned him out of the room. As they exited into the hall, Toni and Jordyn rushed them.

"How is she?" Toni asked.

"She's going to be alright. Noah was the one that assaulted her," Chade explained. "Baylei's sleeping, but I need to know how well you know Noah?"

"Whatever you need on his ass, I got it. He has to pay for what he did to my friend." Jordyn was mad; as she should've been. Noah was wrong on all levels.

"Bet, Chade has my number. Hit me up with that information. For now, I'm gon' get out of here. I have to mentally get myself together so when Juice comes into to town, we can make this problem disappear."

Chade went to say his goodbyes to Baylei's mom and promised to return later. He chopped it up with Wes and his guys as Toni and Jordyn went back in the room with their friend. Chade wanted to find Noah and beat his ass like he did Baylei, but Donovan was right. He had too much to lose and with Donovan on top of the situation, Chade knew Noah would get handled sooner rather than later.

Chapter 26

Baylei was in the hospital four days before she was released. The doctor wanted to monitor her because he was worried about the concussion she'd sustained. Once she was given the okay to be discharged, Chade was right by her side to take her home.

The two of them spent time together in her home while she recovered from her injuries. Toni and Jordyn didn't miss a beat, coming over to make their friend smile. Wes and Donovan came over as well to make sure Baylei was alright. The guys helped Chade change the locks on her doors and installed security cameras throughout the house.

Chade was lying in Baylei's bed on his back while she laid on his chest. Running his hand through her hair, Chade massaged her scalp with his fingertips. With her eyes closed, Baylei smiled and hugged him around his waist.

"Thank you so much for staying by my side during this time, Chade."

"You don't have to keep thanking me, Beautiful. There was no way I would've left you here alone after what that bastard did to you. He's going to pay for hurting you though."

Chade looked down at the woman that had his feelings going crazy every time he thought about her. He wouldn't want things any other way and he knew from that point, he wanted her to be a permanent fixture in his life.

"I'll try my best to stop. What I can't seem to stop thinking about is the fact that you were ChanceLover all this time." Baylei laughed.

"Nah, if I wasn't so smitten with your beauty, I would've put two and two together in the beginning. LeiLeiBay is Baylei all day. It was destined for us to meet in the matter that we did. I wouldn't have it any other way." Chade ran his thumb along her jawline as he licked his lips.

"Well, it's been a week since I've been back in Chicago and my private parts is telling me you are missed," Baylei revealed with a devilish grin.

"Is that so? How do your ribs feel?"

"Fuck these ribs! I need you to make love to me, Chade. I'll take a long soak in the tub to soothe the ache later. Are you going to give me what I've been craving?"

"You do know we have to go to my mother's house for dinner tonight, right? If you're in pain, I'm going to have to postpone."

Baylei pushed herself up on her elbows with a frown. Chade sat back as he watched her every move. Without another word, Baylei reached into his boxers and released the beast that was dying to come out to play. Placing his hands behind his head, Chade waited to see exactly what Baylei had in store for them.

She stroked his length slowly, causing precum to ooze out of the tip. Baylei lowered her head and flicked her tongue over the hole before devouring his pipe. Chade's toes cracked and his legs locked in place. The way Baylei swallowed his member had him fighting to breathe.

"Fuck, Beautiful! You sure know how to make a nigga feel good," Chade growled as he cupped the back of her head.

Baylei eased out of the panties she had on and kicked them onto the floor. She continued to suck Chade slowly as she maneuvered her body into the sixty-nine position. When Chade smelled her sweet nectar, he wasted no time grasping her pearl into his mouth.

"Yes, Chade. Eat your pussy, baby."

Baylei grinded her yoni back and forth on his mouth. The friction of his beard teased her lower lips, bringing her to the brink of exploding. Easing his dick further down her throat, Baylei breathed steadily out of her nose so she could deep throat him expertly. The way Chade squeezed her ass cheeks and sucked hard on her bud, she knew every suckle was making him feel good as hell.

Chade smacked her hard on the ass and Baylei fought hard not to cum. She wasn't ready just yet. There was no stopping what was meant to be when he stuck his finger in her back door.

"Oh shit! Suck my pussy, baby!" Baylei screamed. The mixture of pleasure and pain took her over the edge. Her love juice flooded his mouth while marinating his chin. She rocked back and forth on his lips and Chade drank every bit of it.

"Are you feeling, okay?" he asked quietly while rolling Baylei over onto her back.

"Yes. I'm fine," she said with her eyes closed.

That's all Chade wanted to hear. He parted her legs with his knees before reaching over to grab a condom from the nightstand. He covered his member and smiled. Baylei was snoring lightly, but she started the lovemaking, and he was going to finish it.

Placing his mushroom head at her opening, Chade pushed his way into her love box and almost came instantly. Her walls clutched him tightly, causing him to bite his bottom lip. Baylei's eyes opened slowly. She rocked her hips as she tried her best to fuck him from the bottom. Chade enjoyed the feeling and allowed her to take control of his joint.

"That's right. Fuck me, girl. You better make it good because once I take over, you gon' tap out," Chade said, lifting her legs. "You can do better than that, Beautiful."

Baylei shook her head no and that was his cue. Chade pulled out and tapped her on her thigh. "Bring that ass to me, baby. Arch that back. I want a deep arch too."

Doing as he asked, Baylei assumed the position and got ready for the hurting he was about to put on her. Chade eased into her from behind and her breath got caught in her throat. The first thrust felt like it was in her chest. Baylei used her hand to slightly push him back, but he slapped her hand away.

"Move your hand and take this dick. This what you wanted, right? I'm about to give it all to you too." Grabbing both of her ass cheeks, Chade spread them open and watched as his pipe eased in out of her wet box.

"Oh my God! Just like that, baby." Baylei moaned as she grasped the sheets snatching them from the bed. As she threw her ass back to meet Chade thrust for thrust, the only thing that was heard in the room were their bodies connecting together.

"Throw that ass back," Chade growled. "This my pussy, Lei. Mark my words."

"I'm about to cum!" Baylei panted.

"Let that shit go then. Rain on me, Beautiful."

Baylei couldn't hold back a minute longer. Her stomach clenched as Chade strummed her bud vigorously. She knew the dam was about to break.

"What are you doing to me?" She cried.

"I'm loving you the right way, Beautiful. Now wet me up."

Baylei's body reacted to his command and she came long and hard. "I love you, Chade!"

"I love you too, Beautiful." Chade emptied his seeds in the condom as his back went rigid from the orgasm he had received. It wasn't until he emptied his tank and looked at Baylei as she slept soundly that he realized he uttered the three words he vowed to never say to a woman ever again.

***

"So, you are the woman that did the unimaginable?" Capri asked Baylei as everyone sat at the dining room table of her home.

"What would that be?" Baylei asked in return as she sipped from her glass.

"You got my son falling in love. It's been years since he has brought any woman to my home. The way he looks at you, all I see is love in his eyes. Don't get me wrong, I love seeing my son happy, but he told me he would never commit to a woman. You have changed his mind, and I would love to know how you did it."

"Miss Capri, honestly, I didn't do anything special. If being me is a special power, Chade will never meet a woman of my caliber again in life. Physically, I've known him two weeks, but I actually got to know him in a sense months ago. Chade had this arura about him that many men don't possess. He was a gentleman from the start, and I got to know him on another level in St. Thomas. I wouldn't change anything about our courtship for anything in the world." Baylei looked over at Chade with a smile.

"We didn't meet by chance. It was destined to happen, and I'm glad it did."

Chade kissed Baylei on the lips. His mother didn't miss the sparkle in his eye as he looked at her as he went back to eating.

There wasn't an ounce of doubt in her mind: Baylei was the one for her son. Capri looked around the table and admired what she saw.

Malik was happy and she hadn't seen him in that light for a while. Toni was going to give him the love he needed. Malik needed a woman that would be able to stand beside him every step of the way.

Sanji had always been a sweetheart, but he worked so hard on himself that he didn't make time for a woman to be in life. But Jordyn was the one that would hopefully be able to balance him out in a good way. The attraction they had was more of a physical thing, but somewhere down the line, she was going to change that as time went on.

Vincent and Chaya were a match made in heaven. Capri was on board with their union the day Chaya told her she was seeing him. Knowing Chade was against them being together, she prayed every night since the night they showed up in her home that her son would come around.

"Hey, Vince. Let me holla at you outside, bro," Chade said, getting up out of his seat.

He walked to the back door and opened it with Vincent right behind him. Chade sat in one of the lawn chairs and motioned for his long-time friend to do the same. No words were spoken for a few minutes until Vincent broke the silence.

"Chade, I know you're mad at me. I owe you an apology, man. I shouldn't have been dealing with your sister as long as I've been without coming to you about it."

"I'm over all that, fam. I can't be mad because what's done is done. Vince, I brought you out here to let you know that I love my sister. You already know this. Do right by her. That's all I ask. Fuck over my sister, our friendship is dead and so are you. This is the reason I never wanted any of y'all to mess around with her. Ain't no coming back."

"I hear everything you're saying, Chade. I got Chaya. The love I have for her won't allow me to do her dirty. Hell, we're two years in and she's the best thing that's ever happened to me. She's a precious jewel and she's in good hands."

225

Chade stood to his feet. "I'm gon' hold you to that too. If yo' ass wanted to be my brother on paper, I would've talked to my mom's a long time ago. But I guess being with my sister was a better choice." They both laughed. "You have my blessing, bro. I was just pissed when I first found out about y'all."

"I get it, and thank you, Chade."

They hugged one another and made their way back into the house.

For the next couple hours, there was nothing but laughter and shit talking within the walls of the Oliver residence. Capri loved every minute of the love she felt within her circle.

Epilogue

The bruising was long gone and Baylei's nose was almost completely healed, but she was still being careful. Baylei convinced Chade to go home a week prior because he had a job to go back to. They were officially dating and were taking things slow for the time being. Baylei didn't allow her insecurities to get the best of her. With Chade's playboy ways in the past, she tried not to let that deter her from trusting him to be on his best behavior while he was in California. A long-distance relationship required a higher level of trust and she was ready to put it to the test.

Baylei was finally well enough to go back to work and hadn't missed a beat since she sat at her desk early that morning. Toni texted her to ask if she would be down for a girl's night. It was Friday, so Baylei was all for a few drinks and dancing. As she put the final touches on the project she was working on, there was a light knock on her door.

"It's open," she called out while continuing to work.

"Hey, I'm about to get out of here," Wes said standing in the doorway. "Take whatever you're working on home and finish it over the weekend and have it ready for Monday."

Wes had been accompanying Baylei to her car since Chade left. If it wasn't him, it was Donovan. She had her personal bodyguards since the incident and she didn't complain one bit.

"Sounds like a plan. Give me a minute to gather everything then I'll be ready."

"What's your plans for the night?" Wes was trying to make small talk as Baylei prepared to leave.

"I'm heading out later to meet Toni and Jordyn for girl's night. It's much needed. We haven't truly gotten together since St. Thomas."

"Have fun, and don't drink too much. Now you can get home early and relax before dancing the night away."

"You're always right on time with the early work days, Bossman. I wouldn't want to work for anyone else because they don't make many bosses like the one, I got," Baylei said as they walked out of the office. Heading to the elevator, Baylei pushed the down button as Joe whistled down the hall. When he spotted her, a smile spread wide across his face.

"Well, well, well, there's my favorite lady in the building. How you been? Hello, Mr. King," Wes spoke to Joe in return and stepped back so he could get closer to Baylei.

"Hey, Joe! I'm doing pretty good and yourself?" Baylei and Joe hugged tightly before he released her.

"I'm better now that I've seen you. I heard what happened and I'm so sorry."

"You don't have to be sorry, Joe. It happened, I'm healed, and I'm pretty much over it. One thing I won't do is allow the idiots of this city to paralyze my movements. I have too much to live for and I can't let this break me."

"Sho you right! That's my girl." The doors to the elevator opened and Baylei hugged Joe, stepping inside. "Take care and I'll see you Monday," Joe said, leaning on his broom.

"I will and I love ya, Joe." Baylei blew a kiss at her work dad and smiled as the doors closed shut.

Baylei was the strongest person Wes knew, besides his wife. She was handling what happened to her like a champ, and that was hard for most to do. His phone chimed as the door opened into the garage. He answered as they walked in the direction of Baylei's vehicle and Sage's little voice bellowed through the speaker.

"Dad, what time are you coming home because Faith is doing the most."

"Sage, what is the problem you have with your sister today?" Wes asked, trying not to laugh.

"You know the Kris Bryant jersey you bought for me? Faith put her nasty hands on it, and now it's ruined. Why do she have to always run up on me without warning? I have to stay fresh and you know I don't like being late." Sage was Wes' six-year-old son and he was mature for his age and always called his father to vent. Their relationship was stronger than gorilla glue and Wes welcomed every minute of it.

"Son, your sister loves you and she didn't mean any harm when she messed up your jersey. Did you voice your concerns with Mama Justice? She can get any stain out with no problem. It's not the end of the world."

"No, I just took it off and put it in the laundry and changed because I would've been late for school. I'm mad because my girlfriend Hazel loves the Cubs and I wanted to stunt for her."

Baylei laughed at Sage's rant because it was the cutest thing. He sounded more like his uncle Donovan than Wes in her opinion. Her boss needed to monitor the conversations his brother had around his son. Sage was going to be a mess when he got older.

"I'm on my way home, Sage. We'll talk more when I get there. Love you."

"Love you too, Dad."

Wes put his phone in his pocket shaking his head. "That boy is something else. Get in the car so I can trail you home."

"Wes, I don't need you to do that. I'll be fine. Go home to your family."

"I'm not trying to hear that," he said, walking to his car, which was parked right next to Baylei's.

She knew arguing wouldn't help change Wes' mind so, Baylei got into her car and pulled off. As she drove, Baylei kept checking her surroundings because she was staying strong in front of everyone but in reality, she was scared to death about Noah coming to attack her again. There hasn't been any word from Donovan so Baylei has tried her best to hide her fear.

Twenty minutes later, she pulled into her driveway and noticed Toni's car parked outside. Baylei should've known there would be extra security in place for when she arrived home. Wes exited his car and walked inside with her to make sure everything was safe. Toni was sitting on a stool eating a bowl of fruit.

"Hey, bestie." She waved.

"How did you know I was getting off early?" Baylei asked quizzingly.

"Wes called me," Toni said, popping a strawberry in her mouth. "My girl gotta have someone here to look after her. Plus, we have to get ready for our night out."

Baylei took off her shoes and walked across the room to hug her friend. She turned to Wes and thanked him before putting his ass out of her house. After locking the door, Baylei sat next to Toni at the breakfast nook, stealing a piece of her fruit.

"Where are we going tonight?" she asked.

"We're going to hit the Irie's. You know Caribbean food is our favorite and we have to hit our spot and watch a good game of basketball while we eat. Plus, we haven't seen Mac in a while. Afterwards, we can dance the night away."

"You already know I'm up for a good time, especially with Mac in the building. That man always forgets he's working when around us." Baylei chuckled. "Since I know what type of night we're going to have, I don't know about you, but I'm about to take a nap. What time are we leaving?" she asked, standing up.

"How about seven o'clock? That would give Jordyn time to get home and change. She's going to meet us there though."

"That's cool. I think I'm going to drive my own car as well. It doesn't make sense for you to drive all the way out here then have to drive back to the city."

"Lei, go take a nap because you already know how we do things. Can you say pajama party?" Toni asked, waving her friend off.

"Make yourself at home. I'm not about to go there with you. Mi casa es su casa. See you in a couple hours, hooka."

Baylei went into her bedroom and removed her clothes quickly. Her bed was calling her and she couldn't wait to dive in it. She got her a t-shirt and a pair of underwear to put on after her shower and walked into the bathroom. A short while later, Baylei was deep under the covers after moisturizing her body.

With her phone next to her, she closed her eyes, ready to sleep, but her phone started ringing with a Facetime call from Chade.

"Hello, Handsome," she answered sleepily.

"Beautiful, what are you doing in the bed so early in the day?"

"Wes let me go home early and I wanted to take a nap before I hit the streets with Toni and Jordyn later. How's your day going?"

"My day is great. I'm on lunch, enjoying the sun before I'm holed up in the office again. Well, get your rest and I'll definitely talk to you before you head out. Be careful, Beautiful." Chade blew Baylei a kiss and she returned the gesture with a nod before ending the call.

Drifting off to sleep with Chade on her mind, Baylei had a dream they were married with children. The scenery in California was beautiful and the house they lived in was just as grand. Chade catered to her like a Queen and she soaked it all in. Their daughter was a spitting image of Baylei and their son looked, acted, and wanted to be the smaller version of his father.

Baylei was enjoying the time with her family when the sound of an alarm jolted her from her sleep. Looking around her bedroom, she saw that the sun had gone down and she couldn't see a thing. Turning on the lamp on the nightstand beside her bed, Baylei stretched like a feline. Toni walked into her room dressed in a robe with her makeup already done.

"What I tell you about walking in on me without knocking! You are so damn disrespectful." Baylei swung her legs out of the bed and stretched her arms over her head.

"Lei, this my house as much as yours. Didn't you say earlier, mi casa es su casa? So that means I can do what I want around here. Besides, I was coming to wake you up, with your grouchy tail. What are you wearing tonight?"

Toni knew how to irk Baylei's nerves and never missed a beat doing so. "I'm just wearing a pair of distressed jeans and I cropped top. We are only going to the damn sports bar." Baylei said irritably.

"I just wanted to make sure you don't dress like a nun. You know, the items that reside in your closet. As a matter of fact, we need to choose a day to donate all of that crap to the Salvation Army. There's someone out there who won't complain about looking boring."

Baylei walked to her closet, choosing her outfit for the night. Toni saw how organized her closet was minus the clothes she used to have. The colors were more vibrant and Baylei was back to who she was before she started dating Noah. Toni walked inside the closet with a huge grin and fingered through the clothes.

"Oh, shit! You done went and upgraded without me? I love this, Lei. You must've run a check on the man who shall not be named card!"

"Um, no. I actually shopped online while sitting on my couch. As far as using that man's money, you know as well I, I never needed it. To answer your question, Chade footed the bill."

"Okay. Mr. Lover Man is stepping up his game. He's been dishing out love and taking care of his woman. That's what I'm talking about!" Toni said, dancing around her friend.

"Take your butt in the other room and finish getting yourself together. I'll be ready in about an hour." Baylei laughed, pushing her friend out the door.

***

Irie's was jumping as it always was on a Friday night when they stepped into the establishment. Something had to be going on because half the establishment was divided by dark doors. It was a good thing for the trio because their usual table was open and Jordyn had snagged it for them. Several big screen TVs were hanging from the ceiling so whichever way they looked, they wouldn't miss the game.

"Hey, y'all," Jordyn sang as she hugged each of her friends. "I'm so excited to be out. Work has been kicking my butt and I couldn't wait to let my hair down."

"It's kind of tight in here. What's happening on the other side of the building?" Baylei asked.

"Oh, someone is having a private party over there. I didn't even know they could put up doors like that. I was trying to get a peek inside, but I couldn't see anything," Jordyn replied. "What are y'all drinking? Mac is the bartender tonight and you know how that goes for us."

"Turn up!" Baylei and Toni yelled. Baylei moved to sit on the other side of the table, but Toni stopped her.

"Nah, Lei. I want to be the one watching the door; just in case. I got your back and your front."

Baylei nodded her head as Jordyn went to the bar and ordered their drinks. No one responded when she asked so she took it upon herself to get their usuals. As she waited to be served, her eyes went to the door as it opened. A lot of people entered along with a group of fine men. She locked eyes with one and he smiled at her. His party went into the closed off section and he stood admiring her. Jordyn had to break away from his stare because Sanji was her eye candy for the time being.

"Heyyyyy, Jordyn!" She was saved by the bell when Mac called out to her. "Where the hell you been and where is my other two faves?"

"They're over at *our* table. How you been?" Jordyn asked after sharing air kisses with Mac.

"I'm good. I'm not mixing the same shit y'all usually drink. I heard you heifas went to St. Thomas and didn't invite me." Mac twisted his lips and rolled his eyes.

"It wasn't even like that, but we got you next time. We will be flying high often than not. Just be ready because we're on our spur of the moment shit. Life is too short to just work without serious play. You know what I mean?"

"Oh, you know I stays ready, boo. Let me get these drinks together because some out-of-town folks booked this spot and I'll be bartending on the other side for the night. Liza told me you and the crew were here, so I came over to get y'all right."

"That's why I love me some Mac. Don't be stingy with the alcohol either." Jordyn laughed.

Mac was the first person they met when the trio ventured out to find a new spot for their girls' night. They had such a good time that they made Irie's their designated spot to have fun when wanting to wind down from a busy work week. He was also the one who did everyone's hair too.

"Okay, chick. I have to go, but I'll see y'all later. Tell Toni and Lei I said hello and smooches."

Jordyn made her way back to the table and their night was just beginning. They had been sitting talking, laughing, and watching the game when a breaking news segment interrupted their program. Baylei asked the waiter to turn up the volume when she saw a picture of Noah appear on the screen. The news reporter was standing in front of Noah's home and the pit of Baylei's stomach churned.

"I'm standing outside the residence of high-profile lawyer Noah Connery's home. Police were sent here for a wellness check because Mr. Connery hadn't been seen in a couple weeks. When a friend of the family, Ashley Kennedy, daughter of multi-millionaire Alfred Kennedy, hadn't been heard from as well, both families became concerned. Officers arrived and peered inside a side window, finding both Mr. Connery and Miss Kennedy deceased. The cause of death is an apparent murder/suicide. Miss Kennedy apparently shot Mr. Connery in the chest multiple times before turning the gun on herself. We will have more on this story as details comes in.

Baylei stared at the television long after the segment ended and exhaled. Knowing Noah was no longer able to hurt her was a relief. She didn't have to live her life in fear anymore, but she would be able to prepare herself in case the police came to her home or workplace asking questions. That chapter of her life was completely closed and she could live in peace.

"Do you think Donovan took care of that problem? Or did Ashley actually shoot that bastard?" Toni asked in a hushed tone.

"Get out my head! I was about to ask the same thing," Jordyn whispered.

"I don't know and truly don't care. Noah deserved whatever happened to him. We know what he did to me and there's no telling how Ashley felt about him playing with her heart. I'm not going to sit here and dwell over it a minute longer. It's a relief that he's no longer around to make my life miserable."

The trio sat silently for a few minutes as they made sure Baylei was alright after hearing the news of what happened to Noah. Once they knew she was good to go, Toni finished her drink and placed the glass in the middle of the table.

The melody for "Perfect" by Ed Sheeran started playing and Toni rose to her feet. Taking a blindfold from her pocket, she walked beside Baylei and smiled.

"I have a surprise for you, Lei, but you have to put this on first."

"You must be crazy, Toni. You're not about to have me in the dark for anything!" Baylei's eyes were wide with bewilderment. "Nah, I'm not doing it."

"You trust me, right?"

"Yes, but what do you have to show me that's so secretive that I must be blindfolded?"

"Trust me, Lei," Toni all but begged. Baylei glanced over at Jordyn and she hunched her shoulders with a sly grin.

"Y'all ain't shit," Baylei said, standing to her feet so Toni could place the blindfold.

Walking through Irie's, Baylei's friends each grabbed one of her elbows as they led her to their destination. The doors to the private area were opened by the staff of the establishment. The room was decorated with sea green and white balloons and there was a table full of food. Baylei's family, friends, and co-workers filled the area. They had all came into Irie's without making a sound just to get in without Baylei's knowledge. Toni stopped in the middle of the room and Baylei raised her hand to remove the blinder.

"Nope, not yet," Jordyn said smacking her hand down. "I'll take it off when it's time." Baylei opened her mouth to protest, but her friend cut that short. "Aht, aht, I don't want to hear none of that."

Ed Sheeran's voice filled the room and Baylei stood quietly listening to the lyrics of one of her favorite tunes. The words made her feel some type of way that day and she couldn't figure out why.

I found a love, for me
Darling just dive right in
And follow my lead
Well, I found a girl
Beautiful and sweet
I never knew you were the someone waiting for me

'Cause we were just kids when we fell in love
Not knowing what it was
I will not give you up this time
But Darling just kiss me slow
Your heart is all I own
And in your eyes, you're holding mine

Chade stepped out of a side room with his boys right behind him. Walking across the room, Chade stopped and kissed his mother on the cheek and hugged his sister. Wes gave him the thumbs up and Donovan shook his hand before allowing him to approach Baylei. Jordyn and Toni moved away from their friend with tears in their eyes.

Well, I found a woman
Stronger than anyone I know
She shares my dreams, I hope that someday, I'll share her home
I found a love
To carry more than just my secrets
To carry love, to carry children of our own

Chade reached up and removed the blindfold and stepped back. Baylei opened her eyes that she'd closed since she couldn't see anyway and covered her mouth when she glanced around the room. Tears rolled down her face and of course, Chade wiped them away with his thumb. The picture of Baylei and Chade, hugged up on white sand in front of the crystal blue waters of St. Thomas, hung on the wall in front of her. If one didn't know their story, it would appear the two of them were madly in love at the time the photo was taken. Baylei once again opened her mouth to speak, but Chade silenced her by placing a finger to her lips.

"Baylei Marie Jefferson, you broke the mold, baby. My heart has been fluttering since the day I laid eyes on you in St. Thomas. From your beautiful hair, down to your pretty little feet, I wouldn't want you to change anything about yourself. You are ambitious, hardworking, and a go getta. I need you on my team. As Ed Sheeran said, I found the love for me."

Chade stared deeply in Baylei's eyes with so much love. Donovan walked over and slipped something in his pocket but Baylei missed the exchange because she only had eyes for the man standing before her. Catching the tears before they fell, she fanned her face as the onlookers waited patiently for Chade to finish what he had to say.

"It was destined for us to be together and I'm happy you were brought into my life, not once, but twice simultaneously. The man upstairs knew what he wanted to happen between us and he made sure to see it through. Baby, I've played the field far too long, this is my last stop. Never in a million years would I have thought I would be standing in this position today."

When he got down on one knee, Baylei started bawling. He reached in his pocket and came out with a black velvet box. "Beautiful, I want my last rodeo to be with you. Will you marry me?"

Chade opened the box and inside sat a halo engagement ring with sixty round diamonds set in platinum. The diamond that sat in the middle was five carats and blew Baylei's breath away. She was lost for words because she hadn't expected Chade to propose so soon. The dream she had earlier came back to her and she knew someone in heaven sent that man to take care of her.

"Chade, I would love to be the future Mrs. Oliver. There's a reason we were brought into each other's lives and I can't wait to see what's in store for us. We fell for one another in a short amount of time, but I was told early on, there's no time period for love. Long as you're one hundred percent sure you're ready to be a one-woman man, then I'm ready to be your lifetime unforeseen lover."

Stay tuned for Book 2:
For the Love of You: Malik and Toni

This was a different storyline from what I usually write. I decided to step outside the box and show a softer side of the Ghostwriter. I really hope you enjoyed Chade and Baylei's story. If you would like to read more about Wes and Donovan, please feel free to read about them in the Paid in Karma series. Thank you for rockin' with me, and I appreciate you from the bottom of my heart.

~Meesha
#Iamtheghostwriter

Submission Guideline

Submit the first three chapters of your completed manuscript to ldpsubmissions@gmail.com, subject line: Your book's title. The manuscript must be in a .doc file and sent as an attachment. Document should be in Times New Roman, double spaced and in size 12 font. Also, provide your synopsis and full contact information. If sending multiple submissions, they must each be in a separate email.

Have a story but no way to send it electronically? You can still submit to LDP/Ca$h Presents. Send in the first three chapters, written or typed, of your completed manuscript to:

LDP: Submissions Dept
Po Box 944
Stockbridge, Ga 30281

DO NOT send original manuscript. Must be a duplicate.

Provide your synopsis and a cover letter containing your full contact information.

Thanks for considering LDP and Ca$h Presents.

Coming Soon from Lock Down Publications/Ca$h Presents

BOW DOWN TO MY GANGSTA

By **Ca$h**

TORN BETWEEN TWO

By **Coffee**

BLOOD OF A BOSS **VI**

SHADOWS OF THE GAME II

TRAP BASTARD II

By **Askari**

LOYAL TO THE GAME **IV**

By **T.J. & Jelissa**

IF LOVING YOU IS WRONG... **III**

By **Jelissa**

TRUE SAVAGE **VIII**

MIDNIGHT CARTEL IV

DOPE BOY MAGIC IV

CITY OF KINGZ III

By **Chris Green**

BLAST FOR ME **III**

A SAVAGE DOPEBOY III

CUTTHROAT MAFIA III

DUFFLE BAG CARTEL VI

HEARTLESS GOON VI

By **Ghost**

A HUSTLER'S DECEIT III

KILL ZONE **II**

BAE BELONGS TO ME III

A DOPE BOY'S QUEEN III

By **Aryanna**

COKE KINGS V

KING OF THE TRAP III

By **T.J. Edwards**

GORILLAZ IN THE BAY V

3X KRAZY III

De'Kari

THE STREETS ARE CALLING II

Duquie Wilson

KINGPIN KILLAZ IV

STREET KINGS III

PAID IN BLOOD III

CARTEL KILLAZ IV

DOPE GODS III

Hood Rich

SINS OF A HUSTLA II

ASAD

KINGZ OF THE GAME VI

Playa Ray

SLAUGHTER GANG IV

RUTHLESS HEART IV

By Willie Slaughter

FUK SHYT II

By Blakk Diamond

TRAP QUEEN

RICH $AVAGE II

By Troublesome

YAYO V

GHOST MOB II

Stilloan Robinson

CREAM III

By Yolanda Moore

SON OF A DOPE FIEND III

HEAVEN GOT A GHETTO II

By Renta

FOREVER GANGSTA II

GLOCKS ON SATIN SHEETS III

By Adrian Dulan

LOYALTY AIN'T PROMISED III

By Keith Williams

THE PRICE YOU PAY FOR LOVE III

By Destiny Skai

I'M NOTHING WITHOUT HIS LOVE II

SINS OF A THUG II

TO THE THUG I LOVED BEFORE II

By Monet Dragun

LIFE OF A SAVAGE IV

MURDA SEASON IV

GANGLAND CARTEL IV

CHI'RAQ GANGSTAS IV

KILLERS ON ELM STREET IV

JACK BOYZ N DA BRONX III

A DOPEBOY'S DREAM II

By **Romell Tukes**

QUIET MONEY IV

EXTENDED CLIP III

THUG LIFE IV

By **Trai'Quan**

THE STREETS MADE ME III

By **Larry D. Wright**

IF YOU CROSS ME ONCE II

ANGEL III

By **Anthony Fields**

FRIEND OR FOE III

By **Mimi**

SAVAGE STORMS III

By **Meesha**

THE STREETS WILL NEVER CLOSE II

By **K'ajji**

IN THE ARM OF HIS BOSS

By **Jamila**

HARD AND RUTHLESS III

MOB TOWN 251 II

By **Von Diesel**

LEVELS TO THIS SHYT II

By **Ah'Million**

MOB TIES III

By **SayNoMore**

THE LAST OF THE OGS III

Tranay Adams

FOR THE LOVE OF A BOSS II

By **C. D. Blue**

MOBBED UP II

By **King Rio**

BRED IN THE GAME II

By **S. Allen**

KILLA KOUNTY II

By **Khufu**

Available Now

RESTRAINING ORDER **I & II**
By **CA$H & Coffee**
LOVE KNOWS NO BOUNDARIES **I II & III**
By **Coffee**
RAISED AS A GOON I, II, III & IV
BRED BY THE SLUMS I, II, III
BLAST FOR ME I & II
ROTTEN TO THE CORE I II III
A BRONX TALE I, II, III
DUFFLE BAG CARTEL I II III IV V
HEARTLESS GOON I II III IV V
A SAVAGE DOPEBOY I II
DRUG LORDS I II III
CUTTHROAT MAFIA I II
By **Ghost**
LAY IT DOWN **I & II**
LAST OF A DYING BREED I II
BLOOD STAINS OF A SHOTTA I & II III
By **Jamaica**
LOYAL TO THE GAME I II III
LIFE OF SIN I, II III
By **TJ & Jelissa**
BLOODY COMMAS I & II
SKI MASK CARTEL I II & III
KING OF NEW YORK I II,III IV V
RISE TO POWER I II III

An Unforeseen Love

COKE KINGS I II III IV

BORN HEARTLESS I II III IV

KING OF THE TRAP I II

By **T.J. Edwards**

IF LOVING HIM IS WRONG...I & II

LOVE ME EVEN WHEN IT HURTS I II III

By **Jelissa**

WHEN THE STREETS CLAP BACK I & II III

THE HEART OF A SAVAGE I II III

By **Jibril Williams**

A DISTINGUISHED THUG STOLE MY HEART I II & III

LOVE SHOULDN'T HURT I II III IV

RENEGADE BOYS I II III IV

PAID IN KARMA I II III

SAVAGE STORMS I II

AN UNFORESEEN LOVE

By **Meesha**

A GANGSTER'S CODE I &, II III

A GANGSTER'S SYN I II III

THE SAVAGE LIFE I II III

CHAINED TO THE STREETS I II III

BLOOD ON THE MONEY I II III

By **J-Blunt**

PUSH IT TO THE LIMIT

By **Bre' Hayes**

BLOOD OF A BOSS **I, II, III, IV, V**

SHADOWS OF THE GAME

TRAP BASTARD

By **Askari**

THE STREETS BLEED MURDER **I, II & III**

THE HEART OF A GANGSTA I II& III

By **Jerry Jackson**

CUM FOR ME I II III IV V VI VII

An **LDP Erotica Collaboration**

BRIDE OF A HUSTLA **I, II & III**

THE FETTI GIRLS **I, II & III**

CORRUPTED BY A GANGSTA I, II III, IV

BLINDED BY HIS LOVE

THE PRICE YOU PAY FOR LOVE I II

DOPE GIRL MAGIC I II III

By **Destiny Skai**

WHEN A GOOD GIRL GOES BAD

By **Adrienne**

THE COST OF LOYALTY I II III

By Kweli

A GANGSTER'S REVENGE **I II III & IV**

THE BOSS MAN'S DAUGHTERS I II III IV V

A SAVAGE LOVE **I & II**

BAE BELONGS TO ME I II

A HUSTLER'S DECEIT I, II, III

WHAT BAD BITCHES DO I, II, III

SOUL OF A MONSTER I II III

KILL ZONE

A DOPE BOY'S QUEEN I II

By **Aryanna**

A KINGPIN'S AMBITON

A KINGPIN'S AMBITION **II**

I MURDER FOR THE DOUGH

By **Ambitious**

TRUE SAVAGE I II III IV V VI VII

DOPE BOY MAGIC I, II, III

MIDNIGHT CARTEL I II III

CITY OF KINGZ I II

By **Chris Green**

A DOPEBOY'S PRAYER

By **Eddie "Wolf" Lee**

THE KING CARTEL **I, II & III**

By **Frank Gresham**

THESE NIGGAS AIN'T LOYAL **I, II & III**

By **Nikki Tee**

GANGSTA SHYT **I II &III**

By **CATO**

THE ULTIMATE BETRAYAL

By **Phoenix**

BOSS'N UP **I , II & III**

By **Royal Nicole**

I LOVE YOU TO DEATH

By Destiny J

I RIDE FOR MY HITTA

I STILL RIDE FOR MY HITTA

By **Misty Holt**

LOVE & CHASIN' PAPER

By **Qay Crockett**

TO DIE IN VAIN

SINS OF A HUSTLA

By **ASAD**

BROOKLYN HUSTLAZ

By **Boogsy Morina**

BROOKLYN ON LOCK I & II

By **Sonovia**

Meesha

GANGSTA CITY

By **Teddy Duke**

A DRUG KING AND HIS DIAMOND I & II III

A DOPEMAN'S RICHES

HER MAN, MINE'S TOO I, II

CASH MONEY HO'S

THE WIFEY I USED TO BE I II

By Nicole Goosby

TRAPHOUSE KING **I II & III**

KINGPIN KILLAZ I II III

STREET KINGS I II

PAID IN BLOOD **I II**

CARTEL KILLAZ I II III

DOPE GODS I II

By **Hood Rich**

LIPSTICK KILLAH **I, II, III**

CRIME OF PASSION I II & III

FRIEND OR FOE I II

By **Mimi**

STEADY MOBBN' **I, II, III**

THE STREETS STAINED MY SOUL I II

By **Marcellus Allen**

WHO SHOT YA **I, II, III**

SON OF A DOPE FIEND I II

HEAVEN GOT A GHETTO

Renta

GORILLAZ IN THE BAY **I II III IV**

TEARS OF A GANGSTA I II

3X KRAZY I II

DE'KARI

248

TRIGGADALE I II III

Elijah R. Freeman

GOD BLESS THE TRAPPERS I, II, III

THESE SCANDALOUS STREETS I, II, III

FEAR MY GANGSTA I, II, III IV, V

THESE STREETS DON'T LOVE NOBODY I, II

BURY ME A G I, II, III, IV, V

A GANGSTA'S EMPIRE I, II, III, IV

THE DOPEMAN'S BODYGAURD I II

THE REALEST KILLAZ I II III

THE LAST OF THE OGS I II

Tranay Adams

THE STREETS ARE CALLING

Duquie Wilson

MARRIED TO A BOSS... I II III

By Destiny Skai & Chris Green

KINGZ OF THE GAME I II III IV V

Playa Ray

SLAUGHTER GANG I II III

RUTHLESS HEART I II III

By Willie Slaughter

FUK SHYT

By Blakk Diamond

DON'T F#CK WITH MY HEART I II

By Linnea

ADDICTED TO THE DRAMA I II III

IN THE ARM OF HIS BOSS II

By Jamila

YAYO I II III IV

A SHOOTER'S AMBITION I II

BRED IN THE GAME
By S. Allen
TRAP GOD I II III
RICH $AVAGE
By Troublesome
FOREVER GANGSTA
GLOCKS ON SATIN SHEETS I II
By Adrian Dulan
TOE TAGZ I II III
LEVELS TO THIS SHYT
By Ah'Million
KINGPIN DREAMS I II III
By Paper Boi Rari
CONFESSIONS OF A GANGSTA I II III
By Nicholas Lock
I'M NOTHING WITHOUT HIS LOVE
SINS OF A THUG
TO THE THUG I LOVED BEFORE
By Monet Dragun
CAUGHT UP IN THE LIFE I II III
By Robert Baptiste
NEW TO THE GAME I II III
MONEY, MURDER & MEMORIES I II III
By **Malik D. Rice**
LIFE OF A SAVAGE I II III
A GANGSTA'S QUR'AN I II III
MURDA SEASON I II III
GANGLAND CARTEL I II III
CHI'RAQ GANGSTAS I II III

KILLERS ON ELM STREET I II III

JACK BOYZ N DA BRONX I II

A DOPEBOY'S DREAM

By **Romell Tukes**

LOYALTY AIN'T PROMISED I II

By Keith Williams

QUIET MONEY I II III

THUG LIFE I II III

EXTENDED CLIP I II

By **Trai'Quan**

THE STREETS MADE ME I II

By **Larry D. Wright**

THE ULTIMATE SACRIFICE I, II, III, IV, V, VI

KHADIFI

IF YOU CROSS ME ONCE

ANGEL I II

IN THE BLINK OF AN EYE

By **Anthony Fields**

THE LIFE OF A HOOD STAR

By Ca$h & Rashia Wilson

THE STREETS WILL NEVER CLOSE

By K'ajji

CREAM I II

By Yolanda Moore

NIGHTMARES OF A HUSTLA I II III

By King Dream

CONCRETE KILLA I II

By Kingpen

HARD AND RUTHLESS I II

MOB TOWN 251

By Von Diesel

GHOST MOB II

Stilloan Robinson

MOB TIES I II

By SayNoMore

BODYMORE MURDERLAND I II III

By Delmont Player

FOR THE LOVE OF A BOSS

By C. D. Blue

MOBBED UP

By King Rio

KILLA KOUNTY

By Khufu

BOOKS BY LDP'S CEO, CA$H

TRUST IN NO MAN

TRUST IN NO MAN 2

TRUST IN NO MAN 3

BONDED BY BLOOD

SHORTY GOT A THUG

THUGS CRY

THUGS CRY 2

THUGS CRY 3

TRUST NO BITCH

TRUST NO BITCH 2

TRUST NO BITCH 3

TIL MY CASKET DROPS

RESTRAINING ORDER

RESTRAINING ORDER 2

IN LOVE WITH A CONVICT

LIFE OF A HOOD STAR

Meesha

CPSIA information can be obtained
at www.ICGtesting.com
Printed in the USA
LVHW051234211121
704028LV00010B/1043

9 781955 270328